POINTED
ATTACKS

POINTED ATTACKS

A MEG SHEPPARD MYSTERY

BOOK THREE

VICKY EARLE

ISBN: 978-1-78324-229-0

This book is a work of fiction. Any resemblance to actual
persons, living or dead, events or locales is entirely coincidental.

www.vickyearle.com

Published by Wordzworth
www.wordzworth.com

This book is dedicated to my sister,

Dawn

1

Needled

William and I had our first passionate disagreement this morning, and a residual shiver tingles down my spine, like an aftershock. He told me he purchased a fantastic deal through a last-minute booking site: a brief vacation at a resort in Cuba for both of us, as a surprise. But it was more like a bolt out of the blue for me. And the surprise for him is that I'm not going.

I grind my teeth and grip the oak rail as I do my best to quash the conflicted emotions inside me. But I can't stop my brain from pressing the replay button. I see William arrive at the farm with a smile from ear to ear, a sparkle in his eyes, and loaded with goodies for breakfast. His sudden droop in countenance showed his disappointment and puzzlement at my decision. My flushed face and raised voice conveyed my annoyance at being told a vacation had been planned that I couldn't to go on.

Instead of leaning on the oak-rail fence to watch and listen to my horses as they tear off the fresh, bright green blades with quick sharp snatches, I could be packing to leave on a vacation with William.

It's partly my fault. I'm not a good communicator, although I'm trying to improve.

I hadn't mentioned to William that I plan to go to England. My mother told me, just two days ago, that she's dying and wants to see me one last time. She said she has something incredibly important, as she put it, that she needs to tell me, and she'll only divulge it if I visit her in person.

From William's perspective, he doesn't see the urgency, since he wonders if she can be believed. This is a valid point. In the past, honesty has not been one of my mother's strengths. And that's an understatement.

Not only that, she let me down dramatically as a mother. She stood by and did nothing as my stepfather abused me. Despite all this baggage, we somehow developed the beginnings of a promising relationship after she arrived, unannounced, on my doorstep before Christmas.

But I can see why William is perplexed. He can't understand my decision to cross the Atlantic to see a mother who failed me in every way, and who's likely luring me with another of her lies. He can't fathom why I turned down his generous offer of a vacation with him, a man who cares about me deeply. He's hurt, and his kindness and patience must be wearing thin. And to make matters worse, I don't think there's anything I can do about what's upsetting him. Another tremor prickles me from head to foot.

William has decided to go to Cuba on his own.

And I'm going to England.

I'm not sure how serious this disagreement is. In the heat of the moment, he said that he'll never move to the farm, come what may. We touched on this possibility about a month ago, but neither of us has pushed it since.

Another vexation is that I thought William would take care of Kelly, my beloved border collie, while I'm away. But, of course, I failed to mention this to William until today. So, I have to find someone else. Fast. At least I don't have to be concerned about my horses, Eagle and Bullet, since I know I can board them at the stables located on the other side of Vannersville. And Rose and Speed are back at the racetrack, where optimism and spirits run high as a new season of thoroughbred horse-racing begins.

I leave the horses to graze. Fortunately, the spring grass hasn't grown much yet, so I don't have to worry about them overdosing on the fresh, young blades. Their digestive systems would object to an overload of that juicy stuff.

Kelly and I reach the back door and leave the soft spring air behind us. We enter the kitchen to be greeted by Cooper and his purrs. He weaves around my legs and leaves liberal amounts of his tabby fur on my jeans. He must be the happiest animal alive. It's a feat to get my jacket off and hang it up without toppling over the persistent ball of fluff.

The landline phone rings as I reach for the kettle. Neal Carvey, the racehorse trainer for Rose and Speed, is on the other end.

"You won't believe this," he says.

"Are Rose and Speed okay?"

"Great. I should have said that first. This is something different. But it's a bit of god-awful déjà vu." His voice is sombre and raspy.

"What is it Neal?"

"There's this trainer, he's a friend of mine. I should say 'was', because he's dead and I've just heard that it's being treated as a suicide."

"Oh, no." I gasp. "I'm so sorry, Neal." There's more to this.

"He didn't kill himself. I know he didn't."

"You're saying someone killed him?" A weight lands on my shoulders as my stomach knots. I've barely had time to recover from my investigations into who killed my husband, Frank, and who killed the jockey, Juan. Neither death was considered suspicious at first. And it was assumed Frank had committed suicide. Talk about déjà vu.

"He wouldn't have killed himself. I'm sure of it. Can you and William look into it? You got the guy who killed Juan. Sorry, my voice is cracking up."

"I'm just about to leave for England."

"Oh." I can hear dejection in his lowered, quieter voice. "I don't know anyone else who could help."

"Right. Well, my flight isn't until the day after tomorrow, so I could talk to a couple of people in the meantime, and then follow up when I get back. That's the best I can do."

"How long will you be away?"

"I haven't booked my return flight because I don't know. But I can't leave Kelly and the horses for long. I haven't even found someone to look after Kelly yet. It's all happened rather quickly."

"I'll see you tomorrow then?"

"I'll be at the track as early as possible."

I'm reluctant to take this challenge on, with its inevitable frustrations and potential dangers. But I admit I like to help people by uncovering the truth.

A headache throbs across my forehead.

One thing at a time. The first priority is preparation for my trip to England, despite the probability that my mother has asked me to travel across the Atlantic on false pretences. But I don't have enough conviction to say 'no'.

I switch the kettle on and turn my thoughts back to who'll look after Kelly. Joanna, a neighbour down the road, used to help, but she's busy with her new small business: creating and selling personalized gift baskets. I text her, just in case.

She calls me on my mobile.

"Sorry, can't do. But I have a suggestion. Our landlord, Russell, might look after her. Could be worth a call."

"I didn't realize that Russell's your landlord. He's the guy with the long beard who lives on the big farm opposite the old mill pond, right?"

"That's him. That's one of his properties. He used to live abroad, but he moved back soon after that farm became vacant. He's been good to us. He gave us a chance to get back on our feet, as you know. You'll have to go find him, though. He doesn't have a mobile, and he's nearly always away from the phone."

I'd rather find someone Kelly knows, but I can't think of anyone. And she hasn't been crated or put in a kennel since I adopted her from the Vannersville Humane Society where I used to work. So, boarding isn't an option. I have no choice but to go in search of Russell and hope for the best.

* * *

It takes me about an hour to get organized and into the pickup truck with Kelly. As we venture out onto the road, my sense of unease grows. I don't know this man. I shouldn't be willing to entrust my beloved dog to someone I've not even talked with before. I contemplate turning around at the first opportunity, but catch myself. I've gone over my contact list. There's no-one who could look after Kelly at their place and no-one who could come to the farm to look after her. So, I should at least talk to this guy. And if he doesn't seem suitable, I'll just have to cancel my trip to England.

The location of his farm is marked by a mailbox which looks as if it's been a target for the snow-plow more than once. Two old maples, past their prime and lacking several large limbs, stand on either side of the entrance. I hesitate. Perhaps he doesn't want any visitors. Perhaps he's out. I contemplate reversing back into the road.

But Kelly whines, which, for some reason, encourages me to move ahead. Large cedar trees edge the long driveway and obstruct the view on either side. There are several buildings ahead, one of which is a white board-and-batten house with sky-blue trim and a shiny black front door that overlooks a square yard covered in gravel. There are no pot-holes. It must have been graded recently. Two other sides of the yard are edged by substantial farm buildings with sound walls made of dark, weathered wood.

I'm taken aback by how neat and tidy the farm looks, especially since it must have been rented out by him for many years. He was either lucky with the tenants or has done a great deal of work on it since he moved in.

A rusty red tractor rumbles into the yard and halts abruptly. A man eases himself down and walks over to us. His long white hair and unkempt beard make it hard for me to read the expression on his face. I leave Kelly in the truck and walk towards him. When we meet, he looks at me with pale brown eyes that are surrounded by a myriad of brown wrinkles.

"You must be Meg," Russell says. "Joanna just called, and I was near the phone for once. But I had to get this tractor back to the barn before the rain, you see. Otherwise the rust will take over completely. Is your dog with you?" He looks past me towards the truck.

"Yes. Would you like to meet her?"

"I sure would. Joanna told me her name, but I've clean forgotten it. Senior moment. Get a lot of those." His smile is full of crooked teeth which are not as white as his long hair. "She can run around here. Just let her out."

"Her name's Kelly." She jumps out of the truck, but crouches on her stomach as if she's afraid of the sky falling. Her wide eyes look up at me.

"She's not been here before, you see," Russell says. "She'll get used to it. I'll be glad to have her company. How long are you going for?"

"I'm not sure. But it won't be for longer than a week."

"You're leaving soon, right? If you could bring her food and treats and her blanket when you drop her off, that'll help her settle in."

"Where will she sleep? I don't want her outside all the time."

"She'll be with me and she can use an old duvet for her bed. I'll put her blanket on it so there's something familiar for her to lie on. It's in the kitchen. Come in and I'll show you."

I step just inside the kitchen door and see the folded duvet on the floor in the corner. The place is neat and tidy inside as well as out. Kelly leans against me and doesn't want to go in. She's such a smart dog that she's probably figured out that I plan to leave her. I thank Russell and tell him I'll be in touch once I know my plans, and I don't make a commitment. He gives me assurances that Kelly will be well-cared for and that she'll have a great time on the farm as his companion. When we reach the truck, Russell reaches out to pat Kelly, but she slouches away and sits on my foot.

* * *

Joanna texts me when I get back home, and asks if I found Russell and if it worked out. I reply that Kelly wasn't herself, but I figure it's because she doesn't know Russell or the farm. Joanna responds Russell seems like a decent guy, he's a neighbour after all, and that I shouldn't worry. She adds that she'll visit Kelly a few times while I'm away. Since I can't think of any alternative other than to cancel my trip to England, I decide to take Kelly to Russell's. But I know that I'll worry about her every minute that we're apart.

I wish William would stay, but I understand why he wants to go. He needs a holiday. I'd hoped that one day we'd go on vacation together, and that Kelly would come with us. I don't know where he thought Kelly would go while we were in Cuba. We didn't get as far as talking about that.

* * *

The rain is relentless. I watch rivulets run down the kitchen window as shivers run down my arms. The damp weather penetrates the house and seeps into my pores. I sip my steaming tea and hope that it will warm me up.

I fed Eagle and Bullet first thing this morning. Kelly and I enjoyed the melodious music of the dawn chorus as we walked the well-trodden path to the barn. We led the horses into the field that has a run-in shed since they'll need shelter today. And then I cleaned out their stalls.

Back in the house, the clock tells me I must have moved slower than usual. I planned to get to the track early, since I promised Neal I would. But it'll be closer to ten o'clock by the time I get there.

When I look at Kelly, a queasiness grips my stomach. It's as if I'm letting her down and she knows it. I wish she could come with me. I'll be so glad to get back home and see her wagging tail.

I can't bear to be parted from her in the meantime, so I tell her she's coming with me to the track. I'll smuggle her in. We've done this before and, so far, we've got away with it.

* * *

The activity in the barns and on the training-track is past its busiest when we finally arrive. But there are several exercise riders still around, decked out in various shades of rain-suit. Some horses, back from their gallops, have steam rising from their hot bodies, and mud splashes coating their legs and underbellies. Several have their tails tied into giant knots to keep the long hairs out of the worst of the dirt.

The rain has eased a little but its cold persistence soon permeates my jacket, as I squelch through the waterlogged mixture of sand, straw and mud that lies between the truck and the barn where Neal is. I should have worn something more waterproof.

Linda, Neal's dedicated groom and superb horsewoman, is busy wiping off a horse with old towels so that she can put his blanket on. I can see he's had a bath even though it's chilly. She has a sweat scraper in her back pocket, which got rid of the surplus rinse-water that lingered in the horse's coat. As soon as she puts his thin blanket on, Linda hands the horse over to the hotwalker, who will lead the horse around and around the shedrow until he's dry enough to be put in his stall without the risk of colic or chilling. Knowing Linda, she won't want to stop her work to chat, so I just wave and ask her where Neal is.

He's in his tiny office with a mug of coffee cupped in his hands, which smells as if it's been kept warm since he first came in at about five o'clock.

"Good to see you," Neal says. "Coffee? It's not the best. I'll make some fresh."

"No thanks."

"Okay. Let's not waste time. I'd like to show you where he was found."

"I'm sorry you've lost a friend. Tell me a bit about him first." I step inside and lean against the doorpost as water drips off the metal roof and splashes onto the pitted concrete path behind me.

"We weren't close, but we shared things and help one another out. He has, I mean had, a much bigger operation than mine, with about forty horses. But he was good to me, and if I didn't have company for one of my horses in the morning, he'd have one of his join mine at the training-track, if he could."

"What's his name?"

"Grayson Sloan."

"I've heard of him. Isn't he the trainer there were rumours about concerning the use of performance-enhancing drugs?"

"I don't believe any of it. I've always known him to be a nice, decent kind of guy."

"Do you know of any reason anyone would want to kill him?"

"All I heard was that he recently had issues with a syndicate."

"You mean a group of people who jointly own one or more racehorses?"

"Yep, that's it.

We walk into the barn and have quick visits with both Speed and Rose, who had their exercise much earlier this morning. They grab large mouthfuls of hay and munch as they watch what's going on in the shedrow. As we walk out of the door and across the road into the next barn, we dodge puddles and give way to horses. We do this one more time before we reach Grayson's barn. Neal's such a fit, energetic person that I find it hard to keep up with him, even though I consider myself to be in pretty good shape.

This barn's dreary, silent stillness contrasts with the busy, colourful bustle of the other barns. There's an eeriness now that the owners have transferred their horses out and most of Grayson's stalls haven't been filled by other trainers' horses yet. The shedrow is empty and quiet, except for one hotwalker and his charge, who pass us as they circle inside the barn.

"His office is in a trailer just off the end of the building. It's got yellow tape round it, but I know that people have been going in to get their stuff and medication for the horses and, you know, things they need."

"And you said that you don't believe it was suicide, but the police are treating it as if it was?"

"The police must have their reasons. But I didn't see any signs that he was suicidal. In fact, he told me that there's a stakes race coming up soon for three-year-olds, and he thought he had a good shot at it with a colt he was training."

"Let's see this trailer, then. How did he die?"

"I don't know. I'm not in that loop." He takes off, rubs his closely cropped brown hair. "I can't see how he hung himself in here. That was the first rumour that went aroud.

"Nothing jumps out at me. I'm going to see if Linda knows anything. Sometimes the grooms know more about what's going on than anyone else."

"Good point. I haven't asked her."

We make our way back to Neal's barn. The rain has diminished to a drizzle, and the sky is not so heavy and dark. I slide my hood off and run my fingers through my shiny, dark hair as we make our way to Neal's stalls. Speed and Rose both nicker as I fumble in my pocket and clasp my cool fingers around a couple of smooth, round mints. They crunch on the small treats with relish.

Neal finds Linda in a stall, but she barely lifts her head to acknowledge we're here.

"Neal, I don't remember seeing this horse before," I say as we move closer.

"This is Hector." Neal says. "We're assessing him at the moment. He has a couple of nasty injuries and he's off his food. And he's been difficult to deal with. We have to sedate him to clean his wounds and bandage him."

"I bet Linda's doing a great job," I say. "Linda, I know you're busy, but I wonder if you know anything about Grayson Sloan's death?"

"I've got to finish this. You should talk to Amy. She's one of Grayson's grooms." Her muffled voice is just about audible from her squatted position by the horse's injured back leg. How she manages to do what she does in a day with that rotund body of hers I'll never figure out. She doesn't appear to eat much and she must use up vast quantities of energy.

"That's a great help, Linda. Let me know if either of you think of anything else. I'm going to catch up with Amy right now."

"She's in barn twelve," Linda mumbles.

ked Amy down, I'll need to get
t organized for the trip to England.
cause I like Grayson, but perhaps they
g," Neal says, as he looks at the dusty floor

nk that perhaps it could have been suicide after all?"
ly. I'm just trying to make sense of it. I can't imagine
anyone would want to kill him. I just can't believe he's dead."

"It's a shock. But now you've got me interested, so I'll follow up for sure when I get back from England."

Neal gives me the beginnings of a smile and shakes my hand.

After I take a quick peek at Kelly, who's still lying down dutifully behind the truck's front seats, I stride off in search of barn twelve and Amy.

Mist rolls in and envelops the barns in damp white clouds, which isolate them from the rest of the world. It's a relief to leave the clammy air and walk into the comparative dryness of barn twelve, which is a hive of human and horse activity. I walk along the edge of the shedrow where the stalls are, and five hotwalkers pass me as they lead their blanketed horses. A couple stop to let their horses drink from personalized buckets that each hang on a post. Large tubs filled with straw and manure wait to be lifted up and chucked into the dumpsters outside. Numerous saddles, bridles, bandages (for leg protection) and saddle pads have been flung over the rail, in readiness for the next ride, or waiting to be cleaned or laundered. The colours of the buckets change as I walk from one trainer's area to another. I ask a hotwalker if he knows where Amy is, and, with his help, I soon find her as she scrubs a bright green feed bucket. She sees me approach and lifts her head.

"You must be Meg Sheppard," she says. "Linda texted me to let me know you might be coming. It's about Grayson, isn't it?"

"And you're Amy. Yes. I'm sorry to hear about Grayson."

"It's too awful. Such a shock."

"I've been told he committed suicide."

Amy puts her brush and cloth in the feed bucket and faces me, her light brown complexion enhanced by her vivid yellow jacket. She puckers her lips to show her disapproval of what I said.

"He didn't."

"Okay. What makes you say that? I know nothing about this at all."

"Linda said that you're like a private investigator, is that right?"

"Not officially. Neal Carvey asked me to look into Grayson's death because he thinks it's suspicious and no-one's treating it as such."

"I told the police that Grayson wouldn't commit suicide. He's a tough kinda guy. I worked for him for two racing seasons, so I should know what he's like. The police wouldn't give me details, but the security guard who found him said he was slumped over his desk with a syringe lying next to him. He had his sleeve rolled up. Before you ask, there was no note. That's all the time I have to talk to you right now. I'm working for a new trainer and he's a goddam task-master."

"Can I chat with you some more later? I'll be away for a few days, but I'll follow up when I get back. Perhaps we could meet when you get a break, or after work?"

"I suppose so. I'm glad someone's looking into it." She turns her watery, dark eyes back to the feed bucket.

2

Secret

The day's agenda looms ahead of me as I stumble downstairs to let Kelly out. The mist has lifted and the warmth from the sun touches my face when I open the kitchen door. Pansies greet me with their cheerful faces in the small garden, their colours dancing in the breeze. I'll miss the farm, the horses, Cooper, and especially Kelly, while I'm away. I already miss William.

I haven't seen him since our argument.

I grab my barn jacket and boots and prepare to go to the barn to feed the horses. Eagle and Bullet whinny as I scoop up their grain rations and pour them into their feed buckets. I lug a couple of pails of water out to the paddock and top up the small trough. Kelly follows as I return to the barn for half a bale of hay. The horses work hard on the small shoots of new grass, but there's not enough nourishment to be gained from the time invested, so they wander over to the hay from time to time.

Kelly's happy that the snow and ice have gone but, on our return to the house, she tiptoes around the puddles as if monsters lurk in their unknown depths. Her paws are almost dry, and only need a quick wipe with an old towel as we stand on the mat just inside the kitchen door.

If only William were here. A wave of remorse hits me. I should go to Cuba with him. The flight isn't until early tomorrow morning and it would only be for six days. I could postpone my trip to England. But what if my mother is telling me the truth, and she is dying? What if she was to die while I was on vacation? How would I feel? And, presumably, I wouldn't find out what she wanted to tell me in person. But she has lied many times in the past. My head spins with indecision as I plod upstairs, intending to pack: for England or for Cuba?

* * *

The shipper arrives on time at noon, and Eagle and Bullet load with no issues, although they've not travelled anywhere in a long time. I can't remember how many years they've been rooted at the farm. They'll be in a paddock together at the boarding facility, and will be brought in at night.

After they've left, the stalls and paddock are empty, still and quiet. They lack the movement of life I enjoy watching every day. The barn cats are curled up asleep in the feed room. I'm glad that Joanna will check on them, as well as Cooper, when she can. She's a lot more reliable now that she's shaken off her gambling addiction, but a lot less available since she's started up her business.

* * *

The moment I've dreaded is here. I must take Kelly to Russell's farm. I'm loaded with food, bowls, treats, a blanket, and chews. She senses that something's up. She slinks out to the truck and cowers on the floor behind the seats.

We arrive at Russell's farm. I don't have to drag Kelly out of the truck, which is a relief. But I tell Russell that I'm worried that she might try to run home. He assures me he won't let her out of his sight and that he knows she's obedient and smart. He tells her to lie down on the duvet, which has her blanket on, and gives her a biscuit. She ignores the treat. Her ears are flattened, her head heavy on her paws, and her eyes half-closed. I waver. I don't want to leave her to visit my mother. What am I thinking? Russell squats down beside her and strokes her head with a gentleness that calms me as well as the dog, and she looks at him.

Having received this small dose of reassurance, I leave.

But I feel nauseated as I drive back down to the road, and torment myself again with thoughts that I've made a terrible mistake and I should never go anywhere. I've let down the animals who rely on me.

Nevertheless, instead of changing my plans, I place the last few items in my bag and get into the taxi, and reach the airport well in time for the overnight flight across the Atlantic to Heathrow.

* * *

I can't sleep on the flight with no space to get comfortable and eat only two bites of the inedible food. It's a relief to hit the tarmac, to find the bus and to reach the car rental depot. I sit in the unfamiliar vehicle and take a few minutes to find the switches and levers I need, and to disable the automatic engine shut-off, which would otherwise occur with every halt, however short.

Most of the drive is on smooth, clearly marked motorways, but I'm tired. I grip the steering wheel and fight to stay alert. I stop at a service station for a strong cup of tea, and note the invasion of American fast-food chains. I stick to the cafeteria and find a double-chocolate muffin to add to my caffeine intake. I leave with lighter eyelids.

Eventually, I exit the motorway with about half-an-hour left to drive on winding roads with small roundabouts and zebra-crossings. I surprise myself at how well I navigate all the foreign aspects of driving in England, including being on the left-hand side of the road, given that I haven't been back here for about two decades.

Over four hours have passed since I left the airport, and I arrive at my mother's retirement home exhausted.

I'm directed to the visitor suite and dump my bag there, wash my hands and look out of the window at a familiar landscape. The building is on the side of a large hill. It gives its occupants a panoramic view of the jumble of rooftops and meandering streets, as well as of the park at the top of the cliffs which overlooks the sea. The view, more often than not, is obliterated by a rolling sea-mist which clings with tenacity to the town, until the wind or the sun's rays cause it to dissipate. Nothing much has changed in all the years I've been in Canada. The familiarity disturbs me, and anxiety threatens to take hold. I take a deep breath to brace myself and walk along the dark, narrow corridor to my mother's small apartment. It's more like a bed-sitter with a kitchenette. Her heavy fire-door is held open with a rubber wedge, and I see her profile as she sits in a recliner placed in front of the large window.

She greets me with such excitement and exhilaration that I feel guilty for having considered not coming. She doesn't attempt to get out of her chair, but she has more colour in her face and more hair on her head than my imagination had presumed. She grabs my hand and holds on as if her life depends on it. I'm taken aback by her effusive welcome and, in an effort to quash my awkwardness, I suggest I make tea.

As I pour the boiling water into the small teapot barely large enough to make two cups, I glance out at her and wonder what she's up to. My intuition niggles at me, because things aren't quite as I expected. But I decide not to confront my mother, and to wait and see how things unfold.

"How's William?" she asks and smiles as she lifts her cup.

"He's in Cuba."

"Alone?"

"I had to come here." I tell myself not to say any more.

"Oh, dearie me. I am sorry." She looks down at her lap as she puts the cup and saucer on a small, rickety side table. "But I didn't know what to do."

"How's your treatment going?"

"I told you I'm dying. Don't get angry with me, but I'm probably going to be fine. I told you that for a reason. I'll explain."

"Tell me what's happening with your treatment, then." I stifle a yawn as a wave of numbing tiredness hits me. Now that I know she's not dying, that she summoned me here under false pretences, that I've fallen victim to yet another one of her lies, fatigue takes over rather than the anger I would have expected. And, I admit, there's a sense of relief. I flop back in the armchair and look out of the window as seagulls soar in circles, turning their heads this way and that, looking for tasty bits of abandoned food far below.

"Darling. Oh, you don't like me calling you that. Let me start again." She wrings her hands and seems flustered. Her agitation makes me sit up. "I'll tell you about the treatment first. I had a biopsy, only a small hole in my head. You can hardly see where they did it, except for the bald patch. Anyway, it's not cancer."

"What about the tests you had done in Canada?"

"They didn't do a biopsy. I saw an oncologist for all of about five minutes. She said that it was probably benign, but in the same breath she said she'd heard about the long wait-lists here, as if that was a concern. She made me more nervous because I thought I should have a biopsy and find out for sure, and have a treatment plan. But I tried not to think about it. I wanted to stay with you for longer at the farm."

"You did the right thing to come back to England. And you sold the house and moved into this place. Is it okay?"

"So-so. I'm getting used to it. Back to treatment. Because benign tumours cause symptoms and can even be life threatening, they want to remove it. They think they'll be able to get all of it. If not, they think radiotherapy will be the best route."

"Do they know what caused the tumour?"

"They said head trauma could, you know. Well."

"Ah." She doesn't have to say any more for me to understand. My mother also suffered abuse doled out by Stan, my stepfather, but I didn't know how bad it was. I have a better idea now. "When's the op?"

"In three days."

"Why didn't you tell me? Why weren't you honest? You could have asked me to come because you're having the operation, instead of telling me you're dying." I purse my lips, but then draw a deep breath. There's more, I'm sure. This is not the reason she wants me here.

"I didn't mean for you to come while I was having my op. It just worked out that way. The reason is bigger. Oh dear, I don't know how to tell you."

"Why don't you just spit it out."

"I feel sick."

"Just tell me."

"You have a half-sister."

"What? That's not possible. I don't believe you."

"I thought you might not. That's the reason I wanted you to come, so I could convince you and make sure you knew before the op. Things can go wrong, you know. Anyway, I should have told you years ago, but I didn't have the courage. I need you to believe me." She looks at me with intense but watery eyes. She blinks a few times and then turns away as her lips tremble.

"Tell me about her."

My mother turns towards me again, her face more relaxed, although she has a deep frown that makes her eyes look smaller.

She tells me she found out that she was pregnant soon after I left. She was forty-one. Terrified, she tried to conceal her pregnancy as long as possible from Stan, but, of course, he found out and was angrier than she could even have imagined. This was partly because it was too late for an abortion by then.

His physical attack was like an eruption of vile hatred, in my mother's words, and she felt his assault was an attempt to cause her to have a miscarriage. She woke up the next morning, alive, and could feel the baby kicking. Despite the relief, she spent the entire day in tears and in pain. She knew the baby would have to be put up for adoption. She couldn't face raising another child in that house.

She says that the baby was a girl, born with hardly any hair, and blond.

"I want you to find her before I die," my mother says as she leans back in the recliner, her eyes closed and beads of sweat on her upper lip.

"Hopefully that gives me a long time."

"I mean it. I just can't bear it any more. You need to meet your sister. At least see her."

"I think I'm in shock. It's not sunk it. It's hard to forgive you for not telling me until now."

She opens her eyes and leans towards me. "Look, I can't pretend I've been a great mother, and I can't go back and change things even if I want to." Tears roll down her cheeks. "I need you to search for her."

She has a history of lying and has a brain tumour, but this must be the truth. I can't think otherwise. It sounds too real.

My mother has no inclination to sit in the communal dining-room-come-restaurant, and neither of us feels like food. But we both need to eat. So, I venture out to find the fish-and-chip shop that used to be by the harbour. I'm relieved that my route doesn't take me anywhere near the house in which I was raised. I couldn't cope with the painful flashbacks which the sight of its cold, grey brick facade would inevitably evoke.

The expected walls of sea-mist waft in, and the cold dampness permeates my thin jacket and even my skin. I haven't brought enough warm clothes with me. I forgot how chilly it can be, especially by the sea.

The fish-and-chip shop has fresh paint, but otherwise looks much the same as I remember. While waiting in line, I receive a text message. Joanna has just been to Russell's place and, although she didn't find him at home, Kelly was in the kitchen and came to the door, wagging her tail. Thank goodness. Some of the tightness in my chest, which I hadn't noticed until now, eases as I put my phone away.

* * *

I lie awake all night despite my desperate need for sleep. My mind tosses about more than my body does in this narrow bed, and jumps from one thought to the next. It's as if my brain is a thought-mixer that churns everything in my head, but resolves nothing. It stirs up curious imaginations about what it'll be like to have a sister and what kind of person she is. And William's face pops up, as large as life, as he comes through the kitchen door with his news about the surprise vacation in Cuba. Kelly is mixed up in this image. Her mournful big brown eyes look at me with reproach. Added to these disturbing pictures in my mind, I imagine that Eagle and Bullet have no hay. And I panic about Cooper, and wonder if I've left enough food and water, but remember that Joanna will check when she can. When will that be?

She's already checked on Kelly. Get a grip.

* * *

Morning at last. My mother has found some energy, perhaps because she's relieved that she's finally told me what she should have told me years before. But I still don't understand why she didn't tell me as soon as Stan died.

"See if you can get a flight home. You should go back," she says. Her kitchenette comes in handy for breakfast. She's made some toast and has grapefruit and yoghurt, as well as a pot of tea.

"I don't want to leave until you've had your operation."

"I want you to. If you stay, they'll rope you into looking after me. If I don't have family, social services arranges for help."

"It's such a brief stay."

"That's all that I needed. But I hope you understand why I wanted to tell you in person. I'm sorry it's such a long journey, and all your animals, and William especially. I hope you two will be okay when you get back. See if you can book something for this evening."

"If you're sure about this?"

"I'm sure."

"I hope you'll be able to visit us again soon."

"That's my plan." She gives me a rare smile, pulls her brown cardigan around her shoulders and pours the tea.

I book a seat on a flight that leaves tomorrow evening, at about the time my mother goes into hospital. I'll have to leave in the morning to make sure I get to Heathrow in plenty of time.

My mother doesn't want to do much of anything. I sense she's slid into a dark place, and I want to help her while I can. We walk arm-in-arm down the high street and spend some time window-shopping. I read most of the newspaper to her and I make sure she has her bag packed for the hospital with everything she needs in it.

*　　*　　*

Another sleepless night. As I drive to Heathrow, I'm concerned that I might fall asleep at the wheel. I stop at three different service stations and down several cups of tea and hope that I'll be alert enough to be safe.

*　　*　　*

After hours of monotonous driving, I deliver the rental car back to the right place and in one piece, which seems like a major achievement. My eyes close and I almost fall asleep as the bus delivers me to the terminal. I drag myself through security and flop down into a chair in the departure lounge. William's face pops up on my phone. I assume he's having a wonderful vacation in Cuba. But he says he's at the farm, that Kelly's okay, but he found her curled up on the back doorstep. Just wanted me to know. No need to worry.

My hands shake so badly I can hardly key in my response. I thank him and tell him I'm on my way home, which doesn't convey the self-reproach which has hit me like a slap across the face. I thank him again.

I knew I shouldn't leave Kelly with someone she doesn't know. Russell told me he'd be with her all the time. He lied. But it's my fault. I let my wonderful dog down and broke my promise not to leave her. I make a dash for the washrooms and wretch into a toilet.

*　　*　　*

The flight home was ghastly. I stood for most of the time by the galley at the back of the plane because I was too restless to settle in my seat. My mother's plight in the hospital, awaiting her operation, flits into my mind for only a couple of quick seconds. At least someone's looking after her. But my poor dog.

The taxi ride home seems to take an eternity. I scramble out when we reach the gate and run, as best I can, with my bag banging against my leg, up the gravel driveway. It's close to midnight, but I see lights on and a car parked near the barn. I hope someone is with Kelly. Please let her be okay.

I open the back door and a ball of black and white fur jumps up and licks my face. I laugh with relief as I tussle with her on the floor. Cooper saunters over and rubs against my bag, his tail straight up in the air.

"We're all glad you're home," William says, as he offers me a hand to help me up.

"Is she okay? And why aren't you in Cuba?"

"She's fine now. But I took her to the vet because she had bloody diarrhea. Apparently, dogs can bleed internally if they're under a severe amount of stress."

"Oh. Oh no. That's too awful. Poor Kelly." I crouch down and hold her head in my hands, gazing into her large brown eyes.

"They gave her something and suggested a bath," William says. "I did that here because I thought it would be less stressful for her. She was good about it, even though I know she doesn't like to get wet. But I think she felt a lot better being home."

"And she loves you, William. Thank god you were here. Why are you here?"

"Meg, I couldn't go to Cuba without you. I said I would out of disappointment and frustration, but it would have been no fun."

I swallow hard to stop tears that threaten to erupt from my eyes. I take a deep breath. "What about the tickets and reservations?"

"I gave them to my assistant, Ramona. She was ecstatic. I felt really good about it. But I'm paying a price for it at the office. I did what I could from here today, but I had to take Kelly in for a couple of hours this evening, and I've been working here since then, till you came home. I didn't want to leave Kelly alone."

"Russell seemed like a nice guy."

"He's Joanna's and Ewert's landlord, right?"

"I think it's odd. Not just that Kelly came home, but that he didn't let Joanna know she was missing. I know he doesn't have a mobile, but he can phone Joanna on the landline, and he certainly knows where she lives. He could have left a message on the door or something."

"Perhaps he's not as responsible as you and Joanna thought."

"I don't know, but I'm going to visit him and find out. Wasn't Kelly smart to find her way home?"

"Kelly's very smart. If you're okay, I have to go. I want to pick up some things from the office and then get at least a couple of hours' sleep before I tackle another day without my right-hand person. If Ramona ever leaves, I'd have to hire two people to replace her."

"Thank you. Thank you, from me and Kelly. Thank you."

William gives me a short, gentle hug, picks up his jacket and work paraphernalia, and leaves. There's a vacuum where his warmth and friendship were. I already miss him and he hasn't got into his car yet. I ruffle the silky hair on Kelly's head and pick Cooper up. I don't deserve any of them.

*   *   *

The morning is bright and sunny with a light, cool breeze rustling the fresh green baby leaves on the trees. These shoots are not as fragile as they appear. In contrast, I do my utmost to bury my fragility so as not to give any outward signs of my fluttering heart and jumpy mind.

I arrange for Eagle and Bullet to come home late morning. According to the barn manager, they ate all their food, were happy in the paddock and were easy to handle.

I set the alarm on my phone for later, so that I'll remember to call the nurses' station to find out how my mother's operation went. She should be going into the operating theatre soon.

I call Joanna on her mobile. I bring her up to date on my return and Kelly's unexpected escape to home. She says she didn't want to mention that Kelly had been scratching at the screen door and whining when she checked on her.

"My bad," Joanna says. "I assumed Russell was out on the tractor somewhere and would be back soon, and that she was just missing you. I was in a rush otherwise I would have looked for Russell."

"It's not your fault. I shouldn't have left her. It was a big mistake. Thanks for checking on her."

"At least I saw she was in the kitchen. I could see there was water in her bowl and a duvet for her bed. I thought she was okay."

As we talk, a text comes in from Neal to ask me if I'm back yet and could I come to the track? Rose and Speed are fine, but Amy wants to chat with me again about Grayson, the trainer who is presumed to have committed suicide. I tell him I'll be there tomorrow morning.

* * *

On my way to check out Russell's place, I contemplate Kelly's return home. The more I think about it, the less sense it makes. Something doesn't add up.

Kelly is seldom on a leash, but I decide it would be a good idea during our visit to Russell's farm, just in case something spooked her or hurt her, or if she gets the idea that I'll leave her there as before. Besides, I don't know if I'll ever be able to let her out of my sight again.

And she's such a smart dog that I expect she knows where to look for Russell, and I want her to help me find him.

The farm looks no different from when I brought Kelly for her stay, except that I can examine it under a brighter light. The sun's glare highlights the grey and black streaks on the weathered wood of the old barn, but the house stands up well under the intense sunshine. I can't see a vehicle anywhere, but I can't remember seeing anything other than the rusty red tractor on either of my previous visits.

Kelly doesn't know how to behave on the end of a leash and weaves all over the place, making it difficult to walk in a straight line. Since Russell still hasn't picked up the phone, I assume he's not in the house and aim to check out the big old barn first. But Kelly, much to my intense surprise, pulls me towards the kitchen door, albeit a bit haphazardly. Perhaps she knows I should pick up her blanket, bowls, food, and treats while we're here.

The mesh in the wooden screen door has come out of its moorings at the bottom and along one side. It would have taken some force for Kelly to burst out of the house this way as she made her escape. She must have been desperate to leave, so it's curious that she wants us to go back in. I knock on the doorjamb and call out Russell's name.

Nothing.

Kelly pulls so hard when I open the battered door that I let go of the leash. She darts past the dog bed and barks. I follow at a trot and find Russell in a heap at the bottom of the stairs. I dial 911 as I feel for a pulse. He's alive, but only lukewarm. Kelly licks his face. I see a flicker of an eyelid, but nothing else moves. There's a little dried blood caked into the carpet where his head lies. This looks like an accident, but I'm not sure. If only Kelly could talk.

He has probably been like this for almost 24 hours. I tell Kelly to go to the dog bed, and run up the carpeted stairs to find a blanket or duvet, and take a fleeting look at the banisters on the way. I can't see a trace of blood anywhere. Perhaps there wouldn't be. I find a folded throw on a chair opposite a window that overlooks the fields, and grab it. Nothing looks out of place, as far as I can tell in my hasty sprint back down. I lay the throw over him. He's lying on his side, his face pointed towards the kitchen. I take a few pictures as I talk to him, and assure him that help is on its way. I don't know if he can hear me. Kelly whines. I tell her to wait.

It seems an eternity before the ambulance and police show up. When they finally arrive, almost simultaneously, they bring a flurry of large, hot bodies in uniforms with loud voices and heavy feet. I'm asked a few questions and do my best to make the situation sound suspicious, hoping that what I say will lead the police to dig underneath the surface. My intuition tells me that this is not a simple fall down the stairs. The paramedics take off Russell's running shoes and lift him onto the gurney. He has an IV drip attached through a vein in his hand, and thin white blankets tucked in around his body. I'm right, he is alive, at least for the moment.

The police ask me to leave once I've given them my contact information. Kelly looks as if she hasn't moved a muscle since she laid down on the dog bed, her ears flat to her head, overwhelmed by all the noise and bustle, perhaps. I gather her and her things and, with shaky legs, make my way back to the truck.

3

Injured Horse

We arrive at the farm just in time to see the horse transport truck reverse into the driveway. The trailer rocks and sways as Eagle and Bullet stomp around their box stalls inside. Their raucous whinnies ricochet off the steel walls and reverberate around my head. They must know that they're home.

The driver helps me to unload the filthy specimens: their manes knotted around burs, and their coats caked in mud.

"They look awful," I say.

"They have a couple of muddy paddocks at that place, and at the back there's lots of that burdock stuff. But I reckon they had fun running around with their mates."

"They were with other horses?"

"Yeah. They like putting a whole bunch of them in together. We had to catch them while about fifteen of them ran circles around us."

"Oh. That's not what I thought the arrangements would be."

"You'll have to take that up with the stables. Not my area."

"I know. Thanks for picking them up at such short notice, and sorry it was a hassle." We put them in their stalls, steam rising from their acrid-smelling, mud-caked bodies. I have a challenge on my hands. I could really do with Linda's help, but she's so busy at the track that I can't ask her.

The horses need time to calm down and dry off, so I have a cup of tea and a piece of toast and make a futile attempt to relax in the recliner. Cooper's curled up on my lap, and Kelly's fast asleep on the floor at my side. The moral of these escapades with my animals is that I must not leave them. We all suffer the consequences, with the possible exception of Cooper and the barn cats. Nothing seems to faze them.

* * *

Kelly and I enter the barn in anticipation of spending the entire afternoon in there. The horses are dry and have settled down in their stalls. They munch on their hay as if everything is right in their world. I retrieve my grooming box from the feed room, and get ready to tackle the first dirt-encrusted, bur-infested animal. I lead Eagle to the cross-ties in the aisle and use a metal curry-comb to gently scrape off the dried, caked-on mud. It falls in powdery curtains to the floor, along with wads of shed winter coat. Despite the daunting challenge ahead, I let out a sigh and settle into my work. As I pick up the dandy brush, Eagle snorts and shakes, sending clouds of dust billowing into the air around him that make me sneeze.

I go to the feed room in search of a tissue. The two barn cats are asleep: intertwined and squished into one of the cat beds. I adopted them from the humane society. They were strays who weren't claimed by their owners. They're sisters. Do I really have a sister? The question hangs over me as I hold my breath. I dab my eyes and grab another tissue to blow my nose.

*   *   *

It's late. William couldn't come this evening. His workload is daunting and, to compound his challenges, he thinks he might have caught the norovirus which is making the rounds of the community. He told me to stay away when I offered to help. But, on reflection, my offer might not have sounded sincere. We didn't talk for long on the phone.

I'm apprehensive as I open the laptop and enter the web address of the adoption reunite site that my mother said she'd been told about. My fingers fumble, and my brain jumps from one thought to another. Perhaps I haven't eaten enough today. But I refuse to let myself stop to look for something edible because I might use the interruption as an excuse to put off the whole thing. My mother asked me to find my sister, and, assuming she exists, I think I should try.

But I'm afraid. I'm afraid of what she could be like. Images of a female version of my stepfather, Stan, pop up in my mind's eye, and I grind my teeth. After all, he's her father.

*   *   *

With my mug of tea in my hand, I look out of the kitchen window at the pansies which smile back at me in the early morning spring sunshine. I haven't planted many. Chuck, who was the gardener here, and later was my partner until he died suddenly and unexpectedly, planted trays of pansies in multiple cheery colours each spring. The gardens get much less attention now.

My eyes drift to the paddock, which is erupting with fresh spring greenness. The horses keep their noses to the ground and snatch what they can of the recent growth. Eagle and Bullet look respectable and no longer have caked mud all over them, although I couldn't resurrect the shine in their coats. Their manes and tails are sleek and clear of tangles. My eyes move to the landline phone on the wall. I'm about to call the nurses' station to find out how my mother is doing. It's lunch-time in England, breakfast time here.

I can hear the hubbub of intense activity when the nurse answers. I just begin to introduce myself when she tells me she'll take the phone to my mother.

"Hello," a faint and wobbly voice travels precariously across the Atlantic. It doesn't sound like my mother.

"Hi. How do you feel?"

"Sleepy, but I'm not in any pain. I'm alright. Have you found your sister yet?"

"I've registered on that adoption reunite site but haven't heard anything."

"Alright. How's William? Is he back from Cuba?"

"He didn't go."

"Oh. I see. I'm going to have a nap. It was nice of you to call." Her voice fades and the call ends. I'm not able to get through to the nurses' station the second time. The line is busy and I eventually give up.

*   *   *

Kelly has been smuggled into the track again. Rose and Speed are in their stalls, heads lolling over their metal mesh half-doors as they watch the world pass by. Neal tells me he's happy with both of them at the moment and that he'll review the racing program to see if there are suitable spots for them to run, probably in about three weeks' time. I ask where Linda is, and find her in a stall almost buried under a horse as she cleans wounds, as far as I can make out.

"Is this Hector?" I recognize him as the one she was working on last time I was here.

"Yeah. He needs time off." Linda is too busy to talk any more.

I make my way over to the barn where Amy works. The sunshine pours through the open windows that line the shedrow and illuminates the billions of dust particles dancing in the air. It's almost as if a dirty mist is playing around me.

Amy emerges from a stall and takes a couple of gulps from a travel mug.

"Amy, have you got a minute?"

"You've timed it right. I'm going to have a short break in about five. I could meet you in the cafeteria."

It's a pleasant walk. The air is full of optimism as horses are led, groomed, ridden and talked to. Their snorts and occasional whinnies mix with the riders' banter as they go to and from the training-track. A few of the riders are singing, which must help to relax their mounts. I know the tunes make my spirit smile.

Amy shuffles into the cafeteria, her large, dusty boots scuffing the floor, her shoulders somewhat hunched. I pay for her toasted bagel with cream cheese and we sit down with our mugs of hot chocolate.

"I've been thinking about Grayson a lot, trying to figure out who would want to do him in," she says as she looks at me with unwavering black-brown eyes. "There was a rivalry between him and Bryce, another trainer in the barn. Really, it was about Bryce making weird accusations of all sorts. There was a big stakes race coming up, and the tension got big. Bryce is the only person I can think of who didn't like Grayson. I hope you'll go see him?"

"I'll follow up for sure. Thanks for the lead."

"Someone heard Bryce say Grayson was doping. It's gossip and there's a lot of it around here, so it might not be true. I know Grayson didn't dope, and that's a fact."

"If Bryce said that, why would he make that sort of accusation, do you think?"

"Because, when we had horses in the same race, our horse would beat Bryce's. We didn't always win, of course, but Bryce sure had a bad racing season last year. And the same pattern is repeating this year, although it's early in the season."

"What can you tell me about Bryce?"

"Don't know much, but I don't think he's got what it takes to be a horseman. His poor performance could be all about his lousy training skills. Who knows?"

Amy says she's in a rush and pockets the rest of her bagel.

Bryce isn't hard to find. He's cleaning some leather tack, which he's hung on a hook just outside his office door. He simply nods when I explain who I am, and that I'm on a mission to uncover the circumstances of Grayson's death. He continues to clean a bridle with a sponge and saddle soap.

"What do you want with me?" he asks, his eyes fixed on the tack.

"There's gossip, and I wonder if there's any truth to it, that you believed Grayson was using performance-enhancing drugs, obviously ones that can't yet be detected through the testing."

"I believe it, because it's gotta be true. His horses always out-performed mine. My horses are no worse than his horses. So, I ask myself, how come?"

"Did you accuse him of doping?"

"I talked to him about it. He denied it, of course, so I asked him what his secrets were because he couldn't be doing as well as he was without a little extra help."

"What did he say?"

"He just brushed me off. He laughed and walked away. So, I reckon I hit the nail on the head. He just wasn't about to tell me, that's all."

"Did he make you angry?"

"Sure did. But if you're suggesting I'd kill him over it, you're wrong. We all know he killed himself."

"I don't think he did. I think it was murder."

"That's bad. Now, I'm busy, so can't talk no more."

"Before you go, where were you the night Grayson died?"

"I've got no alibi, if that's what you're getting at."

Bryce walks into his office and slams the door.

During my amble back to Neal's barn, I enjoy the cheery chirps of the sparrows as they gather straw, hay and baling-twine to make their nests. The barns in the backstretch are a haven for birds, which walk close to the horses and fly in and out of stalls without fear, and even sit on the windowsills within reach of barn workers.

I hope to talk to Linda, but she's nowhere to be seen. Neal is sending a message on his mobile, so I stroke Speed's nose while I wait.

"I'm glad you're still here," Neal says. "I have a big favour to ask. You know Hector, the injured horse we have here?"

"The one Linda's been working hard on?" Uh oh.

"Hector was one of the horses Grayson trained. No other trainers were interested, so I said I'd take him on, but he's injured, as you know. The owner wants to sell and, if we can get him back into training, someone might be interested. He showed a bit of promise last season. Came third in his first race, I think. He's only three this year. But he needs a rest. I don't think we have a chance of selling him in this state."

"What are you asking me to do? Buy him?"

"That would be even better, but no, I'm just hoping he can have a needed break at your farm. Linda says she'll come out there first thing each day, and again after she's finished here, so that you don't have to do the bandages or give him meds. I don't want to make it harder for you to find out who murdered Grayson." He smiles. "I know it's a big favour, but he must go to a good place. That's important to us. We'll work something out about costs."

"I think I can do it with Linda's help. She's a gem."

"She knows her horses, and she's a hard worker to boot."

"Who's the owner, by the way? Will he or she be coming over to my place?"

"Actually, it's a syndicate. Mr. Stanley is the contact. Can't remember his first name at the moment. I've never met him, just talked to him on the phone. I have his billing information but I don't know any more than that, except that he wants to sell the horse asap. Come to think of it, you should chat with him. I'll text you his phone number. You could ask Amy what she knows about him."

*   *   *

It's early afternoon by the time Kelly and I get back to the farm. Eagle and Bullet toss the hay about with their noses, having given up on nibbling the short shiny blades of grass, since there aren't enough to satisfy their need for forage. Kelly and I need to do some foraging of our own in the kitchen. I should have picked up something to eat on the way home.

It's been a long, lonely time since I've seen William. Before I grab something to eat, I text him to ask if he feels better and if I can visit. I want to say that I miss him, but I don't key in the words, I'm not sure why. He responds right away and says he'll come over and I sing a few bars of "Hallelujah" from Handel's Messiah until it hits me I have nothing to offer him to eat. To top it off, there might not be enough coffee grounds in the house.

*   *   *

Kelly knows it's William at the door and I let him in. He's wrapped in a charcoal woollen coat, and has a long black scarf wound twice around his neck. A black toque tops the outfit. His face is pale and taut, his lips have a blue tinge, and he's shivering.

"You're still sick. You look terrible," I say as I grab the paper cups and plastic bag out of his hands.

"I'm much, much better. It was only one of those twenty-four-hour things. I've just lost some of my strength and feel the cold."

"Let me hang up your coat. You go into the family room and relax in a recliner, and grab a throw. Cooper likes the fluffy one. He'll help to warm you up." I'm not at my best when someone needs tender loving care, but I try. I delve into the plastic bag and find several goodies, including an oatmeal raisin cookie for Kelly. She sits next to me and licks her lips in anticipation. And there are cheese croissants and honey crullers.

William has a bit of colour in his face by the time we've finished our hot drinks. Cooper is curled up on his lap. I move from my recliner to the sofa so I can be nearer to William. I want to show him the pictures of Russell at the bottom of the stairs, which continue to haunt me and raise several questions in my mind. I called the hospital, and all they told me was that Russell's still a patient there and no visitors are allowed. I wonder if he has any family because they would probably be permitted to visit, and perhaps I could talk with them.

"You see this one? There's a little dried blood caked into the carpet, but I didn't find blood anywhere on the stairs, or any other signs there."

"Did you look elsewhere in the house?"

"No. But I think he was either attacked at the bottom of the stairs, or he was hit somewhere else and dragged there." I flick through a couple more pictures which are similar. "Ah, this is the one I want. He's wearing running shoes. You can see them clearly in this picture. Let me expand it so that I can see if they have any dirt on them."

"You wouldn't know if he wears shoes indoors?"

"I would say it's rare for someone living on a farm to wear their shoes into the house. And his home is pretty clean." I study the enlarged picture of his shoes. "I can't tell if this is dirt or stains, but there's something on them."

"Let me see." He looks at my phone. "I'd say it's dirt, and it's likely that they were worn outside."

"What if there were two people? He could have been struck while he was outdoors and brought into the house."

"I expect the police are doing a thorough investigation."

"Can you find out?"

"I knew you were going to ask me that." His eyes are half-shut and his half-eaten cruller is sitting on the plate that I placed on the coffee table. Kelly shows a fleeting interest in it, but then lies down on the floor beside William.

"When you feel better, I mean."

He falls asleep before I finish my sentence, and I'm relieved. He needs rest. And he could do with someone to look after him for a bit. But I hope he doesn't think I would be any good at it. I can't even look after myself properly. Animal care is different, which reminds me that Hector is due to arrive tomorrow morning and I should prepare.

Neal's right. I should talk to Hector's owner, Mr. Stanley. I wonder what his friends call him? I retrieve the number from Neal's text. No answer and no way to leave a message. I hope that my attempts to track him down won't use up a lot of time. I leave Kelly spread on her side, on the floor next to William, dozing, with her paws paddling, and Cooper on William's lap, with his whiskers twitching. I hope their dreams are of happy, sunny spring days.

Making as little noise as possible, I leave the house to work in the barn. I select a stall which is two down from Eagle's, just in case Hector doesn't like either of the horses, and empty a couple of bags of wood-shavings that emit a clean, pine scent. I unearth water and feed buckets and carry them over to the stall. My phone vibrates.

The message is from the adoption reunite site. The phone wobbles in my hand as I read, but it's just a request for some more information about me and my mother. I'm not sure if I should be hopeful or not. I finish my chores in the barn, lead Eagle and Bullet into their stalls, and make sure they have everything they need.

William sits at the kitchen table with his hair dishevelled. He doesn't have much of it, but what he has could do with a trim. I look at him and feel an urge to give him a hug, but I make him a small coffee instead, with the meagre supply of coffee grounds I have.

"Meg, are we going to make this relationship work or not?"

"What do you mean?" I didn't expect that question, especially not at this moment, but it's probably been simmering inside him since my refusal to go to Cuba, and my trip to England. The fact that my mother lied again doesn't help.

"You know what I mean. We agreed we would communicate, and that we'd get to know each other really well, and I don't think we're doing a good job. I don't blame you. I think we each need to ask ourselves what we want from this relationship. If we care enough, we have to put some effort into it."

"Look, I made you some coffee." I put the mug down on the table in front of him and sit down on a chair with a thud.

"I know you want to make light of this, but it's serious."

I'm saved by the landline phone ringing. It's Neal with the shipping details about Hector, and what the shipper should bring with him to the farm: Hector's meds, bandages and health record. No special feed necessary. That's good because I hadn't thought of it. He tells me that Rose and Speed are doing fine and that Linda will come over mid to late afternoon tomorrow. He asks me what progress I've made in the investigation into Grayson's death, and I have to admit I haven't made much at all, but once Hector's settled in, I'll follow up. I hang up the phone as William gets up and grabs his jacket.

"You're leaving? I hoped you'd stay for something to eat," I say. I don't add that I'd have to go out for supplies.

"I have to get going. I have research to do this evening at the office. Ramona won't be back until the day after tomorrow."

Instead of saying something or giving William a hug, I plonk myself down on a kitchen chair and hold my head in my hands. I seem to be incapable of doing the right thing to get my relationship with William back on track, and I don't know why.

4

The Veterinarian

It was a sleepless night. Images of Frank, Chuck and mostly of William floated around in my head, as if to taunt me, and to point out that I was incapable of loving any of them, and that I lost them all because of that. Part of me thinks it'll be easier just to forget William, to forget the whole lot of them, and to go back to living alone with my animals. I have been content in the past with that lifestyle. Surely, I can do it again.

After I've given the horses their feed, I take Kelly for a walk in the large field, with the bitter wind in our faces as we turn for home. We let the horses out and my normally sedate retirees kick up their heels and canter across the paddock, the wind in their manes and their tails upright. They snort one after another and create puffs of steam that float around their faces. I hope they'll be much calmer by the time Hector arrives.

I'm determined not to think about William. In any case, he's very busy, and so am I. Neither of us have the time to contemplate our relationship. Despite this convincing rationale, my heart continues its relentless thumping.

*   *   *

Hector arrives in one piece but, despite sedation, he has his head in the air, and whinnies, snorts and trots, rather than walking calmly at my side, as I lead him into the barn. It doesn't help that Eagle and Bullet canter over to the fence to see who's arrived. Hector's chestnut coat gleams, and his bandages on both back legs are clean, neat and secure: all evidence of Linda's professional care. I put him in his stall and he tears around in circles, mixing his hay with his bedding, and calls out to his new stable mates. No-one would think there's anything wrong with him.

Kelly and I head for the house, and I hope Hector will settle down enough for us to leave for the track to ask some more questions about Grayson's death.

Blocking William out of my thoughts doesn't work for long, because he texts me to let me know that a lethal level of ketamine was found in Grayson's blood. He doesn't say whether the police are now treating his death as a homicide. I suppose that doesn't necessarily follow. Grayson could have obtained the drug and administered it to himself. I send a brief reply of thanks to William, arguing with myself that I should reach out to him. But I back away, despite the disquiet that tells me how fortunate I am to have him in my life and that I need to let him get closer.

*   *   *

Amy is raking the shedrow floor when I show up. She continues to work as I talk with her, her strong, stocky body using the rake to make long stripes in the sandy dirt.

I'm curious to know more about what happened to Hector. He appears to have good conformation with a strong shoulder and well-balanced legs. I like his bright, intelligent eye and the bounce in his step, although he is rather highly strung and could present me with some challenges. Amy doesn't know his breeding, but I can easily find that out.

"Tell me more about what happened to Hector and how his owner fits into all this," I ask.

"Hector's owner? He's owned by a syndicate."

"Several owners then. I think someone called Mr. Stanley is the contact?"

"Russell Stanley, you mean." Her teeth are clenched as she rakes with more vigour. "I don't like him."

"I see. Do you know his address?"

"Neal would have it."

"Okay, thanks."

Just as I'm about to turn and walk away, she leans the rake against a wheelbarrow and says, "Russell was having trouble with his partners in the syndicate."

"What do you mean?"

"Grayson, if he was here, could tell you a lot more." Her eyes shimmer as the slightest pools of water gather. "The syndicate members were up in arms about all the bills. Last year wasn't good."

"How many horses did they have?"

"Five."

"So, if you include all expenses, vet bills and trainer's bills, jockey fees and other stuff, they'd be paying about $17,500 per month, at least. And that doesn't include what they paid out to purchase the horses in the first place."

"I haven't done the math. It had a lot to do with the vet bills. Russell wanted Grayson to change vets, to someone other than Emma, but she's a member of the syndicate, so I suppose it made sense to use her. They thought she'd keep the bills down, I guess. But they were way up there and that made Russell angry."

"What happened to Hector?"

"I'm not sure. Best to ask Emma. Some kind of skin disease at first, but then he had a nasty stall accident and cut his legs somehow. These horses can be their own worst enemies sometimes."

"Thanks."

"Russell thought Hector was the syndicate's best prospect. I know that much."

"I can see why he'd be upset then."

As I walk to the trailer that serves as an office for the veterinarian partnership to which Emma belongs, I receive an email to tell me that my mother will be discharged tomorrow and there will be some follow-up care provided in the retirement home, whatever that means. I'll call my mother when she's back at home.

When I reach Emma's office, I find out that she's attending to an emergency. I can't hang around because I need to check on Hector at the farm. Kelly and I will be back at the track tomorrow.

I text Neal and find out that the address for the syndicate's contact is for the farm where Kelly and I found Russell at the bottom of the stairs. I thought the telephone number looked familiar. Nevertheless, I nearly drop my mobile when I read the exact same address. I text Neal back to let him know I happen to be aware that Russell is seriously injured and in hospital. Does he know of any relatives? No, he doesn't.

*   *   *

Hector is calmer. He picks through his bedding to find some hay in the stirred-up mess. Now that he's saner, I shake out another flake of hay for him. Kelly and I almost bump into Linda as she lumbers into the barn carrying a fifty-pound bag of carrots.

46

"Let me help you," I say, as I grab onto the bag of orange net.

"Hector loves carrots. Neal got these, but he says Hector will share with Eagle and Bullet."

"That's nice of him. I should have said 'them', both Neal and Hector."

"He looks pretty settled."

"He was uptight at first, but I think he's calmed down. He's had a good roll though and messed up your excellent grooming. He has bits of wood-shavings and hay stuck to his coat. And see his bandages? They looked amazing when he arrived."

"No problem."

Hector lets out a loud whinny, which rumbles through his large chestnut body like a mini-earthquake.

"He'd be happier if he could see the others, though," I say. Horses are herd animals. I know he wants to join Eagle and Bullet.

"You have a round-pen, don't you?"

"It's behind the barn. Good idea. He'd be able to see his stable-mates if I put them in the small field, which would help. I can do that."

"That'd be great. He should be restricted for a couple of days, maybe more."

I tell her what I found out about Russell. She looks away and watches Hector, who paws at his new hay and makes the messy stall worse.

"Not quite as settled as I thought," I say.

*   *   *

I lie in my bed, wide awake, stirring up my bedding, just like Hector did with his. I toss and turn because I don't understand why I don't try to make things work between William and me. I don't understand, despite my attempts at self-analysis. It's a conundrum because there's a gap, a vacuum in my life that I can't ignore, and it hurts.

When I finally get up and see a layer of snow on the pansies outside, I figure it's a sign telling me I have a frosty heart and that I'm not capable of loving anyone. And that must be right, because I'm able to block it all out and go to the barn to feed the horses.

Hector is interested in Kelly, but doesn't snort at her or shake his head. I'm glad that he doesn't hate dogs. That could be dangerous.

Hector's bandages look brand spanking new. I check the garbage in the feed room and sure enough his old bandages are in there, and there are two pots of meds on the counter. Linda's been here and has already left to start her work-day at the track.

Once Hector is settled outside in the round-pen with hay and water, and Eagle and Bullet are in the small field, and the stalls are cleaned and new bedding put in, Kelly and I make another trip to the track. I go straight to the veterinarians' offices in search of Emma and find her, as she's about to have a mug of coffee. She lets me know Neal gave her the heads up that I want to talk with her since I'm looking into Grayson's death.

"I suppose I shouldn't admit that I had an unpleasant encounter with Grayson," she tells me. "It was brought on by Russell Stanley."

"What was it about?"

"All to do with Hector. Russell and Grayson had high hopes for him, but he suffered from several mild conditions last year as a two-year-old, which affected his training. Grayson and I agreed that it's best to be cautious with young ones, and they certainly should not be pushed when they're not well. They need time to mature and to grow the bone, balance and muscle, so that they are prepared, as well as they can be, to protect themselves from injury when they eventually race. The outcome of all that happened to Hector last year is that he only raced once. This year, Russell was champing at the bit, you might say, wanting to get the horse into the first possible race. But soon after Hector came into the track, he contracted a mild flu-like virus and had inflammation in the ankles. The ultrasound revealed nothing, so I concluded it was linked to the virus. My advice was to treat the horse with anti-inflammatories, and antibiotics as a precaution, and to give him stall rest for a week, supplementing that with hand-walking. I said he should not go back into training for at least three weeks, and obviously not until the inflammation was down."

"I don't get the problem here. This sort of stuff happens all the time."

"The trouble started, apparently, when Russell approached Grayson to ask for a change in veterinarian. Grayson told me all about it because he was pretty upset. Russell said that he'd found a veterinarian willing to prescribe a new drug called Testos. Grayson pointed out that it's a banned substance, since it's a synthetic testosterone and builds muscle and strength, considered to be performance-enhancing. I can only guess how long the withdrawal time would be, or how long the horse would have to be off the drug before it would test negative. If I were to make a stab at it, it would be three months because it's a hormone. Grayson told him it would be a terrible decision. Russell remained determined, so Grayson told him he would have to find a new trainer first, because he would lose his trainer's licence if the horse ran and tested positive while he was in his racing stable. That's how it was left. But I was called the next day because the horse had injured himself in his stall. Grayson didn't know what had happened. Russell blamed him, even though he wasn't present to hear my assessment. His absence got Grayson thinking. He wondered out-loud to me if the drug, Testos, had been administered the evening before and that Hector had reacted to it. He asked me if that could be possible. I told him yes, there is always the potential for a drug reaction. The other possibility is that Russell had another veterinarian compound a medication, and the horse had a reaction to one of the components. I'm not accusing here, since

I have absolutely no evidence. I'm just pointing out possibilities."

"If it was a medication compounded for Hector by the veterinarian, it would have been customized for him and could have included a combination of drugs such as an anabolic steroid, a pain-killer, and other things that Russell wanted. Wouldn't this have shown up in the bloodwork?"

"The results didn't give us any answers. If he was medicated, the tests didn't identify the drug or drugs."

"You've been so helpful. Thank you. I've taken up a lot of your time, but I want to ask you something else about Grayson's death."

"I've got about two minutes."

"Grayson died of an overdose of ketamine. How easy would it be for a non-veterinarian, like him, to get hold of that drug?"

"Difficult to steal from a veterinarian, if that's what you're asking. Everything I transport in my truck is double-locked, and when I'm accessing the drugs, my assistant supervises the truck so I don't have to keep locking and unlocking when I'm treating a client. I also keep an inventory. I mark out anything I've taken, or tell my assistant to. And then this has to match the bills I issue to clients which, of course, include all the medications I've administered, or dispensed to the trainer. I think the rest of the veterinarians would follow similar procedures in order to comply with regulations."

"Shouldn't be that easy, then."

"Shouldn't be. But you never know. Have to run."

"Before you go, I just have to ask if you were here the evening Grayson died?"

"No, I was home with my husband. You can check."

"Thanks a lot. I hope you have a good day."

The warm sun is melting the snow, and I dodge various muddy puddles on my way to pick up a cup of tea from the cafeteria. I notice the security office nearby, which prompts me to drop in. I want to know if anyone saw anything the night when Hector got injured.

Although the person I talk to is courteous, I don't get anywhere. There's limited surveillance of the barns at night, since all the gates to the backstretch are closed, and there are no security cameras, other than those installed by individual trainers. I know Grayson didn't have any in his barn.

Just as I turn towards the door to leave, a security guard emerges from the back of the office.

"Hey, are you the one asking about that trainer, Grayson?"

"Yes," I reply, and turn back from the door.

"I called the police, but they've not got back to me. I want to tell someone."

"Okay. I'd be happy to hear whatever it is you have to say. But tell the police too."

"Yup. I was the one who found the poor devil. Just got back to work today. Had some time off. I'll talk to you outside." We trudge down the wooden steps from the security office and stand in the sunshine on the uneven, puddled parking lot. "I've got a good eye. I'm observant, being a security guard, I should be." He straightens his long back and stands with his legs apart.

"I'd say that would be an excellent quality to have in your business."

"I saw a couple of pens on the left-hand side of his desk. That points to him being left-handed. But his left sleeve was rolled up."

"That's a good observation."

"And I heard it was ketamine what killed him. If you don't know already, there's this guy who hangs around outside the south gate. You can get stuff off him. So, doesn't have to be one of them vets what killed him. Could be anyone."

"Thanks."

"That doesn't help, does it?"

"It does, for sure. Thank you. If you think of anything else, let me know."

He's right. It could be anyone. I haven't narrowed the field. In fact, I've made things more complicated by wrapping Hector into all of this. And although I still want to find out how Russell ended up at the bottom of his stairs, that incident probably has nothing to do with Grayson's death. I've learned before that I can mislead myself by a conviction that events must be linked, only to find out that they're not, at least not in the way I imagined them to be. So, proceed with caution, I tell myself. Where do I go from here, though?

*   *   *

As soon as Kelly and I are back in the kitchen after our quick check on the horses, I text William. I don't know why it takes so much courage to ask if he can come to the farm this evening. I get a quick reply saying that Ramona has only just returned, and he's too busy. His cold shoulder gives me the shivers.

Kelly puts her head on my lap as I read an email from the adoption reunite site. They need me to fill out one page of their form again. I can't think what that's about, but it reminds me to call my mother. She should be in her recliner by the window overlooking the sea by now.

"How are you?"

"Much better. I'm chuffed with how I've bounced back from having my head cut open."

"You sound a lot better. What's the next step?"

"More scans I think."

"I hear that you're to start radiotherapy."

"I don't think I will be. I was told this morning that they thought they got it all."

"That's splendid news."

"Enough of this. Have you found your sister?"

"Not yet. The adoption reunite site just asked me to fill out part of their form again. I can't think why. I'm sure I completed it correctly."

"Ah."

"That sounds ominous. You know why, don't you?"

"Oh dear."

"Don't just say 'oh dear', that doesn't help. There's something else I need to know. Let me guess. Stan isn't her father." I chuckle and sit back in my chair, but there's a heavy and revealing silence at the other end of the phone. I lean forward. "He isn't, is he?"

"No."

"Wow. You should have told me."

"I could only cope with one piece of the picture at a time."

"Mm. So, how did you manage that, with Stan's vice-grip on every moment of your life?"

"He went to work, and I had to go grocery shopping. I wasn't under his nose all the time. He'd inquisition me, but he wasn't able to control all that I did. He didn't lock me up."

"How did you meet this other man?"

"It doesn't really matter, does it? But I'll tell you, if you want to know."

"I suppose I do, although he has nothing to do with me."

"I met him in the grocers. Stan had told me not to go out because I had a nasty swollen black eye, and a cut on my cheekbone which looked angry. I put some cream on it but it was getting more painful. I had to go out because I didn't have enough potatoes for Stan's dinner. So, I put a head-scarf on and hoped no-one would ask. It was okay until I was in the queue to pay, and this man was behind me. I had to turn around towards him to empty my cart. To cut a long story short, he said I should get my cut seen to. He talked to me again in the parking lot and I started to cry. I felt so embarrassed as well as stressed. Stan would have been furious beyond belief if he'd known what was going on. Anyway, it started a friendship that developed, over a long time, into more than that. When I got pregnant, shortly after you left, I knew the baby was his."

"Did this man know?"

"Of course not. I couldn't possibly tell him, or anyone, but I put his name down on the birth certificate."

"Honesty prevailed for once."

"I sort of panicked. I just had to put down his name."

"How come Stan didn't find out?"

"He wanted nothing to do with the baby. He wanted me to get rid of it."

"He knew it wasn't his baby, that's what I think."

"So, on your silly form, you'll have to put a different name for the father. It's Joshua Kent."

"Did you love him?"

"Once I knew I was pregnant, I told him I couldn't see him ever again. And you're right, Stan knew it wasn't his baby. That's the reason he beat me up so badly. Long story, which you don't need to hear."

"It must have been so hard to give up the baby for adoption."

"It was. She was beautiful. But it wasn't as hard as living with the nightmare of knowing that Stan had hurt you right under my nose, and that it could happen all over again to this lovely child."

"Let's not go there." I can hear muffled sobbing. This can't be good for someone recovering from having had a brain tumour removed. "So, his name is Joshua Kent. Got it. I will fill the form out again." His name is scribbled in a spidery scrawl on a scrap of paper in front of me.

"How's William?" She sniffs loudly into the mouthpiece of the phone.

"He's okay. He's busy at work."

"Mm. Meg, don't lose someone you love. I have so many regrets. Don't end up like me, wondering what your life could have been if you'd made the right decisions."

"Never mind about me. Let's focus on finding your other daughter."

"Promise me you won't try to find her father?"

"If my sister wants to find her father, we can't stop her. You'll have to brace yourself for that possibility."

"I hadn't thought of that."

"She might already be on that quest."

"Oh."

We end our conversation with small talk about Cooper, who's chewing the cord to the landline phone until I hang it up out of reach. He saunters away with his tail in the air.

5

Hospital Visit

Today is bright, sunny and still. Soft warmth surrounds me and Kelly as we walk to the barn. The ground is spongy, and the grass is perking up and will grow today. Robins and goldfinches sing, but are drowned out for a couple of minutes by a low-flying group of honking geese whose wings sound as if they could do with a spot of oil.

Linda has left me some fuel for my wings: a tea which is still warm enough, along with a carrot muffin, placed on the countertop in the feed room. Hector paces in his stall, and asks for his breakfast. I watch as he eats and wonder if I should offer to buy him. I have a constrained budget for the operation of the farm, for the horse-racing business and for my personal expenses. Finances are tighter than they were because I no longer work at the Vannersville Humane Society. But Murray, Frank's brother (my brother-in-law), is determined to secure at least some of Frank's millions on my behalf. He's facing some challenges, he says, because of the banking laws in the Cayman Islands.

I shouldn't encumber myself with additional expenses in the probably vain hope that Murray will eventually get clearance for me to access the funds.

I sit down at the kitchen table with the carrot muffin and a fresh mug of tea. A knock at the door startles me and Kelly, although she stops herself almost mid-bark because she realizes it's Murray. He must have known I was thinking about him. He visits quite often, which I usually enjoy. After all, he's the closest I have to family in Canada. I let him in and he sets down two large teas and two breakfast sandwiches. I decide to wrap the carrot muffin up for later.

"I came to see how you are, and ask you how your mother's doing," Murray says as he lifts Cooper off the table and puts him onto the floor. William would have brought an oatmeal raisin cookie for Kelly, and she looks disappointed. So I dig out treats for her and Cooper.

Murray stares at me with unwavering intensity as I ramble on and bring him up to date on everything I know about my mother and my half-sister. He asks a few questions to which I don't have answers. We sit for a couple of minutes in silence as Cooper rubs against his legs and Kelly flops under the table, having eaten her biscuit and given up on the appearance of a cookie.

"And how's William?"

"Fine."

"He's living here now, isn't he?"

"What's this about, Murray?"

"You like to get straight to the point, don't you?" He swirls the remainder of his tea around in his cup.

"Why your question about William?"

"I feel responsible."

"What do you mean? You're not responsible for me, that's for sure."

"I feel responsible for ensuring that Frank's money, once I finally get things sorted, goes into your hands and no-one else's, no hangers-on."

"So, you think William is like Chuck, and just after my money."

"Do you know for a fact that he isn't?"

"Murray, I know Frank was your brother and I appreciate all that you're doing to get his money here, but my relationships are my business."

"But Chuck...",

"But Chuck nothing. I don't want to talk about him or William with you, Murray. He and William are completely different."

"Both of them were drug addicts."

"Murray!" He must have done some digging into William's past, because I've not revealed to him that William had an issue with drugs for a while after his wife died. That was several years ago. He's turned his life around since then. He's in good physical shape, has his legal firm back on track and has restored his ethical values and his professionalism. He has recently returned to his beloved hobby of watercolour painting. And I cannot imagine for one second that his interest in me has to do with Frank's money. If he got wind of Murray's accusation, he would be devastated and wouldn't want to see me ever again. I shudder.

"You shuddered. You see, you've come around and realize I'm right to have these concerns."

"You're wrong. I shuddered for the opposite reason. I'm dumbfounded that you could think this way about William."

"You have to agree that I should make sure that Frank's money gets into the right hands, that is, yours."

"If you want the money, you can have it." I pick up the cups, paper bags and napkins, wipe the table with a flourish and toss the cloth into the sink. Kelly has her ears flat on her head and doesn't move a muscle. But her eyes follow me.

"Now you've insulted me. I just want what's best for you."

"If this money is going to cause friction, I want nothing to do with it."

"That's ridiculous. You're just saying that."

"No, I mean it. I don't want you to malign my friends, question motives, spy on people, set rules or any other nonsense, all in the name of protecting me and or making sure the money gets into the right hands as you put it."

"I'm doing it all for you."

"Murray, let's drop this for now, and we'll talk later. I have a lot on my plate, and I'm sure you do too, so let's give it a rest for a bit."

I'm relieved when he goes, and my audible sigh raises Kelly from her spot under the table. I would have preferred to be under there with her during Murray's visit. And he'll be back again soon, no doubt.

As I lean over the sink to rinse out the cloth, I see Hector kick up his heels in the round-pen, and Eagle and Bullet trot along the fence-line closest to him. Hector looks the epitome of the classic thoroughbred. There is a classiness about him, along with a noble spirit, strong bone structure and good muscle. I'd have thought that Russell would want to hold on to him at all costs.

On a whim, I call the hospital and ask to talk to Russell and they put me through to his phone. He answers after one ring, which takes me off-guard. I just assumed he wouldn't want to talk to anyone for quite a while. He asks me how Kelly is and then says he'd like me to visit. He's allowed visitors now, but no-one has come to see him, and he's bored out of his mind.

*　*　*

We make it to the hospital by early afternoon, Kelly dressed in her therapy-dog gear and me with my volunteer badge. I make sure that I have the necessary approvals for us to enter Russell's room, and his eyes light up when he sees us. I should say, when he sees Kelly. She sits next to the bed and Russell pats her head. He rummages in the drawer of his nightstand and finds a packet of crackers for her.

His long, almost white hair looks shorter and thicker than I remember, but his beard is just as unkempt as it was when I first met him.

"How are you?" I ask.

"I'm relieved Kelly's okay. I didn't look after her very well." He pats her head again.

"Kelly's doing fine. But, how are you?"

"Not bad. Neal tells me that Hector is doing well at your farm. That's good. I didn't know you're into thoroughbreds."

"I didn't know you are. What happened to you? Do you know?"

"I fell down the stairs."

"No, you didn't. I found you and that's not what it looked like to me."

"The police told me I was lying at the bottom of the stairs and that a neighbour found me there. So, that was you."

"Don't they think it suspicious?"

"No reason for them to."

"I do. You had shoes on that didn't look like indoor shoes to me. And there was no trace of blood, or anything that looked damaged, anywhere on the stairs."

"I see."

"You must have some idea of what happened."

"You've come to pester me with questions." He leans back on his pillow and I almost feel guilty for spoiling the visit he'd looked forward to.

"I'm the kind of person who gets straight to the point," I say. "And I like to find out the truth, even if it's hard to face."

"That's the trouble. The truth is hard. And I'm too old for this shit."

"What shit?"

"People being angry with me."

"Why are they angry with you? And who are they?"

"Okay, I give in. Stop all your questions, and I'll tell you. You can sit down, bring that chair over. I've been involved in thoroughbred horse-racing and breeding for about forty years, but most of the time it was only in a small way."

"What does 'in a small way' mean?"

"Usually no more than two or three horses at the racetrack at any one time. Before I lived abroad, I bred my own racehorses, but I also bought yearlings from the sale in September."

"No claims?"

"I don't like claiming horses. Also, having my own farm meant I could look after the horses until they were ready to race, and get to know them and make sure they were broken in properly and had the right handling."

"That can make a lot of difference. What's this got to do with people being angry with you?"

"I'm getting to that. You in a rush or something?" I'm not sure if he's poking fun at me or if he's irritated. He has his eyes closed as he leans back onto the pillow. "Because I'm a long-time racehorse owner and known in the business, I was asked to talk to a group of people at some kind of reception, to give an overview of what's entailed in being a thoroughbred racehorse owner in Ontario. Someone else talked about breeding. And other people explained ways of purchasing horses, such as at the sale, by claiming and through trainers who might have an owner looking to sell. They mentioned syndicates and how it's a good way to go because it spreads the risk."

"Was anyone trying to set up a syndicate at the time?"

"No, and that was a problem because there were several people there who were interested and that's how this goddam stuff all started." He opens his eyes and stares at the ceiling.

"You set up a syndicate?"

"I hate partnerships. I've been burned by them before, so I don't know what in hell's name I was thinking, especially at my age. I don't want to deal with difficult people any more, I've had enough of it."

"Who are these people, and what happened?"

"The group eventually shook down to be too small. Two people changed their minds later, when it came to signing stuff, so I had to scramble. We'd agreed on a syndicate of five and that we'd have five horses in training. There were three of us. They'd agreed to use Grayson as the trainer, so I asked him if he'd join, and he agreed, and he suggested Emma, a vet, might join. She'd always wanted to be an owner, but never found the time to do the research and was apprehensive about the risk. After all, she's seen all the god-awful things that can happen to horses."

"So, Emma, Grayson, and you, and the other two?"

"Philippa Woolsey, about my age, was at the session and was the one who talked about breeding. She left the business when her husband died several years ago, and she said she missed racing and wanted to get back into it. They'd always raised their own stock. Her husband had been a fountain of knowledge about lines, conformation, statistics. She thought the syndicate would be a good opportunity."

"The other person?"

"A new, young guy, Oscar Smedley. He's only about 35 years old. He owns an internet financial business, and he drives fast cars. He got very excited about the Ontario Sires Stakes Program. I did my best to explain that the chances of winning one of those races were pretty slim, even if you do all your homework and buy what you think is a superb horse. He would not let his enthusiasm be dampened. And he was the one that propelled me to set up the syndicate. He said if I set one up, he'd be in, and that he'd bring the syndicate luck because he's never failed at any venture he's been involved in.

He also said he would chronicle every step of the journey on his blog. He believes in marketing, and he said this would be good for the horse-racing industry, which, in his opinion, needs a bloody great boost. I couldn't disagree with him."

"I still don't have a sense of what happened to make everyone angry with you."

"Get us some coffee, and I'll tell you when you get back. Kelly can keep me company while you're gone." He turns his gaze to her and pats her head.

I hesitate, but Kelly seems fine with the situation. She's in her therapy-dog mode and is conscientious about her job. It doesn't take me long to pick up a decaf coffee, a tea, and a couple of bananas.

"Picking up where I left off: Grayson guided me in the selection of the five horses. Oscar ruled they had to be Ontario sired, but the others didn't state any preferences. Hector was one of the horses, and I thought he was the most promising. We had five horses in training by about the middle of June last year."

"Then the bills would start coming in."

"Yep. And they all knew this would be the case, about $3,500 each per month, depending on what issues there were. Often more. It wasn't long before things started to go wrong. It began when a weird virus swept through most of Grayson's barn, and the horses had to be kept segregated to help stop its spread. It affected the respiratory tract and set all five horses back. Hector was the sickest. We eventually got over that and then a skin disease erupted. Our five horses suffered by far the most, and Hector was really under the weather. Emma advised Grayson to ease up on the training for five days, I think it was. Do you want to hear all the things that caused us trouble? We had foot issues, colic, eye infections, coughs, girth sores and much more. By November there'd been peanuts in revenue and a whole pile of expenses."

"They blamed you?"

"Sure did. They also blamed Grayson. He was the trainer, and they thought he must be doing it all wrong. Oscar told me he thought Grayson was useless and said that it's all right for the trainer. He still gets paid his training fees while the owners just fork out money and get nothing. I pointed out that Grayson was also a member of the syndicate, but Oscar said that's not the same because most of the expense is the trainer's fees, so he's not actually coughing up as much as the rest of us. He was seeing red. Philippa couldn't understand why things had gone so badly. She blamed me and Grayson. She said her horses had always done pretty well at the track, she'd never owned such underperformers. They wanted out, and Grayson and I wanted no more to do with the syndicate. We got two of the horses claimed by dropping them down to low-level races."

"You had three horses left."

"We couldn't even get them to the races to get a chance at them being claimed."

"Where did they go for the winter?"

"I looked after them at my farm and didn't bill anyone, even though I'm not rolling in it. I think Oscar and Philippa assumed the syndicate had folded. But there's a termination clause, and part of it states that the horses have to be sold for the syndicate to be dissolved. Bills started coming in when the three horses went back to the track, which meant Oscar and Philippa were spitting nails. Now they're demanding that the horses be dropped down sharply into low-level claiming races to stop the bleeding. But, of course, the horses aren't ready to race yet, so the training fees keep mounting up, as well as the vet bills."

"And Hector got injured. When I asked Emma about this, she claimed you approached Grayson asking him to change vets because you wanted Hector to receive a prohibited drug called Testos, and she went as far as to suggest that someone could have administered the drug to Hector the night he got injured."

"That woman has a nerve. If anyone gave him the drug, it was her."

"Why would she do that? She'd be risking her career."

"She's a crafty one. Don't believe everything she tells you. I wouldn't be surprised if she can mix that stuff with something else, making it hard to detect."

"You think Emma was responsible?"

"That's right."

"Mm. It didn't do any good because he's not going to race for some time."

"That's why I said I would sell him. And that's what I'm trying to do. Neal took him on when Grayson died and said he'd help to find someone. But it will be hard to find someone who has the patience and resources to take him on, given the state he's in."

"What are you asking for him?"

"Five thousand. It's peanuts for a horse of his breeding. I'm sure he'll race one day, just not soon, that's all."

I almost tell him right there and then that I'll buy him, but I have some more questions.

"Do you have any idea who might have wanted to kill Grayson?"

"Wasn't it suicide?"

"There's a possibility it was murder."

"Shit. I hope it wasn't anything to do with this syndicate. That would be tragic. After all, trainers can only do so much, they're not magicians. The quality of the horse, both physical and mental, is by far the major factor. You know that."

"It helps to have a good trainer, though. Bryce, a trainer in the same barn, accused Grayson of using performance-enhancing drugs. He was convinced of it because whenever he raced against him, he lost."

Russell shuts his eyes, lies back and chuckles. "Don't make me laugh, it makes my head ache. That no-good loser, Bryce. He has no idea what he's doing. He has zero horse-sense."

"Do you know why he'd accuse Grayson?"

"Envy, jealousy. I don't know." He turns his head to look at me. "I'm very tired now. You should talk to Amy about Grayson's training program. I'm sure she'll enlighten you, you know, his lead groom." His eyes water, and he shuts them, and that's that. I leave with several other questions I should have asked.

Kelly and I visit a couple of other patients on our way out, and I'm sure my dog has a swagger as we walk out to the truck. She loves her work as a therapy-dog and I should come more often.

I don't have any idea who would want to hurt Russell. He's trying to sell Hector and I can't see a member of the syndicate doing anything to hinder that. I know they're angry with him, but what would they have to gain by seriously injuring the man?

Back at the farm, with everyone fed and watered, except for me, I sit down at the kitchen table with my laptop and rework my budget. I would like to be able to afford to buy Hector, and most important, to restore him back to health and get him to the races. His big, bright eyes and gleaming chestnut coat, as well as his energy and vibrancy, have made me a fan. But my finances don't look good. Cooper tries to help by chasing the cursor. I can't allow myself to be distracted. I need to get creative about how to trim expenses.

Nothing miraculous happens. I fold my arms on the table and put my head down.

A syndicate is a good idea, but I don't want to be partners with anyone. And the new tax laws have made it harder for small-time racehorse owners like me. I must remember these new rules when I draft various scenarios. One thing in my favour is that I can bring any racehorse home if I have to: where it costs a lot less to care for the horse than at the racetrack or a boarding stable.

I give up on my budget. I got nowhere.

William hasn't contacted me.

I can manage without him or anyone else. I don't need partners in my life or in my racehorse business.

Why do I feel unsettled, and even a little queasy, whenever I think of William, then? I'm saved from my thoughts by a timid knock at the door. Linda is here very late in the day.

"I came back because I want to talk to you," she says. "I hope that's okay?"

"Of course it's okay."

"Here's a tea and carrot muffin. I've just had my dinner."

"That's thoughtful, Linda. I haven't had anything. What's up?"

"I didn't want to send a text 'cause it's not my business."

"What isn't?"

"Hector."

"Are you concerned about him being here?"

"Nope. I'm worried about him not being here. Neal and I think you should buy him."

"Why?"

"We like him. Neal can't buy him. He's got too many parts in too many horses and he hasn't got a farm where Hector can go to get better. He'd have to pay a lot."

"I like him too but I'm not sure I can afford him."

"Russell might come down. Amy says the syndicate guys want out, like, yesterday."

"It's ongoing expenses that would be the kicker."

"He's only three. He could have this year off. And Rose and Speed might make enough to pay for his training next year."

"You know I can't count on that. But, Linda, I will think about it. In fact, I was thinking about it just now. He is rather stunning and I have to admit that I do like him."

"That's good, then."

"Hector's coat looks wonderful, by the way. Do you groom him every morning?"

"Only a quick brush. I don't have time for Eagle and Bullet though."

"Goodness, no. I'll have another go soon. They were in a terrible mess when they came back from their brief stay away." They're not groomed up to Linda's standard, that's for sure.

"Is William around? I didn't see his car, but was hoping to say hello."

"No, not here this evening. Did you need him for something?"

"Mom wants to do her will. I thought William could tell her what to do."

"There are lots of resources on-line."

"Mom doesn't have a computer and doesn't want me to have to bother with it. I'm sure it's simple, but she wants a lawyer."

"Okay, I'll let William know."

I don't want to let William know. I want to pretend he doesn't exist because every time I think of him, my stomach knots.

It takes determination to eat the muffin because I don't have an appetite. I'm tempted to offer it to Kelly, but she's had her dinner and doesn't need it. I pick a bit off the top and the sweetness tastes good and perks up my taste buds. I finish it, shut my laptop and tell Kelly we're going out for a short walk.

6

The Syndicate

The dawn is dark, dismal and drizzly. The sun must be just above the horizon, but I can't see it. As Kelly and I step out of the kitchen, I marvel at the daffodils with their tall, pointed shoots poking up to the sky. How these bulbs survived being frozen in the ground for the winter, I don't know. I'd forgotten Chuck had planted them in the bed near the kitchen door, at the base of a few scraggy shrubs that were put in when Frank and I bought the farm.

Hector will have no shelter from the drizzle if I put him into the round-pen, so he'll have to stay in his stall until the weather improves. The air, while warmer than it has been, still has a bite to it, and if he gets wet, he could get chilled. Eagle and Bullet have a run-in shed in their field. Hector isn't happy when I leave the barn, but I can't help it. I tell him I'm doing the best I can and trying to help him, but it doesn't sink in.

The live people behind the adoption reunite site give the impression that they're doing what they can to assist me. I've had a few emails with more questions, and one earlier this morning that asked if I would permit my email address to be given to someone in their database who they believe is a match. I gave my okay, but not without some trepidation. What is it like to have a sister? What if we don't get along?

William's face appears on my phone. I think he's asking me to do something, but I don't answer. I've worked extra hard this morning at pretending he doesn't exist. It's as if I can't cope with the stress of making our relationship work. I've convinced myself that going to the track to delve into my investigation into Grayson's death will calm the turmoil.

*   *   *

Amy has a few minutes to talk with me while she waits for a horse to come back from a timed work.

"Can you tell me more about Hector's injuries?" I ask as I hand her a coffee.

"Some. Soon after the horses came back to the track this year, another one of these viruses hit some of them. Hector seems to be sensitive to them. He was out of sorts and had swollen ankles. With so much pressure from the syndicate members, Grayson asked Emma if there was anything she could do to help him get over it. She prescribed a compound she made up herself. That night is when Hector got injured."

"You look like you're about to cry."

"You would too, if you were me. I miss Grayson so much." Her mouth curves down at the corners and she looks away.

"I'm sorry. It must be difficult for you. I'm glad you're helping me to find out what happened to Grayson. He must have blamed Emma for Hector's injuries?"

"Yes. Grayson believed Hector had a reaction to the meds, perhaps colic. The pain must have made him roll and thrash around, and that's how he got so badly injured. Grayson was furious about it and told me that Emma's bill for the meds was crazy high, which made him even madder at her."

"I don't think it's any secret that another trainer in this barn, Bryce, accused Grayson of using performance-enhancing drugs."

"That's a laugh."

"Can you tell me more?"

"Bryce doesn't know one end of a horse from the other. Grayson was in a different league. But you know it can be a bit of a vicious circle. Bryce has poor horses and gets poor performance, so owners aren't going to give him good horses to train, are they?"

"True."

"Grayson was ahead of his time." She turns away, her lip trembling. "Sorry, I just can't believe Grayson's not here any more."

I wait until she turns to face me again.

"What do you mean by he 'was ahead of his time'?"

"He believed in training the whole athlete. He offered a premium package for those owners willing to pay extra. Before those horses came to the track to do regular training, they went through a course of basic dressage at a farm down south. They learned balance, focus, trust, and developed their back muscles. He believed in it. He had them on a special diet with vitamins and supplements, just natural stuff. He wanted Russell to have the syndicate's horses in it, but there was no money for it. Grayson especially wanted Hector to go through it."

"Do you think it made a difference?"

"You never really know, do you? Because you can't compare the same horse. But the horses that came in from there sure looked great. Dappled coats, good weight and eager to work."

"It sounds like it was probably worth the investment then."

"Grayson was a real horseman, not like that Bryce guy." She turns away again, as a tear drips down her left cheek. She watches a horse, with his exercise rider on his back, walk down the shedrow and into a stall, the rider being careful to duck his head in the doorway. The rider dismounts and Amy's there with a lead rein, and takes the horse out to the waiting hotwalker. It's time for me to leave.

I try to find Emma, but I'm told she's busy with an emergency case and isn't likely to be available for an hour. My chat with Amy has put Emma at the top of the list of suspects, which grows daily. Other possible suspects include Philippa and Oscar, since they're members of the syndicate and were angry with Grayson. I call Philippa and, once she understands that I'm looking into Grayson's death, she's eager to meet with me and invites me over for a coffee after lunch.

Lunch hasn't crossed my mind, but Kelly's need for a walk and drink has. I drive away from the barns and head for home. The drizzle has fizzled into a fine mist, and the grey clouds race across the sky as if eager to find a new place to soak with the rest of their contents.

Kelly runs around the paddock as Eagle and Bullet watch from the small field. I enter the barn and snap a lead rein onto Hector's halter. He prances at my side, but doesn't yank or pull, as I lead him to the round-pen. He kicks up his heels twice after I let him go, but then stands, with his head held high, to watch Eagle, Bullet and Kelly. After I've tossed a couple of flakes of hay over the rails, I call Kelly and we take a break in the house. It seems quiet and empty despite Cooper's loud purring. I've had no visitors today. As I hang up my barn jacket, I notice one of William's scarves draped over the peg. I have a yearning to take it down and wrap it around me, as my eyes water and my stomach flutters. I'm just hungry, that's all.

* * *

After a quick break, Kelly and I get back in the truck. I have time to pick up a sandwich on the way to Philippa Woolsey's place. I'll feel better if I eat.

An avenue of aged, stately maple trees leads up to the front door of Philippa's stone house. A demure, uniformed maid answers the door and shows me into an expansive sunroom that overlooks acres of rolling fields, with a forest in the distance. Although the day is dull and damp, the sunroom is bright and airy. Wicker furniture with vibrant-coloured cushions is arranged around six glass tables. Fresh tulips in yellows and pinks fill a white vase placed in the middle of each table. This house was built for entertaining.

Philippa greets me with a firm hand-shake and asks the maid to make coffee, and tea for me. I'm glad she asked me what my preference is. But as soon as we start to talk about Grayson, Russell and the syndicate, the lines on her face become more pronounced, her eyes narrow and her voice deepens.

"I'm not at all surprised that trainer, Grayson took his own life," she says. "He ought to be ashamed of himself."

"What do you mean?"

"What do I mean? I mean the results were appalling. He selected five horses which he assured me had great potential, and not one of them won a race last year. When my husband was alive, we bred and raced, and we never had terrible results like that."

"Trainers can only do so much, though."

"Trainers, who are given the job of selecting quality racehorses, can do a lot. Grayson didn't have what it took. And Russell Stanley pushed me into becoming a member of the syndicate. I'd given up all involvement in breeding and racing. No horses out there any more." She waves a hand towards the view of the fields.

"I heard that you'd expressed an interest in continuing to be involved in racing, that you missed it."

"Who'd you hear that from? Let me guess, that Russell man. He had a bee in his bonnet about setting up syndicates. He made quite the pitch for it at a session I went to. I gave a short talk on breeding, but in his spiel, he went on and on about syndicates. He approached me afterwards, and I got bamboozled into joining."

"How did that happen?"

"I let my guard down." She looks down into her lap where she wrings her hands. "The memories of good times at the track swirled around me and I got caught up in the excitement of the evening. But it was a big mistake. Neither Russell nor Grayson had a clue what they were doing. And we, the other members of the syndicate, paid dearly for it out of our own pockets. Nothing to show for all the expense. Nothing."

I ask her about the horses she and her husband had owned and races they'd won. Her eyes light up as she relates some highlights of their breeding and racing history. She offers to show me around the house and stables, and invites Kelly to accompany us when we're outside.

The stables echo with our voices, the stone walls damp and cold. Each stall door has a plaque with a horse's name etched into tarnished brass. The emptiness and silence, the dinginess and dankness, make me think of ghosts, of lives passed, of loneliness and emptiness without animals. Without people. Without William. I move towards the door to leave, and Philippa follows with Kelly close behind.

*   *   *

I'm glad to be on my way home. Perhaps I'll be back in time to see Linda.

But she must have come and gone. Hector is back in his stall with fresh bandages on. He looks less agitated as he stands, more or less still, and chews on his hay. I find another large bag of carrots in the feed room.

But, despite the reassurance that all the animals are okay, and the comforting warmth of scattered rays of sunshine that pierce the patchy skies, I have a grey cloud hovering over me that follows me everywhere. The farm has been my haven, the animals my companions, but there's something lacking. It's not enough any more.

* * *

I pick up a message from my landline phone. My mother's voice rambles on with muddled words, but I decipher that she's talking about money from the sale of the house, that she's only permitted to send a certain amount each year, that she'll check it out, and that she needs my banking information. Since it's getting late in England, I tell myself that I'll call her tomorrow. I have no energy to even think about a conversation with her right now.

After a walk around the large field with Kelly, I lead Eagle and Bullet into their stalls, feed the dog and Cooper, grab a piece of toast and a mug of hot chocolate, and sit in a recliner in the family room. But I can't relax. I get up and give the rest of the toast to Kelly in the kitchen. I make myself finish the hot chocolate and grab my jacket.

* * *

Kelly and I walk into Russell's room in the hospital where the lighting is subdued and silence reigns, in stark contrast to the brilliant light and the incessant noise that intrudes from the corridor. Russell rouses from a nap and tells me he'll be discharged tomorrow.

"I meant to ask you what your diagnosis is."

"Just a blow to the head. It needed stitches, but the reason they have me in here is that I had some signs of concussion. Since I live alone, they kept me in for observation. No big deal."

"You told me you fell down the stairs. That's not true, is it?"

"So, this isn't a social visit. This is more of the inquisition."

"It's both."

"You can get me a cup of decaf coffee then."

When I return, he's patting Kelly's head as she looks at his nightstand.

"Your dog remembers I had some crackers in here last time. I'll see what I can find. Ah, a cookie, a plain one. That should be okay. Here you go." He gives Kelly her treat, which she takes gently from his hand. "Such a nice dog."

"So, what happened to you?"

"I'm embarrassed, if you want the truth."

"I do."

"It was a woman."

"What do you mean?"

He inhales deeply. "A woman came into the old barn. It was dark in there, you see, and she was dressed in black, but I could tell it was a woman. But I couldn't make out who she was. As she walked towards me, she yelled something. I can only remember one word and it sounded like 'Grayson' and then I felt a whack on the side of my head, probably with something like a baseball bat. I fell through the trap-door in the floor and hit the cold stone floor of the barn down below. I remember Kelly licked my face, which might have helped me come around. I was able to get up and stumble into the house. I must have collapsed at the bottom of the stairs. I was trying to get to a phone, I suppose, although I don't recall reaching the house. That's it."

"Have you told the police?"

"No. There's nothing to report. I fell through the trap-door. I only told you because it might help you find out what happened to Grayson since I think my attacker believes I had something to do with his death."

"Did you?"

"Only inasmuch as I set up that goddam syndicate. There's gotta be a link. One of the members must have killed him."

"To me, it doesn't seem like a sufficient motive to murder someone."

"Money can turn people into monsters capable of doing terrible things."

"I know, but there wasn't that much money involved, really."

"It's also a matter of pride. Oscar bragged to everyone in the world that he owned racehorses and that he was going to win big. He told me he'd set up a blog. I guess that's a site on the internet. Anyway, he made a big thing of it even though I warned all of them, and especially him, that horse-racing is a chancy business."

"What about Philippa and Emma? Philippa told me you bamboozled her into joining the syndicate. She's mad at both you and Grayson."

"She said she was bamboozled, did she? Interesting. Philippa approached me after the talks and questions were over, with a drink in her hand, and told me she missed being involved. She wanted me to know how successful she and her husband had been, but she admitted she didn't have the eye for conformation or the knowledge of pedigrees that her husband had. So, the syndicate idea was attractive to her, she said."

"What about Emma?"

"She came on board later. Grayson suggested Emma. She was aware of the risks. But I don't think she realized how expensive it can be to have a racehorse in training."

"You think that there could be a link between Grayson's death and the attack on you?"

"I don't know. My attacker said something like 'Grayson' before hitting me, but didn't explain, or check on me after I fell as far as I know, so I don't know what to make of it." He closes his eyes and tells me he's not talking anymore.

* * *

Yet another day dawns without William in my life. As I lie in bed, Cooper licks my ear as if he knows I should be feeding the horses. Kelly looks at me, and wags her tail in slow motion revealing her confusion that I'm not out and about, but expecting that I'll come to my senses at any moment. Cooper sits on my stomach and starts an elaborate grooming ritual, but it only lasts two minutes because I sit up, pat Kelly and get out of bed, albeit with little enthusiasm.

The sleet slaps me in the face as we leave the house for the barn. Winter's attempt at a comeback. The icy wind rattles the barn door and rushes past me as I open it. I pull the large door shut, using most of my strength, and let the warm barn air wrap around me. The horses are keen for their feed. Whinnies echo off the barn walls as Hector paws at his rubber mat. Linda hasn't been here because his bandages are dirty and have slipped a bit. I hope she's okay. I feed them all and, taking advantage of Hector being distracted, I take the bandages off. The wounds are deep and raw. It will take a long time for them to fill in and for the skin to grow back, but they don't seem to constrict his movement or affect his mood.

Linda appears at the stall doorway.

"I'm late. Neal had an emergency. One of the other horses Grayson trained, and Neal has now, was down in his stall and they couldn't get him up. Neal wanted me to help."

"Is the horse okay?"

"Emma's checked him and they can't find anything wrong."

"What do you think?"

"I don't think Emma should be compounding meds. She gave Grayson a med she made up for that horse because he had a cough. He'd only coughed once or twice. It would've been better to wait and see. He didn't seem to be congested. But I'm not a vet, so what do

I know?" Linda dumps her bag on the floor with a thud and walks into the stall to check Hector.

"I just took the bandages off because they'd slipped a bit. I took advantage of the fact that Hector is food-obsessed."

"He is, yeah."

"I am thinking of buying him."

"That's great. He's happy here. I'm sure he likes you. You got his bandages off!"

"I told you, Linda. You must be upset about that horse."

"I am. Sorry. I wish you'd buy all those horses."

"Which horses?"

"The three that syndicate group still own. Neal has the other two now. They seem to keep getting things wrong with them. I'm thinking something fishy is going on."

"The horse that Emma treated is also one of the syndicate's horses?"

"Yeah, and she looked at the other one this morning and said she needs bloodwork. Emma said she might have a thyroid deficiency. Doesn't look like that to me. But, hey, she's the vet." Linda stomps into the feed room and I follow.

"I'll have a chat with Emma. I planned to, anyway."

Linda puts the kettle on to warm up water to dilute the antiseptic wash and gathers the ointment, dressings and bandages out of her bag. Her experience pays off. She doesn't drop the dressings, the bandages don't unroll out of her hands, and no wood-shavings end up on the wound: all things that would have happened to me. Hector looks quite smart in his clean outfit.

"Shame he can't go out," Linda says as she gets rid of the garbage and puts the soiled bandages in a plastic bag.

"The sleet is horrible. But it might clear up later. I'll let him out if it does. Come inside and have some hot chocolate. You can tell me more about what's happening."

"I can't stop. Neal is so stressed about what's going on with the horses."

"Why does he still use Emma as his vet?"

"'Cause Emma's in the syndicate. He doesn't for any of his other horses. If he wasn't so worried about them, and didn't want so bad to find out what's going wrong, he'd ask Russell to find another trainer. He's that upset."

"But the vet's the issue, by the sound of it."

"That's what I think. But, hey, I'm not the boss. Have to go."

The sleet hasn't let up. It melts on my face as Kelly and I go back to the house. I shake my jacket over the mat and shiver. My fingers are cold. I need some warmth in my life. Someone here to talk to would help.

I call my mother.

"How are you?" I ask.

"Doing better than expected." Her voice sounds faint and distant, and a little breathy.

"I'm not sure what to make of that. What did you expect?"

"That my brain wouldn't work. How's my friend, Cooper?"

"He's curled up on my lap at the moment."

She insists I give her my banking information. She wants to send me a 'little money' from the proceeds of the sale of her house. I tell her she should keep it all for herself, but she insists she has enough to come and see me occasionally, as well as to treat herself to a few things, such as a new handbag, modern hairdo and colourful wardrobe.

I tell her I've not heard anything from the adoption reunite site since I don't want to build up her hopes. I don't tell her I'm expecting to hear from someone who might be my half-sister. There's been no message from her yet, although I've given my permission for my email to be shared with her. I almost feel relieved, because I'm uncertain how to handle it. There are so many questions and so many considerations and so many complications that adding a sister to the mix of my life would bring. It's easier to be alone.

"What about William?" she asks. "Still busy at work?"

"I expect so."

"Meg! You're letting him slip away. Why?"

"I don't want to talk about it. I've got to meet someone about a murder in a minute. It gets more complicated every day."

"I know I've said this before. Don't be like me and create a ton of regrets." Silence. "But I hope you get your man. Don't your Canadian Horse Police say that?"

"The RCMP or Royal Canadian Mounted Police. They always get their man. I hope so too."

We end our conversation on safe territory, talking about the weather. My mother says the daffodils are over and she can see some trees in blossom now that the sea mist has curled up and gone away. All I can see is driving sleet.

7

Confrontations

The animals have been fed and watered this morning, but I forgot to eat anything before I left the house. I wonder if I've caught the virus William had. My insides gurgle as if to confirm the theory, but my brain reasons that there's nothing physically wrong.

I have a meeting set up with Oscar Smedley, the only member of the syndicate I have yet to talk to. He lives in a condominium on the top floor of a high-rise building that overlooks the river. It has golden glass sides that give it the appearance of both opulence and vulnerability. I guessed correctly that Oscar's condo faces the river. Its expansive windows frame a wide panorama.

The décor could be described as minimalist: I think that's the trend these days. I can't see a speck of colour. Perhaps that's the in-thing too. A large irregular slab of glass, which lies on a spiral of dark metal, serves as a coffee table. It sits heavily in front of a spongy white sofa which I have sunk into. Two large black-and-white photographs of historic buildings hang on the pale grey wall opposite me.

"I'm a busy man, so let's get on with this. You want to know more about the syndicate, why?"

"Because I think there's a real possibility that Grayson, a co-member and your syndicate's original trainer, was murdered. And there might be a connection."

"He committed suicide. You're wasting your time, and mine for that matter."

"Let's put that aside for a moment. Tell me about how you got involved in the syndicate."

"Just brief. I went to a special session at the racetrack for people interested in getting into horse-racing. Russell Stanley, you know him, right?"

"Yes."

"I liked the sound of the Ontario Sires Stakes Program. The purses are good. Russell laid it on thick about syndicates. When we talked afterwards, he said he was setting one up. I told him I'd bring him luck because I've never failed to excel at everything I do. I wouldn't be living like this if I wasn't a success." He opens his arms wide as if to bring attention to the vastness of his home.

"So, what happened?"

"Long story short, we got five horses and then the bills started coming and coming. I'm not one to have expenses without revenue. A good return is what I'm after."

"Horse-racing is a risky business."

"I was hoodwinked by that pompous Russell. He really sold me on it. And nothing went right. Grayson was a shitty trainer. I wanted to fire him, but he was a member of the syndicate, so we were stuck with his useless methods."

"What about Emma, the veterinarian?"

"She should be gone. Robbing us blind. Nothing she ever does seems to make a difference other than to make things worse. I reckon she deliberately makes them sick and poisons them."

"But she's a member of the syndicate, so if one of the horses wins, she profits."

"But they're all useless horses, thanks to Russell and Grayson, the so-called expert horsemen."

"What about Philippa Woolsey?"

"She's effing furious, like me. We think alike. I just want the horses sold asap. Stop the bleeding, is what I say. It's like a black mark on my copybook. I never do badly at anything."

"Do you think Philippa or Emma would have reason to want to kill Grayson?"

"Might think about it, but I doubt they'd do it. And I didn't kill him. So, don't know who that leaves. But I can see why he'd kill himself."

"So, you have someone who can vouch for your whereabouts on the evening Grayson died?"

"No, I was alone here, working. But that doesn't mean I killed him."

I'm glad to leave Oscar's austere, stark condo, which should be a picture in a magazine and nothing more. It's good to get home but, although Kelly and Cooper are with me, the absence of human beings makes it seem as if I'm living on a desert island. Until now, I've believed in my self-sufficiency and independence, and have relied on animal companionship rather than on human relationships. But cracks have appeared, and I'm less sure of my convictions. Perhaps it's because I've had a taste of something different, and it's created a hankering for human kinship that lingers in my being.

On a whim, I get back in the truck with Kelly at my side and drive to William's office. I hope that Ramona, his assistant, will squeeze me in between clients so that I can talk with him. It worked before, so perhaps it'll work again.

I open the front door of the renovated house that serves as William's office and stop dead in my tracks. William's left hand is flat on Ramona's desk, and his right arm is behind her head, as he bends over and kisses her. I can't believe it. Right in the reception area. He turns. His brow is furrowed, and there are droplets of sweat on his upper lip. He opens his mouth, but I don't stay a second longer. I wheel around and slam the door behind me as my face burns and my heart races. I get back into the truck, and Kelly licks my cheek.

It's hard to accept that it's over, just like that, whatever it was between William and me. I spend the rest of the day trudging around the farm and barn, doing chores. In the evening, I groom Kelly and Cooper. I clean the kitchen. I lie back in a recliner in the family room and doze on and off during the long, lonely night. Serves me right. I have a propensity to self-destruct in relationships. I brought this all on myself.

* * *

I struggle to get going in the morning, but force myself to get a move-on because I want to see Linda. And during my unsettled night, I remembered that I'd said I would tell William that Linda's mom would like help with her will. And I haven't done it.

"I took a chance and brought you a tea and a muffin again," Linda says as her rotund body comes through the barn door laden with bags and the cup of tea. "I've already had mine."

"That's so nice. I can't remember when I last ate. I think I'm running on empty."

"I have to run on full, as you can see." Linda smiles. She's looking at me with an intensity which makes me fidget and look at the floor.

"How are the horses?"

"Neal has bought Emma out, so she's gone. About time, is what I say."

"But I bet that was a hard decision for Neal?"

"Neal isn't happy. He says he's stretched too thin. But he cares about the horses so much he told me he had to do something."

"The members of the syndicate are now Neal, Oscar, Philippa and Russell."

"And Grayson's estate till that gets settled."

"Yes, of course. Grayson had twenty percent ownership."

"By the way, Neal's found someone who'll buy forty-nine percent of Hector, if you'll buy the other fifty-one percent, but Neal can't tell you who it is right now."

"Do you know who it is?"

"My lips are sealed."

"Would you buy fifty-one percent of Hector if you were in my shoes?"

"For definite."

"Interesting. I could do with a lift in my life at the moment. Perhaps I'll do it. I'll let Neal know by lunchtime."

"That's good. It would help Neal out a lot. He wouldn't have assholes breathing down his neck every day, at least not about Hector. Hector, you have a great new home! Lucky boy." She strokes his nose, gives him a light groom and new bandages, and then picks up her things and leaves.

What an odd thing. I can't think who would want to own forty-nine percent of Hector. No-one comes to mind. Neal must be really hustling to make something happen towards the disbandment of that syndicate.

A text message comes from William as I sit down at the kitchen table with my carrot muffin and a mug of strong tea. Caffeine is needed this morning. I ignore the text. What can he possibly want to say to me? There's nothing to be said. I get up, blow my nose, put a coat on, grab my muffin and tea and sit out on the verandah in the howling gale that has built up without my noticing. Kelly's silky coat is ruffled up and my hair blows in my eyes, but somehow the bitter wind feels good, as if it's taking away some of the hurt. I stay until I'm cold and Kelly looks at me with an expression that clearly asks if we can go in now, please.

It's nearly lunchtime. I phone Neal.

"Hi, I hear you've found someone who's interested in Hector. Who is it?"

"He doesn't want his name to be known at the moment."

"Do you know him?"

"I know who he is, and you know him. I'm sure you'd be okay with it."

"Why doesn't he want me to know who he is?"

"Your guess is as good as mine. You'll find out who it is eventually, because you'll have to sign partnership papers for when Hector races. And he's going to race, I'm sure."

"Well, I suppose it's not a huge risk when I would have fifty-one percent."

"And I've been able to negotiate a better price, for you and your partner, with Russell. He must like you. He said he'll take four thousand. As you know, the syndicate members really want out."

"I can make that work. Thanks, Neal. It seems like a lot of people want me to have Hector."

"It's like one of these things that's meant to be."

It could mean a lot of additional expense and no revenue. Oh, I sound like Oscar. But that's my reality. I don't have extra cash to throw around. I have to be responsible.

But my decision to purchase Hector brings a glow to my face. Despite the gale, I take some carrots out to him in celebration.

He hates the wind. He's standing with his rear towards the gusts, and his tail is blowing between his legs. I decide he'd be happier in his stall. Eagle and Bullet are in the run-in shed and sheltered from the worst of it.

I toss the carrots into his feed bucket and he munches on them. He would prefer the other two were in the barn as well, but he's got used to being on his own from time to time. I stand in the stall and just watch this large, flashy chestnut as the wind rattles the siding, bangs the barn door, and sends pieces of trees bouncing over the metal roof. Despite all the threatening turmoil around us, it feels safe and cozy in here.

After a few restorative moments, I leave him to finish his carrots.

Russell left a message on the landline phone to tell me he's home at last. Kelly and I will visit soon.

Fearing another message from William, or perhaps hoping, I pick up my mobile. There's an email from someone called Melissa Andrews who says that she was given my email address by the adoption reunite site. She asks if there is a time when we can talk. She says that it's the weirdest thing, but she lives in a town only an hour from Vannersville and could meet me for coffee in the city if that would be better.

She can't be my half-sister. That would be too strange, her being only one hour away. I email my adoption reunite contact and ask what information they have on Melissa.

That gets me thinking about my mother, so I pick up the phone. A strange voice answers after a few rings.

"Who is it, please?"

I explain who I am.

"I'm Jane, your mother's physiotherapist. She's making good progress. She can now walk from her chair to the bathroom."

"Oh. I didn't know she was having trouble with walking."

"Miriam, haven't you told your daughter how you're doing?" I hear some mumbling in the background. And now I can't hear anything. I am tempted to hang up, but I hold on.

"Are you still there?" Jane asks.

"Yes."

"I didn't realize that Miriam didn't want you to know that she has some trouble walking. I shouldn't have said anything to you without her permission. So, I've apologized to her and I apologize to you. But she's now agreed that I can talk to you and let you know that her experience is not an unusual result of the surgery given where the tumour was located. She wants me to stress that she's doing well. But she gets fatigued. She says she'll talk to you later. She needs to rest now."

"Thanks for the update. I wasn't aware."

"I'll give her your love and I'm sure she'll call you soon."

"Thanks." I've never sent my love or conveyed my love in any way to my mother. But I don't correct Jane.

I'm in danger of making the same old mistakes I've made in the past. I don't listen, I don't ask and I make assumptions. William's face appears on my mobile again. He's phoning. Perhaps I should hear what he has to say.

"Meg. I'm coming over." He ends the call before I can say anything. My bottom lip trembles for a couple of seconds.

I busy myself and tidy up the kitchen: I empty the garbage, wash the boot trays, clear the counters, shake the mats outside in the chilling wind, and put the coffeemaker on. Kelly wags her tail by the kitchen door. How does she know it's William? I open it, and Cooper comes out of nowhere and rubs against William's legs as he takes off his shoes.

I pour out some coffee and make some tea. I don't know how to break the silence. I want him to speak first.

"Meg, for once, will you listen?" The tone of his voice is sharp and feels like a spike pricking me. I say nothing and stay standing as he sits down at the table. "It would be better if you sat." I sit down. A headache takes hold of my forehead like a vise. "Now, let me tell you what happened. To be quite honest, I have thought of giving up on this relationship more than once. You don't seem to want to give me a chance. No, don't say anything."

I shut my mouth, literally.

"You opened the door to my office a couple of minutes after Ramona collapsed in her chair. I didn't know idea what was wrong. I called 911. I don't know how to do CPR, but I tried to recall what to do from seeing a booklet on it once. When you came in, I thought you could help me move her. I thought she should be lying on the floor. But you had no trust in me, no faith in our relationship. You must have assumed that I was doing something improper and unprofessional in my reception area, and you just turned on your heels. I asked myself what kind of relationship we have when you jump to conclusions about my behaviour, won't answer texts or emails just like a sulking child, and don't follow up. You quite clearly don't care about me or anyone else. You can talk now. I've learned enough in my legal career that it's important to hear both sides. Crying won't help."

Tears blur my vision. I've done it again. I've destroyed a relationship because I don't communicate and I don't give back. And I reckon I must have trouble with trust, too. I have to face the fact that I don't know how to make a relationship work with anyone, even someone as wonderful as William.

"How's Ramona?" I blow my nose.

"I'm glad you asked." His tone softens a little. "They don't know what it is, but suspect that she contracted something in Cuba, which makes me feel partly responsible since I gave her our tickets."

"It's not your fault." I blow my nose again. Kelly sits on the floor next to me, leans against my leg, and rests her head on my lap. Cooper is nowhere to be seen. William doesn't touch his coffee, and I stare into my mug of tea. What's the point of me trying to find my half-sister if I can't make any relationship work? Especially one with a genuine, smart, supportive and caring person like William.

"Well, I suppose I might as well go." He gets up. I imagine little seeds of regret taking root inside my heart. The ones my mother has warned me against.

"William, please don't go."

"Why?" He turns towards me and looks at me with an unblinking stare. His mouth is a straight line, his eyes dark and penetrating.

"Thank you for coming. Please let me say something." He sits down. "I'm sorry that I misjudged you and didn't trust you. I know how caring and considerate you are. I'm not sure what made me behave the way I did but I think I'm scared."

"We all have our fears." He doesn't look at me.

"I care about you a lot but I'm scared I'm going to blow it."

"Well, you have."

"You're not helping. This is difficult for me."

"And for me."

"Okay, William, shut up. You've made your point. You know that I'm terrified of relationships, of intimacy. Give me a break."

"I've given you too many breaks."

"I suppose I can't argue with that." The clock ticks so loudly I feel like throwing something at it. The silence between us is painful and awkward. The seeds of regret are in danger of germinating. I need to do something. I stand up. "Stand up," I tell him as I walk around to his side of the table with Kelly close on my heels. Trembling, I put my arms around him. I've never done anything like that to a man. He doesn't move, but he doesn't push me away either. I let my arms drop and return to my chair, trying not to let the tears run down my hot cheeks again. At least I tried.

I'm about to sit down when I see William is next to me. He wraps his arms around me and kisses me. His lips are soft and warm. But my body wants to explode into convulsive sobs. I suppose this is what extreme relief feels like.

We talk for a few more minutes. He says he has to leave to finish some work for a court case and he's without Ramona again, which increases the challenges and workload. I hope it won't be long before I see him again. This house has an aura of emptiness about it. It's as if Kelly, Cooper and I just aren't enough to satisfy its appetite for occupancy any more. We can't fill the rooms.

I wander upstairs and enter each of the three spacious bedrooms that reek of vacancy. I pat one of the duvets and a cloud of dust particles wafts up. The furniture looks okay, but the décor in all three rooms needs to be spruced up with more cheerful and paler colours, and new bedding is required. Even with my tight budget, I should be able to buy a few cans of paint. Perhaps William would stay sometimes if I had a pleasant room for him. There would be no pressure on either of us. And what if I really do have a half-sister? She should have a room. I imagine what it would be like to have two of the bedrooms occupied, and the house with more people in it, at least from time to time. And my mother could have a place that's her own and feel welcome to visit. These possibilities energize me. I plan to get paint the next day and start a search for new bedding on the web.

* * *

Awake with a start, I realize I must have fallen asleep in my recliner last night. Kelly's sitting next to me and Cooper's curled up on my lap. It's only five o'clock, so perhaps I'll catch Linda again.

I make it into the barn just as Linda finishes Hector's bandages.

"I'm so glad you're his owner," Linda says as she pulls the end of a long, sticky bandage around the horse's leg and smooths it down.

"I am, too. But I'd like to know who my partner is."

"Not allowed to tell." Linda gets up from her crouching position, unclips the horse from his tie as I gather up all the old pieces of dressing, bandage, and gauze. "As soon as the weather is dryer and warmer, we can leave the bandages off. Air will do these wounds good now that they're not quite as deep."

"I hope it warms up soon. I'm fed up with the cold."

"We'll be complaining of the heat soon. I will be. I prefer the cold." She grabs her bag. "I almost forgot. Neal wants me to ask if you'd talk to Russell again. He thinks he lied about his attack."

"What makes him think that?"

"He wouldn't tell me. Got to run. Lots happening at the track."

"I've got to pay you for all the tea and muffins you keep bringing me. It's just as well you do. I think I'd starve to death otherwise."

"It's okay. I like doing it. You're nice to me, and you've given Hector a good home. See you later."

I have more energy today and my appetite has improved. I enjoy the carrot muffin as I sit at the kitchen table and read the email from the adoption reunite site. Melissa Andrews sounds legitimate from the information they've provided. There's a photo in which her broad smile reveals perfect white teeth. Her face is framed by long, blond hair, a stark contrast to my long, black hair. Her green eyes are large and remind me of horses' eyes, in a good way, kind and honest. I hope this isn't just wishful thinking. I postpone reaching out to Melissa. It won't hurt to delay a day or two. My hand wobbles a little as I put the phone back onto the table.

Kelly scrambles up off the kitchen floor and dashes to the door. It's Murray. He almost pushes his way through the door and, with a dour face, he puts his coat on the back of a chair and sits down.

"Hi, Murray. How are you? Would you like some coffee?"

"No. I've come to talk about Frank's money."

"Oh. Okay."

"I saw William leaving here yesterday."

"Am I under surveillance or something?"

"You know I feel responsible for my brother's money." He folds his arms and stares at me. "I've told you this before. I want to make sure that the money gets into the right hands and that other people aren't hanging around you, or trying to get near you, so that they can get their mitts on the dough."

"And as I've told you before, William is not after money. And the last time you came, you insinuated that my half-sister is after the money too. How would she even know?"

"Everyone knows."

"That's not true. If everyone knew I was about to inherit ten million, I'd expect more attention. Most of the time there's no-one here." Why is there a lump in my throat?

"I'm going to be straight with you."

"I would hope that you've always been honest."

He unfolds his arms and leans towards me across the table with a half-smile.

I lean back. "What do you want?" I ask.

"I want to live here with you," he says. "I could then make sure that Frank's money is managed responsibly and ensure that no-one exploits you. I need to do this for my brother's sake as well as yours." No words come out of my mouth. "You must know that I care about you and want to make sure you're okay, and not just because you're my sister-in-law." His mouth lifts at its edges. But I have goose-bumps down my arms.

"That makes no sense to me. What is this really about?"

"You're not making this easy. I'm opening my soul to you. I care about you a lot." He leans back and folds his arms again. His face is flushed and his eyes are partly closed.

"You're drinking again, aren't you?"

"Whether I am or not has nothing to do with this. You're trying my patience."

"To save your patience being tried any further, my answer to everything is no. I don't want you to live here. I don't want your protection. I don't want you to manage the money, if there is any. And if I want a relationship with someone, that's my business and nothing to do with you. And I won't let you stand between me and my half-sister. The sad thing is that I've grown to enjoy your company and now you've ruined that. You can't come here again with your threats. You're not welcome." I yank his coat off the back of his chair and hand it to him, and open the back door, letting cold air in which bites at my ankles.

He leaves in silence. I sit down, my legs unsteady underneath me, my palms sweaty. Although I'm angry with him, I am concerned for him too. I think my guess that he's drinking again is right. His relationship with Frank was ruined by his alcoholism and his incessant begging for money from his brother. And it's started all over again. I hope I don't get any of Frank's money because that will mean that Murray will be here every day to ask for more.

I have to use my best blocking-out skills to bury this confrontation with Murray and get ready to see Russell.

8

Partnership

Kelly sits on the front seat of the pickup truck as we drive up to the house. Kelly's hole in the outer screen door has still not been fixed. I knock, and Russell lets us in.

"Nice to see you." He pats Kelly on the head. She wags her tail and goes to one of the cupboards lining the far wall. Russell rummages in a box and finds a couple of small dog biscuits which she accepts with relish. Her experience here must have been okay before Russell was injured. "How's Hector doing?"

"Thanks for selling fifty-one percent of him to me. He's doing well. I think he likes his new home and Linda's wound management is superior, of course. Who has the other forty-nine percent?"

"Lips are sealed."

"I want to know more about the attack on you. I've not come up with any good suspects so far, so need more information."

"I don't know what I can tell you that I haven't already said."

"Let's start from the beginning again. Maybe you'll remember something more."

"A woman came into the old barn."

"What made you think it was a woman?"

"I suppose it must have been her build or way of walking."

"Which was it? Can you tell me more about her build and how she walked?"

"Not really. It's dark in that barn." He turns his attention to Kelly, patting her head. "Do you want more treats?" He seems to wobble as he gets up to retrieve more dog biscuits.

"Are you okay? Are you still feeling shaky?"

"I'm fine." He sits down again.

"I'm determined to find out what happened to you. You said she walked towards you."

"Yes."

"Did you see anything in her hand?"

"No."

"But you were hit with something?"

"I think so."

"You're not sure. Did she say anything?"

"I can't remember. This bang on my head has probably affected my memory, you see. I'll get some tea. You drank tea when you visited me in the hospital."

"That's observant."

"I was hoping this was a social visit. I don't feel like answering questions." He plugs in the kettle with his back to me.

"It's partly a social visit. I have to find out the truth about your attack for two reasons. One, your attacker should be brought to justice and two, she might be linked to Grayson's death, and I'm getting nowhere fast on that one. I need a break to help me figure out what happened to that man."

"The attacker has nothing to do with Grayson's death."

"But you said this woman yelled 'Grayson'. How can you be so sure there isn't a link?"

"I just am. Okay?" He turns to me. His hands tremble, and he grabs the edge of the countertop.

"What's wrong, Russell? You're not telling me what's going on, are you?"

"It's embarrassing."

"You said that last time. I don't want the same old made-up story. I want the truth."

"It's messed up."

"I don't care. I just want to find out who attacked you and who killed Grayson."

"I'm not a good person."

"I'm not here to judge you."

"It was Amy. Amy was Grayson's groom. I tried to cultivate a friendship because I like her."

"Okay."

"But my attempts to reach out to her failed. I think she despises me." His bottom lip quivers just a little.

"So, what happened?"

"I was throwing hay bales from up in the loft through the trap-door down to the floor of the barn. I know the old wooden floor is uneven up there, but I tripped and couldn't stop myself as I went tumbling down to the stone floor. I landed on my head."

"Why would she push you?"

"I didn't say she did. Don't put words into my mouth."

"How did you get into the house?"

"She must have dragged me in here."

"There was no evidence of someone dragging you. And you'd be pretty heavy for a woman to drag that far. And why wouldn't she have called an ambulance?"

He doesn't answer. He stares at Kelly.

"Okay. Truth this time." He draws a deep breath. "When I saw her at the track, after Grayson's body was found, she glared at me and refused to talk with me. She walked away. I know she really liked Grayson, and I think she believes I killed him. She came to the farm and found me up in the hayloft, throwing bales down. She yelled at me that I shouldn't have killed Grayson and pushed me as I stood on the edge of the trap-door. I tumbled down and must have hit my head. The blood's still there if you want to check it out. I don't think she meant for me to get hurt like I did. I came to, with Kelly licking my face. I don't know when, and she was nowhere in sight. I stumbled into the house and that's all I remember."

"What do you think would make her believe you killed Grayson?"

"Because the syndicate was going so badly and I wasn't happy with him. I liked Grayson, but whatever he was doing wasn't working, and I had unhappy syndicate members. Amy must have heard some of our discussions, and likely got the impression that I was furious with him and wanted him out of the equation. I have to tell you I've been reeling from the hurt. How could she possibly think that I would contemplate killing someone, let alone someone basically good like Grayson, and for such a pathetic reason? It's devastating." He covers his face with his hands.

"We could put her suspicion to rest if you have an alibi for the evening."

"I wish I did. I went to bed early that day. I'd been at the track all morning, you see, and working on the fencing here all afternoon. I was beat."

"Who do you think killed Grayson?"

"You really want to root out the truth, don't you?"

"I do."

"I honestly don't know. You're sure it wasn't suicide?"

"I'm almost certain."

"Both Grayson and I had words with Emma. Her bills were out of line. Grayson believed she made up things that she had to check on, or tests, or meds. Something wasn't right."

"She might have thought she could recoup some of her losses by overcharging."

"That's what Grayson thought, I'm pretty sure."

"When did you both talk with her?"

"Grayson confronted her at the end of the last racing season but, because she was still in the syndicate, she remained as the vet. Grayson and I agreed we needed to keep a closer eye on things. You should talk with her."

"I've chatted with her already. But I'll give it another shot."

"I don't think either Oscar or Philippa would be capable of such a crime, particularly Philippa, but they were both angry with all three of us: Grayson, Emma and me."

"They both say that you were pushy about the syndicate."

"Mm. Interesting."

"Why?"

"I wasn't pushy." He turns away.

I think I believe him, but I'm not absolutely certain, because he's lied to me before.

Life would be so different if people were honest.

"I can't think of anyone else except that god-awful trainer Bryce," he says. "He thinks everyone's cheating because he never wins races, or hardly ever. But why he'd bother to kill just one trainer rather than try to gas the lot is beyond me."

"If I knew the motive, I think it would be obvious who the murderer was."

"I'll give it some more thought. I might come up with something."

"Okay. Thanks."

"Say hello to Hector for me. I like that horse. He'll do something for you if you have the patience to let him heal."

"Not rushing, that's for sure."

*　　*　　*

Kelly is behind the passenger seat in her usual, concealed position as we enter the backstretch. It's a cool day, but the warmth of the sun through the windshield is making promises of hotter days to come.

I follow Amy as she works, which she's not happy about, since I confronted her with Russell's story as soon as I saw her. I stand in a stall as she brushes a horse in readiness for saddling up. He's the last one to be exercised this morning, so I hope she'll have more time to talk once he's out on the training-track.

"I'm not admitting anything," she says, as she swipes together two brushes she has in her hands.

"Why didn't you call an ambulance? He could have died. The fall could have killed him." No response. "And why did you tell me you didn't know his address when I asked you a few days ago? It would really help if you told me the truth."

"Because I think Russell murdered Grayson." She bends over double again, and I wonder if she's going to be sick.

"I don't believe that Russell killed Grayson," I say. "I think it was someone else."

"What if you're wrong?"

"I'll find out the truth, but I need anyone who knows something to tell me about it. This is serious. The police still think it's suicide despite being told that Grayson was left-handed and his left sleeve was rolled up."

"Who told you that? Grayson wasn't left-handed."

"Oh. Then it could have been suicide. And that's why the police haven't looked into it further."

"It was not suicide." Amy startles the horse with her shrill voice and coughs.

"Tell me exactly why you believe that."

"Because he was such a lovely person." She bends over and sobs. The horse curves his neck down towards her and snorts.

"Amy, let me finish grooming the horse. You just tell me what to do." I know she's on a deadline. The rider will be here soon to take him out and won't want to hang around. "There's more to you and Grayson, isn't there?"

"I've been trying so hard to hide it. We were having a bit of a relationship. Just brush his mane and tail with this. It shouldn't need much."

"What do you mean by 'a bit of a relationship'?"

"We were dating, sort of. It was very relaxed. Neither of us wanted any pressure. We just wanted to see how things went. But I really fell for him. I miss him so much. I hate the trainer I'm working for now. I'm a wreck." She sits down on the straw bedding and tears roll down her cheeks. "I was doing such a good job of controlling myself until you asked your goddam questions."

The rider pops his head round the stall door.

"New groom I see."

"Amy doesn't feel well. Can you saddle up?" I ask. "I'm taking her to the cafeteria."

"No problem."

By the time we're seated in the cafeteria, Amy has composed herself, although her eyes are red and puffy. I get coffee and tea and some cookies.

"Tell me anything you think might help," I say.

"I don't have any proof of anything."

"That didn't stop you hitting Russell."

"I didn't hit him. I didn't even touch him. He tripped and fell down that hole."

"Let's start over. Tell me what you know about Grayson, and your theories about what might have happened. Don't hold back.

It won't be held against you. We're just theorizing, just exploring."

"All I know is what Grayson told me. I've not wanted to tell anyone because I work here and people know people and the next thing I'm out on my ear. I lost my temper when I saw Russell. I've lost my cool with everything since Grayson's been gone." She clasps her hands together in a tight ball. "Will I be in trouble about Russell?"

"That depends on Russell. I'd say he's not eager to press charges. Anyway, you were saying that Grayson told you stuff?"

"You know he was unhappy with Emma. Grayson thought she over-medicated and over-billed."

"That must have been concerning. What did Grayson make of all this?"

"That she was incompetent." Amy looks down into her lap.

"Anything else you can think of?"

"Only that Bryce, the trainer who's in the same barn, hung around a lot. He only has a few horses, so he'd wander around our shedrow. It gave me the creeps. I mentioned it to Grayson in case he hadn't noticed, but he didn't think it was anything to worry about."

"Did you talk to Bryce?"

"I asked him why he was hanging around and he sort of sneered and said he was just trying to learn from the best. The way he said it sounded sarcastic to me. I told you, he gave me the creeps. That's one good thing about being in this barn, I'm away from him."

"You say you don't enjoy working here?"

"I hate this trainer I'm working for. I miss Grayson. He's not a horseman like Grayson was. He's just a puppet for the demanding, greedy, impatient owners who've never touched a horse in their lives."

"That sounds rather harsh. I'm an owner." I smile.

"I know. I'm not saying all owners are like that, but this trainer attracts them. He has a reputation for getting results with poor horses, but no-one's been able to prove he's doping. I want out of here. I hate it."

"Have you talked to Neal Carvey? He's got more horses now and he could be looking for help. I could ask him now if you like. I'm going to see my two horses he's training right now."

"Thanks. It sure would make me feel better about things. Otherwise I might just quit altogether."

"I'll talk with him."

* * *

Neal tells me he's looking for another groom and Amy would be a suitable candidate, and adds that Grayson wouldn't have put up with sloppy workers. I leave it in his hands.

"Glad you popped around," he says, as he gathers the tack together, ready for the saddle soap. "If you agree, I'd like to enter Speed into an allowance race which runs in four days' time. Has to be entered tomorrow."

"He's ready earlier than I expected."

"Don't forget we did that early training. It gave him a head-start. He's in good condition and the race is six furlongs, not long. I think he should handle it well."

"That sounds good then."

"Rose is doing well too, but I want to wait a little while longer because there's a stakes race coming up which would suit her."

"Patience is a virtue in this game."

"It usually is."

"How are your other horses doing?"

"What I don't understand is that the two horses in the syndicate are not doing well at all. But the other horses in my stables are okay."

"Emma isn't the vet anymore, right?"

"Since I bought Emma out, Russell and I agreed that we'd use Edwin since I've been using him for my other horses. He's ethical and a good communicator. I've asked Edwin to do more bloodwork on the two syndicate horses."

"You're the one who puts out the feed, right?"

"Yes. I have a small enough stable that I put it out myself. I might have someone else put it in their stalls, but I have the feed ready in each horse's covered bucket before feed time."

"Sounds good. Hector's doing very well at home. I understand he was pretty sick when he was here?"

"He seemed to catch everything going, especially skin diseases, and had frequent mild colic. I'm relieved he's got a good home. I hope I'll be his trainer when it comes time to send him back?"

"Of course."

"Good. But I want all this cleared up first before he comes near this place again."

"Agreed. I'll track Emma down now. I have some questions about a drug called Testos. Emma and Russell have given me different stories." I follow Neal to his office, carrying some of the tack.

"Testos is a prohibited drug."

"I know. But Emma told me that Russell approached Grayson because he wanted to use a veterinarian who would prescribe and supply Testos. That was just before Hector got badly injured. Emma said that Grayson wondered if Hector had been given the drug the day before and he'd suffered a reaction to it, and that's why he got injured. Also, Testos could have been part of a compound medication."

"I don't know Russell all that well, but I've not heard that he's ever been accused of cheating, and he seems to care about his horses. I find that hard to believe."

* * *

Emma is bent over at the back of her large SUV as she opens and closes various drawers in a storage unit.

"Hi, Emma, I hope you have some time to talk."

She keeps on with her search. "I'm tied up for a while."

"When will you have a few minutes?"

"Not today."

"Okay. How about tomorrow at lunchtime? When do you stop for lunch?"

"Sometimes I don't. But if I do, I eat in my office. You can try there at about eleven."

"Thanks. I'll be there."

The many sparrows dart in front of me, strut on the dirt around my feet, and sing in my ears as I walk towards Bryce's stable. My intuition tells me that Bryce is involved. But I might feel this way because he's an unpleasant sort of guy, dishevelled and resentful. He's sitting outside his office eating an apple.

"Warm enough to sit outside today," I say as I walk towards him.

"Yep."

"I'm trying to find out who killed Grayson, as you know."

"Not guilty. I told you that before."

"I'm talking to everyone I can think of."

"Not getting anywhere then."

"Making progress. I hear you liked to hang around Grayson's area."

"That brown girl tell you that?"

"It doesn't matter who said it. I just want to know why you hung around there, and if you saw anything that might be helpful."

"Nope."

"You thought Grayson was cheating, right?"

"Yep."

"Did you do anything about it?"

"Nope."

"But you hung around hoping to catch someone doing something?"

"Yep. You got it."

"Ah. Did you catch anyone?"

"Nope."

"Did you hear anything?"

"Yep."

"What?"

"You're like a dog with a bone."

"Well, did you hear anything?"

"Emma and me talk sometimes. Emma told me that Russell wanted to use Testos."

"What did you do about it?"

"My lips are sealed."

"Okay. You're protecting someone, probably Emma."

"Not Emma." He gets up, goes into his office and slams the door.

*　　*　　*

Kelly and I flop down in the family room. The horses are fed, and in their stalls, and both the cat and the dog have had their dinner. I'm hungry. Instead of preparing anything to eat, I garner the small amount of energy I have left and set up a meeting with Melissa, my possible half-sister, for tomorrow at 9am.

*　　*　　*

The dawn chorus rings around my ears as if the tunes are being sung by an improv choir, sometimes discordant, sometimes harmonious, but always beautiful. I try to breathe it in, along with the crisp air, to help clear the fog in my brain from too little sleep. The early sunshine glints on the speckles of frost and bounces off Kelly's silky coat.

Whenever I think about my meeting with Melissa this morning, little spiders crawl all over my skin. I've picked up my mobile four times since I got up, intending to cancel. I can't remember when I last ate, and my low fuel level can't be helping my brain function. It flits all over the place, unable to settle.

I'm relieved to find Linda in the barn as she inspects Hector's wounds.

"They're good enough for him to go without the bandages today," she says, as she gets up from her crouch. "They need air, and the weather is on his side."

"What are the next steps?"

"I don't need to come any more if you can put cream on once a day. That will save you some money. I'm sure Neal has been billing you for my time after you bought most of him."

"Which part I wonder? To be honest, I don't know. I haven't received a bill from him yet for Hector."

"If he doesn't let you put on the cream, I have this spray. It's gentle, and it helps the healing process."

"These wounds take time, I know."

"If it gets dirty, you'll need to wash it with this antiseptic soap. That'll be tougher. If there's no-one around to lift up one of his other legs, I'll come, because he might kick if it bothers him, although he's more behaved than he was."

"I'll miss you coming every morning."

"This is the last muffin I'll be delivering." She gives me a big grin as she picks the brown bag up off the counter in the feed room.

"I'll probably starve to death."

"We all need fuel. I'll see you at the track. Just let me know if you want me to come out. Got to run."

9

Elusive Truth

I needn't have been concerned about recognizing Melissa. She looks just like her photograph. Her creamy skin is clear with the freshness of youth, and her eyes sparkle. Her smile reassures me. She has a coffee and a toasted bagel with butter. I buy my tea and sit down. She tells me all about her childhood. Of course, she has no memories of our mother and this makes it even odder to think that we have the same parent. I have to concentrate to hear everything she says, because the words tumble out of her mouth in quick succession, her voice hushed as if she's telling me deep secrets.

The adoptive family didn't work out. She doesn't explain what happened. She was moved from one foster home to another and got into a mess. What the mess was, she doesn't say and I don't like to ask.

"When I was about sixteen, I thought I'd find my real parents. I was so miserable I decided it was worth a try. I hoped I'd be able to live with them, or at least one of them. Things change, you know.

Although I wasn't able to connect with my father, some good came of it because I found out that he's Canadian. This was my ticket out of England, so I could leave all the terrible memories well behind me."

"It doesn't really work though, does it?"

"Not really, but it's helped."

"When did you come to Canada?"

"I didn't leave right away. I didn't want to mess it up, like so many other things in my life, so I decided to finish high school and then go to college in Canada. I worked evenings and weekends and saved."

"Sounds tough."

"Not really. It got tougher when they chucked me out of the foster home when I turned eighteen. That's how the system works. I lived in a bed-sit for a few months. I finished high school and left for Canada soon afterwards."

"That took courage to come on your own."

"That's what you did, didn't you?" She raises her bright eyes and looks at me over her coffee cup. "Anyway, I didn't know what I wanted to do in college. I thought I'd be a nursing assistant, so I enrolled in the program, but realized I wasn't keen. College didn't start until September, so I looked for volunteer work and found an opportunity with the Vannersville Humane Society, helping with a special therapy program. Tell me if I should shut up." She puckers up her face and flicks her long, shiny blond hair behind her shoulders.

"No, don't. I'm interested in your story."

"It's an amazing program. Young offenders can choose to participate in it instead of traditional anger management counselling."

My eyes open wide when I realize that this is the program that I launched at the Humane Society a few years ago. But I don't let on.

"Each youth was assigned a shelter dog that needed training in order to become adoptable. Both a social worker and a dog trainer ran the program. The participants learned so many things, including how better to empathize, to be patient, to be tolerant, to use positive reinforcement rather than punishment or violence, and what it meant to be successful at something and make a difference. And this is what the youth told the evaluators, not what the people running it said. They actually used words like 'empathy'. It was wild."

My eyes tingle with the start of tears, not of sorrow, but of joy at hearing good things about this program, which had been so dear to my heart for so many reasons.

"The biggest difference it made for me," Melissa says, "was that I realized I wanted to work with animals, and I would never have guessed that before. I just adored how the dogs loved the youth, whatever they looked like, whatever mood they were in, however they behaved. No judgement, just love. Brilliant. I was lucky, I could change my registration and got into the vet tech program. And I completed it. I'm pretty proud of that. I have a job as a vet tech in Molehill, the small town where I live now. Don't you think that's awesome?" As Melissa talks, her voice becomes bright, almost tuneful with a hint of staccato. She radiates exuberance.

"I do. I think that's amazing, actually."

"So, how about you?"

I give her a synopsis of my life. I tell her a bit about why I left England, my marriage to Frank, my work with the Humane Society and the deaths of both Frank and Chuck, and a bit about the farm and the horses. I start to talk about our mother, but I cut it short because Melissa's frequently distracted by her mobile phone, and our eyes don't meet for most of the time.

She looks up. "Can I see the farm?"

"I'd love to show you around. How about tomorrow morning?"

"That'll work. I start late tomorrow. I can come about nine. Okay?"

I give her directions. She gives me a hug, which takes me by surprise but doesn't overwhelm me. My desire to have a warm relationship with my sister must be stronger than my discomfort with physical contact. She feels soft and warm, and smells of citrus. She tells me how excited she is to have a sister. She buys a sandwich and we part ways.

Kelly licks my face when I get into the truck. I should have introduced her to Melissa.

I'm puzzled over Melissa's relative lack of interest in my life and in our mother. Perhaps she's one of these self-possessed people. But her youthful positivity, and her love of animals, make me feel more enthusiastic about things generally. That's a good thing.

*   *   *

I find Emma's office in a cramped beige trailer, a little before eleven. It seems like I've waited for an eternity, but she arrives only ten minutes after the hour. She notices me and snatches her gaze away. I think she's forgotten I'd be here. Or perhaps she assumed I wouldn't show up.

"Got to eat my lunch. Don't have much time."

"That's okay. Thanks for meeting with me. I'll get straight to the point. There are allegations that you over-medicated and over-billed for treatment of the Russell Stanley syndicate horses, and I want to give you a chance to tell me your side of the story." I expect her to get angry and indignant, but she continues to eat her sandwich, and answers me with her mouth full.

"I can see why they'd be saying that. Of course, in this business, people are always looking for someone to blame. But there's likely no-one to blame for what's been going on with those horses, and certainly not the veterinarian." She takes another large bite.

"Did Grayson talk to you about the horses' recurring ill-health?"

"He was contemplating installing security cameras. Several trainers do that. Often they're not even connected to anything."

"He must have had reason to believe that someone was tampering with the horses and that's how they got sick so often. Even so, members of the syndicate thought you over-medicated and over-billed. Something was going on, and I have to assume you have a good idea what. Who do you think would want to harm the horses and why?"

"The horses suffered from a range of mysterious symptoms like skin rashes, mild colic, foot soreness and some respiratory issues. I was in Grayson's barn just about every morning. I was only doing my job at the request of the trainer, and Grayson could back me up if he was still around. I billed for my time and the medications. I admit I sometimes threw mud at the wall, hoping it would stick. We weren't able to understand what was going on most of the time. But I didn't over-medicate or over-bill. You ask who would tamper with the horses and why? I have no answers."

"But do you think it likely that someone was tampering with them, as Grayson suspected?"

"I have no evidence one way or the other. But it's true that all the syndicate horses had issues, and none of the other horses in the same barn experienced any of them, at least not to the same extent. There were a couple that had a skin condition similar to the one Hector had. That's all. I have to go."

Emma grabs a couple of small boxes and a bag and disappears out of the trailer. It was hard to assess her body language while she ate her sandwich and apple, but I picked up a level of agitation that I didn't notice before. She was calm and professional during my past couple of chats with her. Perhaps she's just having a bad day. She must have quite a few of them with all the challenges racehorses bring.

As I review my chat with Emma, I remember something I should have pressed her on. Russell denied he approached Grayson to ask him to change veterinarians to one who would agree to administer

Testos to Hector. But that's exactly what Emma told me previously. I should have remembered to ask her about it again.

If only people would tell me the truth, and all of it. It would save a ton of time and cause much less frustration and confusion.

Speed and Rose won't realize that I haven't stopped by. I'd like to visit with them, but I need to go to Russell's farm. On the way back to my truck, I walk through the shedrow where Bryce stables his horses. He emerges from one of the stalls in front of me and we come close to a collision.

"Sorry, just passing through," I say.

"I want to tell you something that's been on my mind."

"Okay."

"One member of that syndicate is called Oscar Smedley, right?" He takes his hat off and scratches his head. "His odd name stuck with me."

"Yes."

"I don't like cheats. I want a level playing-field around here. Never going to get it, but do my bit."

"Okay."

"So, I'm letting you know that Oscar guy approached me. He wanted to fire Grayson and hire me as the trainer for the syndicate. He was an uptight, stuck-up kind of guy. He said he wasn't happy with the performance of the horses."

"What did you say?"

"I told him that all the owners, including Grayson, would have to be willing to transfer the horses to me for me to consider it. And, I said, Grayson won't agree because he sneers at my race record."

"Why do you think Oscar approached you rather than some other trainer?"

"With a better record, you mean? Exactly. I didn't like the smell of it."

"What do you mean?"

"Just a gut-feeling that the guy isn't on the straight and narrow, too desperate, wanting to be a big-shot, something like that."

"I still don't understand why he'd go to you."

"You should ask him. Perhaps he assumed I was hungry and would do whatever it takes to get a buck. I reckon he's that kinda guy who measures success by what you got in the bank."

"And while I'm here, were you with anyone during the evening when Grayson died?"

"No alibi, if that's what you mean."

"Anything else you think of, just let me know." I hand him a card in case I didn't give him one before. I feel less aversion to this man. At least he talked to me in sentences this time. Perhaps he's genuinely concerned about the fairness of the racing industry, as well as the welfare of the horses.

* * *

It's about noon by the time we reach Russell's farm. Kelly is keen to get out of the truck, and I let her run around as I search for Russell. He doesn't answer my knock on the door to the house, so I assume he's out and about on the farm somewhere. Kelly turns her head around to look at me and trots towards a small shack behind the house. Sure enough, Russell is there, scooping grass seed into a small bucket.

"Hello, Russell."

"Wasn't expecting to see you again so soon. Just going to spread some seed where the horses trampled the ground along the fence-line."

"Don't let me stop you. I can follow. How's your head?"

"Okay, I guess. I get the feeling this is another of these non-social visits."

I have a struggle to keep up with his long strides. His well-used muscles have recovered, it would seem, from his stay in the hospital.

"You're right. I want to ask you about Testos again."

He puts the bucket of seed down, leans on the fence, and scratches his beard. He stares at me with unblinking eyes and I look away. I'm not sure what to make of his body language.

"You've come here to accuse me again of wanting to use Testos. Why would I do that when I was bent on selling Hector?"

"I'm not accusing you. I want you to tell me why someone would say that."

He picks up the bucket and opens the wide, barred gate. The cedar gate posts were once large and solid, but are now well-chewed and need replacement. Russell catches me looking at them.

"The price I paid for looking after those three syndicate horses. And to think I didn't charge them and now they accuse me of trying to cheat by using something harmful. I'm sick and tired of all this damned nonsense." He slams the bucket down on the soft earth and it topples, almost losing the seeds which look like small grains of sand.

"Why would someone say this then?"

"Because they want to divert attention away from themselves. You said that Emma told you this. I'd go after her and challenge her, if I were you." The pale skin of his face is flushed and his eyes are narrowed.

"I'd like someone, just one person, to tell me the truth and to tell me everything they know. Could you be that one person?"

"I've told you what I can." He turns away from me, lunges at the bucket, picks it up and cradles it in one arm.

"That's not everything though, is it?"

He grabs a large handful of seed and wafts his arm to one side and then to the other as he walks, letting the seed shower down onto the dark, wet earth.

"Don't you want to find out why Grayson was killed and who did it?" I ask. I traipse behind him with Kelly at my heels, and seed sticks on to my boots. "You know, don't you?"

"I have no goddam idea."

"I'm sure you know more than you've told me."

"Some secrets are best kept as secrets. I'm too old for this harassment. I've got bigger things on my mind."

"I need your help, Russell."

"This could have been a pleasant visit. Kelly's such a nice dog." He quickens his pace, spreading the seed with quick, sweeping movements. I give up and turn to go back to the truck.

* * *

Melissa's on the doorstep promptly at nine o'clock with coffee and toasted bagels.

"Your farm is awesome," she says as I open the door for her.

"I'm lucky to have this as my home."

"Yeah, you are. And the horses. And this must be Kelly. She's lovely, aren't you?" Melissa rubs her hands up and down Kelly's ears.

"How did you know her name?"

"You must have mentioned her yesterday. You said you have some cats?"

"Cooper is the house cat and I have a couple of friendly barn cats as well."

"Where's Cooper?"

"He'll show up soon, I'm sure."

"After coffee and bagels, I'd love to have a tour of everything."

I make myself some tea while Melissa talks about her job. She loves the work, but it sounds like she doesn't have much respect for the veterinarian she works for. She hopes to get something closer to here.

"I'll show you the house first."

Kelly and Cooper tag along. The house seems larger as I conduct a thorough tour. We walk upstairs and Melissa detects the smell of paint.

"These bedrooms are nice," she says.

"As you can see and smell, I'm sprucing them up a bit. I've ordered new bedding."

"Why aren't you painting this one?"

"That was going to be for someone I thought might come here, but I'm not sure anymore."

"A man, I bet."

"This one is the one I thought you might like to use if you stay."

"Awesome. I can see the paddock and the woods at the back. Wow."

"And this one is for my, our, mother. I'm hoping she'll be able to come in the summer."

"Oh, I see." She walks back towards her room "What a neat idea to do up these bedrooms. I love mine. When can I move in?" She giggles and pats Kelly. I just smile in response.

The three of us amble towards the barn as Eagle and Bullet raise their heads and freeze. Just their large eyes follow our movements. Anyone would think they're lawn ornaments except for their size and flared nostrils. They know that someone different is here.

Melissa says the right things about the barn, the paddocks and fields, the horses, the barn cats and even the classical music which wafts around us, emitted by the radio in the feed room. And by the time we walk back towards the house, Eagle and Bullet have agreed that Melissa isn't a threat, and resume nosing their hay, snatching large mouthfuls.

Back inside, I unearth a couple of photograph albums out of Frank's office, so I can show Melissa what the farm looked like when Frank first bought it. I open the first one as there's a knock at the door. Kelly knows it's William.

"Hi, Meg. Ah, I see you've hired a cleaner at last." He laughs.

"William! What an awful thing to say. Now's not a good time." My face is red hot. I can't believe William would say such a tactless thing, especially about my sister, who I've only just met. He opens his mouth to add something, but I shut the door in his face.

"It's all right," Melissa says.

"No, it's not." I sit down with a thump. "He's a good friend and knew you were coming this morning, and he shouldn't have said that. Sorry, I didn't mean to shout."

"I don't think he meant anything by it."

"I can't believe William would say such a thing. He's usually kind and polite."

"You're upset. Sit down. I'll make you another cup of tea before I go. Sorry to leave you like this."

A few minutes later, I sit and stare at a lukewarm mug of tea. I think back to how I reacted. I didn't give him a chance to explain. That, more often than not, proves to be a mistake. There are always two sides to the story. But I try hard to imagine what the other side could be, and come up with nothing.

The irony is that, in my eagerness to create a sisterly relationship with Melissa, I've pushed William away and caused my sister to wonder why I reacted to what William said with such venom. Perhaps I'm over-sensitive and touchy about Melissa because I don't know how to be a sister, and because I don't know if I'm capable of loving anyone. It's a lot of pressure. But it was stupid to react in such an unkind and inconsiderate way to William. I deserve top prize for messing up relationships, some of them before they've even had a chance.

My phone pulls me out of my self-pity and self-criticism to remind me I have a meeting scheduled with Oscar and Philippa. It provides me with the incentive I need to get cleaned up and changed. We're to meet at Oscar's condo since he says he's too busy to go anywhere else.

* * *

The condo doesn't look as if it's been lived in since I visited last. We help Philippa lower herself onto the soft sofa. She'll need help to get out of it too. Oscar has carbonated spring-water, with lemon slices, poured out for us, so he's proven that he can play host if needs be.

"Your eyes look puffy," Philippa says as she peers at me.

"I didn't sleep well last night. Don't know why." I give her a half-smile and sip some water.

"I've got no time for chit-chat," Oscar says. "Let's get on with it. Meg, you're the one who asked to meet with us, so you can go from here." He crosses his legs with a flourish.

"Thanks for taking the time to meet with me. I know you're both busy. I'll get straight to the point. I need the truth about your dealings with Grayson and with Emma."

"That's easy," says Oscar. "The horses were doing so poorly that Philippa and I wanted to change both the trainer and the vet, even though they were members of the syndicate."

"How did you plan to do that?"

"We hadn't got a plan worked out." He shifts his gaze to Philippa. "I hoped you would buy them out, Philippa."

"Not a chance. Even if I had the money, which I don't, those horses aren't worth it. I've always believed that the quality of the horse is paramount. There's only so much that the trainer can do."

"But I thought we agreed we needed to change things up because everything was going wrong. I spoke to Bryce. You know, the trainer who's in the same barn where Grayson was. I heard he's a hard worker and would do a good job."

"You talked to Bryce?" Philippa squirms and lunges forward, as if trying to launch herself out of her soft nest. "He's a no-good useless piece of shit. Didn't you think to look at his race record? Who told you he was good?"

"Emma."

"So, the useless vet told you that Bryce is a good trainer. This would be funny if it wasn't so terribly sad."

"I thought we'd agreed." Oscar unfolds his legs and leans forward with his arms on his thighs.

"I don't know where you got that stupid idea from." Philippa flops back on the sofa as if exhausted. "Bryce would be my last choice. All he ever says is that he wants a level playing-field and that he reports anything that isn't fair. What it boils down to, is that he has sour grapes because he can't get results."

"Philippa," I say, "what do you think is at the root of the problems? For one thing, I've heard that the syndicate horses get ailments of all sorts, when other horses don't appear to."

"They seem to get everything going, but I think the real issue is that the horses don't have what it takes to be runners. I blame Grayson for selecting those horses in the first place. He obviously doesn't have a good eye or good horse-sense. Useless."

"They do get sick a lot," Oscar says as he puts his glass down on the table. "That's why I wanted someone else to look at them. I asked the vet, Edwin, to examine them, but he wouldn't unless I got Russell and Grayson to agree."

"Now, that I'd agree with. I respect Edwin," Philippa says. "He's the new vet now anyway, so that's good."

"Have things improved?" I ask.

"Not enough to satisfy me," Oscar says as he clasps his hands behind his head and leans back. "I want out. I've had it with this business. It shouldn't be called a business, it's just one big gamble and the owners usually lose while the trainers, vets, jockeys and barn crew do okay. We take all the risk."

"But if you have the right horses…" Philippa says.

"You need the right people too," Oscar interrupts. "And we have nothing right. Rehashing all this isn't getting us anywhere. I just want out of the whole thing, and frankly, I couldn't give a damn who killed Grayson. I still think it was suicide. He should have killed himself. It was the honourable thing to do."

"Oscar, hang on," Philippa says. "That's a terrible thing to say. While I'm angry and disappointed and frustrated, I wouldn't say he should have killed himself. I don't think that five under-performing horses is enough to die for, personally."

"Well, I do," Oscar says. "It's a disgrace."

"I'm going to end this with one last question," I say. "Assume that Grayson was murdered. Who do you think could have a motive to want him dead?"

"Bryce," says Philippa. "He's scum, and I know he didn't like Grayson. Amy told me he hung around the barn a lot. That's not right. There's something odd about that guy. I'd guess he wanted to get rid of the competition that he had a hate-on for."

"No, it was Emma," says Oscar. "My theory is that she was trying out new drugs that she made up herself. Let's face it, we got enough bills for medication. I think she thought she was going to come up with some dope that wouldn't be picked up in testing, but would make the horses run faster. But all she did was make them sick."

I thank them both for their time. It's just as well that I made notes since my mind is misty, as if my silent tears have leaked into my thoughts. I lack the will or the energy to do anything else today, so drive home with Kelly with no other ambition than to make sure all the animals are looked after.

*   *   *

"I told you that you're not welcome here," I say, as I stand on the threshold of the back door and stare at Murray.

"I need to come in to give you something. It's important."

I let him walk past me. A frown deepens the furrows of my brow as I catch a whiff of alcohol.

"Murray, I wish you weren't drinking again."

"I'm fine. But I would be a lot better if you showed some compassion towards me. You're all the family I have here in Canada. Remember, I'm your brother-in-law. Not some person pretending to be a relation."

"I take it you're referring to Melissa, my half-sister."

He sits down and I remain standing.

"She was here yesterday," he says. "I imagine she has her claws into you."

"You've been watching me again. Honestly, Murray, this is ridiculous. It's all about the money, isn't it? You can have all of it. I just hope Frank isn't looking down on you as you drift back into alcoholism and spend his money on booze."

"You're a self-righteous bitch, aren't you? You act like a judge and jury. You just criticize other people You do nothing to help them. You're plain selfish and uncaring. No wonder Frank faked his death. I see it now. It was a way to escape the hell that he was in, living with you. Clever, really."

"Murray, you can be so charming and pleasant to be with, when you're not drinking."

"You're not charming or pleasant at any time, so I reckon that's one for me, no two."

"Enough. What did you want to give me, other than cruel words?"

"This." He slaps an envelope down on the table. "I don't know why I'm doing this. It's a hard copy to show the transfer of one million into your account. You won't get any more until you come to your senses. I'm going overseas. You can email me when you change your attitude and you can hope that some of the rest of the money is left."

"Murray, I wish you'd go back to the Lighthouse Rehabilitation Centre."

"There's nothing wrong with me. It's you that's the problem."

"And I don't want to make things even worse between us, but that money is Frank's. You don't have a right to take it."

"Says who? He would have expected you to let me live in his house. His own brother. And he would have expected you to show some care. You don't give anything, do you? It's all take with you. I can see that. I'm looking after Frank's money, that's what I'm doing."

"No, that's not what you're doing."

Before I can say any more, he stands up and lets himself out, leaving me both saddened and astounded.

I look at the envelope as if it might bite me. And I contemplate what Frank would think if he was around. He would be apoplectic if he knew Murray was drinking his money, the very thing he'd fought with Murray about so many times. Perhaps it wasn't just for tax reasons he banked his millions overseas. He didn't want Murray to know about his wealth. So, no-one could know. He wanted his brother to get well. And Murray had finally got well after Frank disappeared, using money from a trust fund, set up by Frank, to pay for rehab. I wish with all my heart there was a permanent cure for alcoholism and that I could stop Murray from self-destructing. But what he wants me to do, I cannot possibly do. He can't live here and I can't give up my half-sister. And William.

I ache inside when I think of William.

My mobile warns me it's time to get ready to go to the races. I can't be bothered to make much effort with my appearance. A sullen face confronts me when I look in the mirror, so I turn away. I pull on some slacks and put on a thin sweater. That's all I have the energy for. Everything seems pointless.

10

Another Victim

Linda's excellent grooming shows as usual. Speed's coat gleams. If there was a 'groom of the month' award, I would nominate her every time. As I watch Speed, with his jockey, being led out by the pony to the post parade, my intuition gives me a prod. It alerts my senses and pulls me out of my self-indulgent funk. He doesn't have the usual spring in his step and his ears aren't pricked forward as they should be. I find Neal.

"You noticed it too," he says. My face must look glum and pale, and more so because my horse might not be well.

"I can't put my finger on it. The vet hasn't said anything?"

"No, he's sound. I don't think anyone else would notice it. He's just a little under his form and there's no reason for it unless he's catching a virus, or something else is brewing. He's shown no signs until now and he passed the vet check this morning."

"Should we scratch?"

"I don't think that would be a good idea. We have to have a reason otherwise he'll be penalized. I've told the jockey to go easy on him."

"Okay."

We stand at the rail by the track. Our expectations have never been so low, and our concern for Speed has never been so high. He comes second from last and looks much more tired after the race than he should be.

"I'll get some more bloodwork done. I can't make sense of this," Neal says. "Last time his bloodwork came back fine."

"He must be getting real sick," Linda says as she leads him back to the barn. "He's not himself."

* * *

The birds and I are up early this morning. Their cheerful songs and the bright sunshine should lift my spirits but they have the opposite effect. I feel miserable, so everything and everyone around me should reflect that. I don't care who killed Grayson, so I won't do any more work on it. All I care about are my horses and Kelly and Cooper, and the barn cats, of course.

I give the barn a thorough cleaning: I sweep the aisle, clean the counter in the feed room and scrub the buckets. Kelly spends most of the time sprawled on her side in the doorway, sunbathing. She must be hot to the touch by now. I sit down on the floor next to her and lean against the large, solid doorpost. She lifts her head, glances at me, and lays her head back down.

Just as I take a deep breath to help me relax, she scrambles up and runs full tilt towards the house. I didn't notice a car come up the driveway. It's William. My heart misses a beat. I wish I'd taken a shower. He has someone with him. I get up slowly, wary of what this visit is about since I told him to leave, and I know my anger showed. I stay standing by the barn.

Melissa jogs over to me.

"Don't say anything," she says, catching her breath. "It's very important that you listen to me. Please."

I look at her. Her eyes remind me of Kelly's when she's asking me for something. I can never resist them. Besides, I should at least listen. I've made so many mistakes when I haven't listened.

"Can we go into the house?" she asks.

William stands by the car. Stupid tears threaten to run down my cheeks which have flushed like crimson beacons, betraying the emotion I won't even let myself acknowledge.

I lead the way to the house, and we all sit at the kitchen table. Kelly has her head on William's thigh and gazes up at him with adoration. Cooper is on Melissa's lap, purring so loudly that it's the only noise I hear other than the thumping of my heart.

"Okay, this isn't going to be easy," Melissa says as she squirms on the chair. Cooper jumps down. "Sorry, Cooper."

William gets up and puts the kettle on and gets the coffee maker going.

"It's going to be really difficult for you not to say anything," she says, "but it honestly would be good if you could just listen. It's ever so important. I'm sorry to do this, but I have to. Okay?"

"Okay," I say. I can't imagine what she can say of such import.

"Our mother," she says.

"Ah. I should have guessed it would have something to do with her," I say.

"This is going to be impossible if you don't just listen."

"Okay."

"Our mother connected with me a while ago. I registered on that adoption reunite site. I think it was when I was fourteen. She registered sometime later, don't know exactly when. She told me she had to use one of the computers in the library and set up an email address that she only used there. She's not tech savvy, but she was determined to find me. I was still in England, so we met. There was a large part of me that didn't want to meet her, ever. After all, she abandoned me. She did nothing for me as I was growing up, being bounced about from one foster home to another. But I wanted to know something about her, about why she tossed me aside. After Stan died, she told me about you. And she told me that my father's Canadian and urged me to move to Canada to be near you, so that we could get to know one another and become family. She said that she wanted us to be sisters more than anything else in the world. Then she told me she'd been having some weird symptoms, headaches and dizziness, and she thought she might not have long to live. But she asked me to wait for you to find me. She wanted it that way. But the other really odd thing is that William found out about me. Mother had blurted it out when he met her here, when you were in Kentucky, I think it was. She told him everything. And it was the truth, which you know can be a challenge for Mum. She's a dab hand at lying. William tracked me down and I told him that Mum wanted you to find me, so he said he wouldn't say anything. Neither of us wanted to damage whatever relationship you have with Mum. So, when William saw me here, it was a big surprise, and he was taken aback and…"

"Said an idiotic thing," William says. "It was a sorry attempt at a joke, I guess."

"But, Meg, why did you react so angrily to what he said? It really wasn't that bad. Why didn't you give him a chance, especially since it's obvious the two of you love each other?"

Like a spoilt child, I run up the stairs, slam my bedroom door, flop onto my bed, and pound the pillow with my fists. Tears flow as if they've been bottled up inside me for most of my life. They erupt like the lava from a volcano, which has tricked everyone into thinking it was dormant for good, but then it spews its molten rock and covers everything around it.

I can't cope with these people who want to be close to me. It's overwhelming and suffocating. I don't have what it takes to be a friend, let alone a lover. I need to live alone. My beloved animals are enough company and give me unconditional love. No complications. No pressure. No expectations that I can't live up to.

I hear someone coming up the stairs and dread my door being opened.

"Just letting Kelly in," says William.

Kelly gets up on the bed. She licks my face, although she knows it isn't usually allowed. I suppose this is one of those exceptional circumstances. She stops, sits up, and looks at me. Sometimes I think she's half-human and perhaps smarter than I am. At the moment, that's probably not a high bar to achieve. She jumps off the bed, goes to the door, turns her head to look at me and emits a soft whine. I don't move. She jumps back onto the bed. I want to stroke her but she jumps down again and repeats her move to the door with another whine. She wants me to go with her downstairs.

"You're right, Kelly. I'm being stupid." I get up, pull a clean, thin sweater over my head and brush my hair. I dab a light coating of face powder on, but I can't do anything about my red, puffy eyes. But the release of those tears, that letting go, has allowed calmness to grow and, perhaps ironically, resilience and resolve to re-surge.

As I walk downstairs, I can't hear anything. Perhaps they've both left. It's as if I'm entering a vacuum, being sucked into nothingness. I fight it, but despite all that I do in my attempt to convince myself otherwise, I know I don't want to be alone. I want to be loved and to love. I always have. I walk slowly towards the kitchen, dreading seeing an empty room. Kelly's tail wags, so I think someone must be here.

"Kelly brought you down, I see," William says. He pats her and finds one of her treats for her.

"I'm sorry," Melissa says as she comes into the kitchen from the family room. "I shouldn't have said what I did. I can be far too abrupt. I really want to be a wonderful sister to you. I mean it. Can I give you a brief hug?"

I walk towards her and we have a quick hug. She's warm and smells of citrus. My tears are close to the surface again. I sit down.

"Just made a pot of tea, but I'm not the greatest at tea, as you know." William pours me a mug.

"I'm the one who should say sorry. I don't understand my own emotions sometimes," I say. "I'm over-reacting to everything."

"Let's put this behind us and start again," William says.

"I can't believe our mother didn't tell me about you," I say as I look up at Melissa, who's standing with Cooper in her arms.

"Let's not worry about that." William says. "We know your mother works in mysterious ways." He puts two mugs of coffee on the table. "Let's just see if we can move forward with a fresh start."

"Well, I want to know sometime, but I agree. I would like a chance at a fresh start." I try to smile, but not sure if all I've done is straighten my mouth.

"What I want to know is how you're getting on with this murder thing," Melissa says.

"I've decided that I'm not pursuing it," I say.

William ignores what I said. "I have an idea," he says. "Why don't we all go for lunch to the nice Italian restaurant you like, Meg? Kelly can keep an eye on us from the front seat of my car. We can talk about the murder and figure out how we can help you. Okay?"

As William drives us all to the restaurant, I think about the three others in the car. I look at Kelly, who's at my feet, and see her unconditional love in her eyes. I look at William and see his large hands on the steering wheel, which I find comforting. I don't know why. And, as I listen to Melissa's warm, bubbly voice behind me, a smile grows inside me.

In the restaurant William and Melissa have lots of questions about the people I've talked to about Grayson's murder and Russell's fall, and it helps me to get my thoughts organized. As we get up from the table, my mobile rings. It's Neal.

"You won't believe this," Neal says. His voice is edgy and shaky. "But Emma is dead."

"What? Oh no!"

"She died the same way Grayson did. Injection. Syringe found. Word is that it's suicide. Like a copycat thing."

"That makes no sense at all."

"I'm real worried. There's a murderer here. Who's he going to kill next?"

"I wish I knew the motive."

"Can you gear up your investigation? I don't think the police consider either to be murder. But I'm sure there's a killer on the loose, and lots of other folk around here feel the same way. We need answers."

"I'll do what I can."

"Another thing: I can't understand it, but Speed's bloodwork came back okay. But Edwin's convinced there's something in his system. I didn't notice anything in the days before the race but, as you know, he tends to be an under-achiever in his training, doing better in races. Anyway, Edwin's having more tests done. I think whatever it is, it had to have been deliberate."

"Why would someone harm Speed?"

"Perhaps someone thinks you're getting too close."

"It would be awful to think that Speed is unwell because of something I'm doing."

"Please don't give up. I'm sure, once whatever it is gets out of his system, he'll recover quickly. And stopping other people being killed and other horses being hurt is pretty important."

"Absolutely."

As we drive back to the farm, I tell William and Melissa what Neal said.

"Wow, that's tragic. Shocking, actually," William says. "I wish I could be around this afternoon, but I have an appointment with a client that I can't cancel."

"I can stay around," Melissa says. "I didn't tell you, but I resigned from that vet clinic. I wasn't happy working for him. I thought I'd be able to focus more on my job search. I want something in Vannersville."

"That's a big step."

"Yeah, I suppose it is, but it feels right. Vet tech jobs aren't that difficult to get. Even if I just get a maternity leave, that's okay."

"Would you like to stay in your freshly painted bedroom at the farm?" I look out of the side window, hoping that this isn't the wrong thing to suggest for either of us. Change is happening faster than I'm prepared for. But I need to smarten up and face it, and enjoy what comes. I take a deep breath.

"Awesome. I thought you'd never ask!" She pats my arm.

* * *

Kelly and I go to the track to talk with Neal before he leaves for the day. I find him and Linda in silence, with their heads down, in his cramped office. The sunshine can't come through the door, but hot and stuffy air hits my face as I enter. They both look up at the same time. Linda's face is flushed, whereas Neal's is pale.

"This is awful," Linda says.

"Two suspicious deaths. At least that's what we all think," I say.

"I mean about Speed." Linda looks at me, her round, red cheeks glistening with fresh tears.

"Could it be that he's caught a virus?" I ask.

"The bloodwork results don't support that," Neal says.

"How's he doing?" I ask.

"He seems to be okay," Neal says. "But I'm giving him a rest from training for at least three days. I've asked security to keep an extra special eye on this barn."

"Who could do that to him?" asks Linda as she looks down at her hands which clasp tissues and lie on her lap.

"I can't understand anyone wanting to harm an animal, let alone a beautiful thoroughbred racehorse," I say.

"Neither can I," Neal says. "Whoever did this killed two people, so watch out because this person is a monster."

"It might not be linked, and perhaps it's just a coincidence and has nothing to do with anything that's been going on." I say. Linda's eyes meet mine with a defiant stare. "But I'm not ruling out foul play. Any idea who might want Speed out of the picture?"

"I've gone over it all," Neal says, "the horses that were in that race, their owners, trainers and even their grooms, but can't find anyone that I think would do something like that to him. And none of them used Emma as their vet and none of the horses were ever trained by Grayson."

"And no links to Bryce, Oscar, Philippa or Russell?" I ask.

"Don't mention Russell to me. He's driving me crazy," Neal says.

"What do you mean?"

"I've got some stuff to do before I go," Linda says as she chucks her tissues in the garbage bin.

"I'll be there in a bit," Neal says. He turns to face me. "Russell has been here first thing the past couple of mornings asking me to find buyers for the last two syndicate horses. I don't know what's making him this desperate. He sure wants to get rid of them."

"How are they doing?"

"Poorly. Not sure why because they have good breeding and conformation. I like both of them, but they're not showing talent. Grayson had a good eye for a horse, so I'd be surprised if they didn't have some promise. It's a bit of a puzzle."

"What about the two which were claimed last year? I mean, how are they doing now? Do you know?"

"Funny you should ask. I thought it'd be interesting to follow them. And they've each won their first race out this year. Mind you, they were both optional claiming races, nothing fancy, but I'm pretty sure Russell and his pals would've been happy with that if they were still theirs and none of this other stuff had happened."

"That's interesting."

"And I'm in shock about Emma. It's like a nightmare."

"It's tragic. It's beyond belief. Tell me what you know."

"It's not much. She was found by the security guard. I think he's the same one who found Grayson. He's off on stress leave, not surprisingly."

"Poor guy. Did you talk with him by any chance?"

"No, but his mate gave me this envelope for you, from him."

There's a small piece of paper inside with scratchy writing: "Noon, tomorrow, at coffee shop over the street."

I show it to Neal.

* * *

My bed feels comfortable and safe as I nestle myself deeper into the soft, puffy bedding. Despite the alarm having sounded, Kelly continues to snore, her paws twitching. Cooper's nowhere to be seen and must have got up early. There are no other humans in the house, but I'm not lonely. William's coming over this evening and promises to bring food for the three of us. Melissa plans to move in if she can make all the arrangements, whatever that means, tomorrow afternoon.

But, despite all these good things, it's as if the wind has been knocked out of me. I've been on a roller-coaster ride of emotions. My insides feel as if they've been tossed about and refuse to settle.

Spending time in the barn with the horses yesterday evening and taking a walk with Kelly in the back field afterwards made no difference.

I'm shaken by Emma's death: perturbed and even distraught by the thought that, if I'd been more diligent in my investigation, I might have been able to prevent it. She could still be alive.

I don't believe for one minute that it's a copycat suicide. My intuition refuses to accept that as a plausible scenario.

My stomach is too upset to accept food, but the thought of it conjures up the image of a carrot muffin, which reminds me of Linda's early morning visits and how much I miss them. Her absence has left a hole. I didn't realize how much I enjoyed and appreciated her coming and how she gave Hector extra love and attention. But he's okay. Access to the flourishing spring pasture has given him a shiny coat, and his freedom has calmed him down. No more round-pen and confined spaces all day long.

Knowing I must eat something, I nibble on a chocolate cookie as Kelly crunches on a dog biscuit. I summon up enough energy to call my mother.

She picks up the phone before I hear the call go through.

"I was expecting you to ring," she says. Her voice sounds stronger, but agitated.

"How are you doing?"

"Alright. Well, I'm not sure. How are you doing?"

"Melissa's talked to you, hasn't she?"

"She has. I think she and William told you everything."

"Why didn't you tell me everything?"

"Because I didn't have the guts to tell you about your sister. You'd been hurt enough. I knew you'd see it as another one of my failures."

"I'd much, much, rather you told me the truth. It would make things so much less complicated and prevent a lot of misunderstandings and hurt."

"It's all very well for you to say that, but it was hard. My visit to see you was meant to be the opportunity to introduce you to Melissa. But I messed it up, and I was scared witless about my headaches and dizziness, and I was weighed down by money worries."

"Did you see Melissa while you were here?"

"Only a couple of times, since you want honesty. She's not forgiven me for anything. And finding out that I hadn't told her about you right away, hasn't helped. Then she wanted so much to meet you, but I said she couldn't until I told you. I don't know why I blurted out the whole caboodle to William when you were in Kentucky. He just happened to be in the right place at the right time for me to spill all the beans. Or the wrong place at the wrong time. Since I'd told him about Melissa, I thought I might as well tell you, but I lost the courage. I hoped William would keep it all confidential, but most people can't keep secrets, except me. I seem to be pretty darn good at it."

"You hid Melissa from me for years. I could have got to know her, especially after she came to live just an hour away. You never know, our relationship could have made a difference in our lives."

"Don't make this even harder. There's nothing I can do to make this better for you."

"What made you tell me in the end?"

"Despite what the doctor said, I was afraid that I might die, and I knew I should do the right thing and tell you and try to explain."

"But you still didn't tell me the whole truth. You had me deal with that adoption reunite site when you were in contact with Melissa."

"But I thought you'd be hurt and angry if I told you I'd seen her and spoken with her and not told you."

"But you've admitted that you thought William would let the cat out of the bag, so I would have found out. You must have realized that it would be better for me to hear it from you and the earlier the better."

"You have a point. Don't suppose I think clearly about these things sometimes. I just couldn't tell you the truth, not all of it in one go. Look, this is exhausting me and we're not getting anywhere. Can't we just go on from here?" Her voice has grown raspy and has a discernible tremble.

"It's not easy." I'm sure mothers are supposed to tell their children if they have sisters or brothers, even if by a different father. And I'm certain that someone who acts as if they love you shouldn't be in cahoots with your mother, aiding and abetting (as William himself would put it) in a conspiracy of silence.

"I've got to get some rest. Just remember, Melissa's your own flesh and blood. Family." She hangs up the phone before I can respond. I rest my head on my arms, which are folded on the table.

Kelly's whines wake me up from my dose. My arms are stiff and my neck aches from being in such an awkward position. Perhaps Kelly needs to go out. I look at my phone and there have been four text messages sent by Oscar over a period of an hour. I must have been in an unusually deep sleep, oblivious to my phone's beeping. A strong cup of tea and some food would help, but I can't think of anything I'd like to eat. Besides, there are hardly any groceries in the house. But there is half of a large, dark chocolate bar at the back of a cupboard, saved for emergencies, and this classifies as one.

Five minutes later I feel better and get hold of Oscar.

"Sorry I couldn't get back to you right away," I say as I stifle a yawn.

"Have you just woken up or something? I thought you horsey people were up with the chickens." He sounds annoyed.

"I've been up for quite a while. Just had a lot on my plate. What did you want to talk with me about?"

"I wanted to make sure that you understand I was right."

"You were right about what?"

"You wouldn't last a minute in the business I'm in." He coughs. "I was right about my deduction that Emma murdered Grayson. She's committed suicide, hasn't she? That proves it."

"But I thought you said that you believed Grayson committed suicide. It was only when I pressed you, asked you to assume that Grayson was murdered, that you came up with the possibility that Emma murdered Grayson."

"Emma's given herself away now, hasn't she? It's obvious."

"Perhaps it's too obvious."

"How can something be too obvious? It's clear cut, that's what I say."

11

Missing

My chat with Oscar shook me into action. I'm in the shedrow feeding Speed some carrots as I wait for Neal. He's in a conversation with Edwin and hasn't noticed me. I don't like to interrupt.

"Meg, I didn't see you. We're talking about Speed's bloodwork. Edwin had more tests done." He and Edwin walk towards me. "Some odd results."

"I told Neal that I can't come up with an explanation for the data," the veterinarian says. "There are no prohibited drugs in his system but my assessment points to some contamination. It'll be a new drug that there's no test for yet. That's my guess."

"I can't believe it," Neal says.

"It could be contamination of the stall or bedding," Edwin says. "It only takes a small amount, depending on what it is."

"I moved some of the horses around," Neal says. "This is bad." He turns to face me. "Speed and Rose should go home for a while until we find out what's going on."

"I agree," I say. "I have a feeling that Speed's condition is linked to the murders somehow."

"Murders?" Edwin's eyes widen. "I suppose I shouldn't be surprised that you think Emma didn't commit suicide. I have to say that I'm pretty cut up about losing her. We had a good professional relationship."

"Meg," Neal says. "This gives me the opportunity to ask you for a big favour. Russell doesn't want me to do this because he wants to sell them asap, but I'd like you to have the two remaining syndicate horses at your farm until this clears up. They're still not doing well. There's weird stuff going on and it's giving me the creeps. Before you say no, Linda has offered to help you look after them all since you'd have five horses plus your two retirees."

"Goodness, that would be almost a full barn," I say, as my mind whirs and I contemplate all the ramifications.

"Before you ask. I don't want them to go to Russell's. Something's going on with him. He's acting strange since he had that accident at the farm."

"I wondered."

"I'd appreciate it. I could rest knowing the horses are in good hands at your farm, with Linda's help."

"For the sake of the horses, I'll make it work. Linda's the clincher. Also, someone else will be at the farm for a while and she's a vet tech." I turn to Edwin. "You're not looking for a vet tech at the moment, by any chance?"

"Not right now, but one plans to start veterinary college in the fall. Ask her to send in a resume."

"So, I can ship all four horses out to you tomorrow?" asks Neal.

"Tomorrow, wow. I suppose that'll be okay if Linda comes and helps set up and unload," I say. Although I'm saddened that the horses aren't well and horrified that there have been two murders, I confess I'm looking forward to the carrot muffins, but especially to seeing Linda again every morning.

* * *

The coffee shop is stark. Everything is angular and colourless, mostly grey, but it looks clean. The staff are dressed in dark-grey uniforms and each wears a white baseball-hat. It's noon and there are only three other customers. One is the security guard who I almost fail to recognize, since he's in blue-jeans and a hoodie. He's slouched over the table with his arms encircled around a mug of something. I nod to him and order my tea, which isn't simple since they have so many varieties and several choices of milk and containers. I take the easy way out and have orange pekoe with two percent milk in a mug.

As I approach the small round table, he straightens his tall body and stretches out his legs.

"Thanks for coming," he says as he leans towards me. "My name's Des. Not sure if you know."

"Hello, Des." I smile and sit down.

"I admit I'm a mess. Finding two dead people, people I know, has shook me up."

"Have you got anyone you can talk to who might be able to help?"

"I can't see what they can do but I'm going to see this counselor person: included in my benefits. I didn't know, but someone told me."

"I hope it's helpful."

"Yeah, well."

"So, you want to tell me something?"

"I want to say that I'm bloody angry that another person has died. Why haven't you or the police caught the shit who did this?"

"From what I've heard, the police believe both deaths are suicides."

"Do you?"

"No, I think they're both murders."

"Got to be the same killer. Emma could be alive if you'd found out who killed Grayson." He leans back again and rubs his hands on his thighs.

"We're all upset and stressed and concerned. Des, I don't see the point of this conversation. Do you have information which might help me find out who the killer is? If you don't, I'll leave."

"You see, it's not just you and the police I blame, I blame me too."

"Why do you blame yourself?"

"Because I saw someone go into Emma's trailer that evening but didn't think nothing of it. I should've been suspicious."

"Have you any idea who it was?"

"I've done a rough drawing of what I saw. It's not much."

"This is a good sketch."

"I like to draw. It's sort of a hobby, I guess. Do you have any idea who it could be?"

"I can think of a couple of people. Can I keep this? I'd like to show it around."

"Yeah, sure. I don't want it."

"I'll make a copy and keep the original safe in case the police eventually take some action and want it as evidence."

"Yeah."

"Anything else?"

"Remember I told you there's a guy who hangs around outside the south gate and sells stuff?"

I nod.

"On my day off I told him I'd heard a trainer had been murdered by injection of ketamine. He said he doesn't deal in that stuff. He said there'd be no demand here because the vets all have it. He reckoned it would be easy enough to get some in the backstretch. He didn't say, but I'm sure he's into pot because it's popular at the track. I don't think he's a high-end dealer because the guys here don't have much money."

"Okay."

"Not much help?"

"I don't know. It's helpful to know that he didn't supply the drug, I suppose. So, a vet or someone with access to a vet's supplies, must be the murderer. I'd sort of come to that conclusion."

"I hadn't. I was sure that this guy was the supplier. When he said he wasn't, I asked my mates if they had ideas."

"Did you come up with anything?"

"They said it would be a piece of cake to get hold of ketamine in the backstretch."

"Oh, I see."

"You don't know much, do you? If you don't do something soon, my mates and I are going to raise funds to get a proper PI. I'm not the only one who's pissed off that there's a murderer still free to go about his business in the backstretch."

"No, you're not the only one," I say. "I promise I'm on it."

"Okay then."

"Thanks for this sketch. Let me know anything else you find out or think of."

"Yeah. But I'm lying low for a bit."

"Good idea."

*   *   *

William texts and suggests that we go out for a meal this evening instead of eating at the farm. When he receives my vague answer, he responds that I've lost weight and that we need time to talk, and that it might be better for both these reasons if we went to a restaurant. It's hard to argue with either of those realities.

I plan to take most of the afternoon to organize the barn for four more horses, and then I'll pick up feed and arrange for the delivery of more wood shavings and hay. I have enough buckets for water and feed.

Under normal circumstances, the four coming from the track would be full of energy and at the peak of fitness, but I expect them to be below par because of the odd things that have happened to them. I'll be cautious, though. They won't be let out into a large field where they could gallop frantically, enjoying their newfound freedom, and run into a fence or slide and fall, or kick up their heels with such zeal that they hurt themselves on a gate or fence. They'll each get time in the round-pen until they calm down, and then they can go into the paddock. The workload and responsibility involved in the care of seven horses is a little daunting, especially since they aren't all mine. But once I get to know the new syndicate horses and work out a routine, it should be fine.

* * *

Time has flown by this afternoon, but I have everything ready for the horses' arrival tomorrow. I've just had a quick shower and am surveying my wardrobe. I push hangers this way and that, scraping and clanking, but nothing looks right. It doesn't help that I can't focus. I have my mind on William. I'm surprised how excited I am about going out for a meal with him. Is it because I'm starving? No, I know it's because I want to be with him, and it seems such a long time since we had a good talk and spent time together, just the two of us.

William invited Melissa, but she said she was too busy packing. I'm relieved he mentioned her because I'd forgotten that she's also coming tomorrow, as well as the horses. I'll have to get her bedroom ready after we come back from the restaurant. The new bedding has been washed and dried, but is folded on the bed. There are no towels or toiletries out in the bathroom. I should do something about that as well.

Kelly enjoys the ride to the restaurant and sits bolt-upright on the back seat of William's car. He's a sensible, defensive driver, and she thinks it's safe to gamble that she won't be tossed off the seat by an abrupt maneuver. When I get out of the car, she squeezes between the front seats and sits on the passenger side to get a clear view of the restaurant.

"I've reserved a table by the window," William says. "Kelly will be able to keep an eye on us."

Although we're at a different restaurant, seeing Kelly on the seat as she follows us with her eyes brings back a vivid, unsettling memory. It was in a similar situation that William pulled the plug on our relationship without warning, saying that from then onwards he would see me in a professional capacity only. I was more devastated than I could admit at that point. Surely that can't happen again.

"You gasped. What's wrong?" William asks. How did that gasp get out? "Ah, I know. That's not going to happen." He reaches for my cool hand with his warm one, melting the frosty crystals coating my insides. A soft glow of warmth envelops me and reminds me of the coziness and safety of my puffy bedding. I smile and squeeze his hand.

* * *

I had a full heart as well as a full stomach when I went to bed last night. Perhaps that's why I had such a good sleep. When the alarm went off, it took me a second to realize where I was and what day it is. A busy day, full of arrivals. William wanted to help, but he has two challenging court cases on the go, and doesn't have the time. Ramona, his assistant, is getting better and started back to work at half-time this week which helps a lot.

William and I talked about anything and everything last evening. Eventually, we discussed the murders. William has some good police contacts, so he offered to check with them to find out if they've launched investigations into either death and, if so, what information has been gathered that they can share. I've seen nothing

149

in the media, but I'm not a reliable reader, listener or viewer of the news, although I peruse the local paper most weeks (if I can retrieve it from the deep, soggy ditch where it is usually chucked).

I throw on some barn clothes and sprint down the stairs. Kelly hears Linda's car crunching its way up the gravel driveway, so I grab my lightweight barn-coat. It's breezy and unsettled, but the air has no cold bite to it. A decent spring day. We greet Linda as she gets out of her car. My appetite is back with a vengeance. Visions of carrot muffins pop into my mind's eye. I'll be sorely disappointed if Linda hasn't brought me one.

"I won't be long this morning. Just dropping off stuff," Linda says.

There's no carrot muffin.

"Is there anything I need to know about?"

"There's some skin medication for Fay, a vitamin supplement that Neal wants them all to have, and he asked me to drop off their health records. I'll help keep track of worming and shots and that stuff."

"Sounds like they're going to be here for a long time."

"Neal says until the killer's caught he doesn't want them in his barn. He thinks there's a link. He doesn't want them hurt any more than they've already been."

"I hope I don't have to hire a security guard again. Will you be here when they arrive?"

"I'll help Neal load first, and then I'm going to follow the truck."

"That's good. I'm not sure if Melissa will be around in time."

"I'll be here. See you then."

As we watch Linda close the gate at the end of the driveway, my stomach rumbles so loudly that Kelly looks at me and cocks her head.

Back in the kitchen, I put a piece of frozen bread into the toaster and give Kelly a biscuit. Cooper wanders in, stops, stretches out his front legs and reaches back with his behind, and yawns, revealing a cavernous mouth that looks as if it would be capable of swallowing a whole mouse. I give him a couple of treats.

Kelly yips and runs to the door, which I open to reveal Melissa, laden down with bags, much earlier than expected. After a quick hug, I help her get her things up to the bedroom.

"I have other stuff in the car," she says. She runs down the stairs with Kelly close on her heels. They both disappear out of the kitchen door, but they're back before I have time to sit at the table. Melissa is weighed down by groceries this time. "I have tea and coffee in the car as well, and some bagels." She dashes out again. I open the various plastic bags and put some of the groceries away.

"Thanks for all this," I say.

"You're welcome. I would have been here earlier, but I went to the track to give my resume to Edwin, as you suggested. He acted as if you'd never spoken with him, but that didn't matter. He seemed fine about it, so that's what counts. But when I was there, I heard that Amy's disappeared. That's the groom who worked for Grayson, right?"

"Disappeared?"

"She hasn't been seen for a couple of days and no-one seems to know where she is or been able to connect with her. The trainer she works for is hopping mad."

"There's a shortage of workers because of new restrictions affecting foreign workers, so I can see why he'd be annoyed, but I would've thought he should be concerned more than angry. I wonder if something's happened to her?"

"Gosh, I hope there hasn't been another murder."

"Don't say that. I can't bear to think of it. As it is, I'm being blamed for the second murder because I haven't found the killer."

"That's hardly fair."

"Perhaps, but it's shaken me up. They know I'm investigating. They think I should be doing a better job and perhaps they're right."

I look at Kelly. She wags her tail and her eyes make her look as if she's smiling at me, telling me it's okay, that I'm not to blame. I know she's not, really. She's just saying she loves me regardless of what anyone else thinks of me. I need her unconditional love. I ruffle her ears.

"I'll help," Melissa says.

"That would be great. I hoped you'd offer. I've something you can do. I have a drawing of a person who was seen entering Emma's office trailer. It was sketched by Des, the security guard, who's the guy who found both bodies. He saw this person enter her office but doesn't know who it is. See if you can find out."

"That sounds like a fun assignment." She folds up the copy of the sketch and puts it in her back pocket. "What can I do to help out here?"

"Are you any good at preparing meals?"

"Not very. But I'll try."

"Because not only do I have to find a murderer, I'll have seven horses to look after. Linda's going to help, but she won't be here much since Neal has other horses at the track which need her attention as well."

"Wow. Seven. I don't know a lot about horses, but I'd like to learn. I've only worked in small animal clinics, but I have some training in large animals."

"Edwin won't take you on if you don't have equine experience."

"Good job I'll get some here, then. Did you have a nice meal with William yesterday evening?"

"Yes, it was great. How did you know about it?"

"William told me. He's been good to me. Hasn't he told you?"

"Told me what?"

"That I've been staying at his place."

"Why didn't you come here?"

"It just seemed like you had a lot going on. We thought you prefer to be alone."

152

"Oh."

"What are we going to do about Amy?" Melissa picks up Cooper and strokes him, wisps of fur floating around him. "Don't worry about the cat hair. I'm good at cleaning."

"So, you are a cleaner, then?"

She laughs. My internal frown melts as she throws back her head and chuckles some more.

"Good one! But what are we going to do about Amy?" she asks.

"I plan to visit Russell. There's something about his relationship with Amy that's niggling at me. I don't think I have the whole story. The horses should arrive in about an hour, so I'll go to his farm and make sure I get back in time. It'd be good if you could help unload. I'll put them in their stalls and then rotate them out into the round-pen until they've settled down enough to let them out into the paddock and small field."

"I can open doors and gates and things."

"That'd be great. Linda will follow the truck on its way here, and she'll lead one horse while I lead another, so we'll do two at a time. Anyhow, I'll leave now so that I have time to talk with Russell."

"Okay. I'll get a light lunch. I bought some salad stuff. I'm not an adventurous salad maker, though."

"I eat poorly nearly all the time, so it'll seem like a feast to me. Thanks. And can you look after Kelly?"

"That's something I'm good at, looking after cats and dogs." She smiles and strokes Kelly's shiny head, as the dog lies her ears flat on her head, enjoying the attention. Cooper rubs against Melissa's legs. "Can I give them each a treat? Then they'll love me forever. I have some in my bag."

"You haven't had a chance to unpack."

"No worries. I can do that later. I'm just so happy to be here, you can't imagine." She does a little jump on the spot as if she's three years old and full of the joys of life, and then she rummages in a large nylon bag and pulls out two bags of treats: one for cats and one for dogs. Kelly sits politely to receive hers while Cooper jumps up onto the chair to be closer to the source. Both want more, but Melissa puts the bags on the counter. She claps her hands together. "Okay, salad, here we go!"

I smile and leave. It's as if I've just been soaking in a warm bath. If it wasn't for a murderer being on the loose, I'd be feeling pretty darn good.

12

Ambulance

Russell sits at his table. His head hangs down as if he's dropping off, his hands clasped around a mug. It's dark in the kitchen. Only a little natural light makes its way through the two small windows and screen door (which still hasn't been repaired), because the clouds have darkened the sky. There are no lights on.

I knock on the door jamb, but get no response, so I walk in and stand in front of him.

"Are you okay?"

"Just tired," he says, but doesn't look up.

"Is your head bothering you?"

"No."

"Russell, what's going on?"

"Nothing."

"I don't buy that. There's something wrong."

"Is this a social visit or another one of your interrogations?" He looks up. His face is grey and his wrinkles look deeper. His beard is straggly.

"You look ill. Is there something I can do?"

"No."

"I wondered if you knew where Amy is?" Did I notice a slight twitch under his left eye?

"What do you mean?"

"They haven't seen her at the track for a couple of days, so people are worried. Two people dead and she's missing. It has everyone on edge. Do you have any idea where she might be?"

"She might as well be dead."

"Russell!"

"She might as well be dead."

"I heard you, for God's sake. Why did you say that? Last time I was here, I was sure you knew more than you told me. What if Emma, and now perhaps Amy, have died because you didn't tell me or the police what you know?"

Silence.

"Has it got anything to do with who owns forty-nine percent of Hector?"

"No. Of course not. Some Ontario registered company. I dealt with someone called Ramona. That's it."

"I know who it is. Thanks. And it has nothing to do with this."

"That's what I said. So, it's someone you know, then?"

"Yes. Back to Amy. Please tell me everything. It could save some-one's life."

"Grayson was killed. Emma worked with him and she's dead."

"But what has this to do with Amy?"

"Amy worked for Grayson, and she'll be next."

"What makes you believe this?"

"There has to be a connection. Before you ask, I don't know what it is, yet."

"I can't think of any reason why anyone would want to harm Amy, and I just can't imagine what the connection could possibly be. Why are you looking so ill?"

"Because I'm sure Amy is next."

"What makes you so sure?"

"She posted that she's being stalked by some guy. It came up on my phone."

"I thought you didn't have a mobile."

"I got it to follow Amy on that social media thingumajig."

"Does she know?"

"No, I use a false name."

"Why are you following her?"

"Because I worry about her."

"I thought she tried to kill you because she believed you murdered Grayson? When am I going to hear the truth from you?"

"I think she's in danger."

"Do you know where she is?"

"She's here."

"What? Is she okay?" I have a headache.

"Yes, but she could be the next one, to be murdered, I mean."

"Russell, you're talking nonsense. For crying out loud, if she's here, look after her. Do something. I've got to unload horses now. The two other syndicate horses are coming to my place. I'll be back."

"I need to sell all three of them. Have to get rid of them. They should stay at the track."

"Remember, look after Amy. I'll be back this afternoon to talk to both of you." I wonder if Amy is with him. I didn't hear or see anything to suggest she is.

Damn. I'm more than frustrated that I can't stay. Russell isn't making sense. Neal's right, he's acting strangely. Perhaps the bang on his head was more serious than was thought.

I get back home with about five minutes to spare before the

horses are due to arrive. Melissa and I do a double-check that four stall doors are open, water buckets full, hay shaken out in stall corners. I decide to put Hector, Eagle and Bullet into their stalls because they could create a ruction outside, and make it harder for us to lead the track athletes into the barn.

*   *   *

Its diesel engine rumbles as the truck pulls up at the end of the driveway, right on time. Linda parks behind the truck. Melissa and I walk down to greet her and the shipper, and I hand a lead rein to Linda. Stomping hooves accompanied by loud whinnies shake the horse-trailer, and muffled replies, almost like echoes, come from the barn. Rose and Speed should soon settle down, but I don't know what to expect from Fay and Basil. The fact that they haven't been here before could exacerbate the situation.

The shipper lets down the large ramp on the side of the truck to reveal the space between the two pairs of horses. All four of them are in standing-stalls having been backed into areas where there is enough room for them to stand, but not to turn around. Rose and Speed have their backs to the engine and on the other side of the ramp, with their backs to the rear of the trailer, are Fay and Basil. Each is tied at the halter, which stops the horse from reaching its neighbour, but allows it to nibble from a hay-net.

Linda reaches for Basil, and I take Fay. Basil stops dead at the top of the ramp and it's hard for me to hold on to Fay. I like the look of both of them. Except for the small, circular patches of dry skin, the aftermath of skin disease, Fay's bay coat gleams and her large, dark eyes sparkle. She arches her neck and shows off the white flash on her face. Basil is a large, majestic-looking grey.

I have fallen in love with both of them before they've even come off the trailer.

Basil clomps down the ramp, having decided he might as well co-operate, after all he can smell pasture. Fay follows with a bouncy step. Basil spins around Linda a couple of times, but Fay is content to do a collected trot.

As we release each horse inside their stall, Melissa closes the doors. We return to the trailer for Speed and Rose. I thought they'd be more laid back about their return home, but they're not. Rose lunges towards the front lawn and almost wrenches the lead rein out of my hands. I was taken off-guard. Speed rears up. Linda lets the lead rein run through her hands, but not out of her grip until he comes down, then she has him back under control. This display is despite his recent race and suspect bloodwork results.

Once safely in their stall, all four new arrivals whinny and paw at their bedding. The other three copy them, but with less exuberance. Time will calm them down.

Melissa asks Linda if she'd like to stay for some salad, but Linda says she has to get lunch for her mother.

"Neal's uptight. There's something else wrong," Linda says as she leaves the barn.

"Won't he tell you what it is?" I ask.

"I think he'd talk to you. Got to go."

"Thanks, Linda. You'll come tomorrow, right?"

"Yeah. It'll be early so I can do my work at the track after."

"Whatever's good. Thanks."

Melissa and I walk towards the house, as the chorus of whinnies continues to erupt from the barn.

"I must talk to Russell and Amy now," I say. "I'm very concerned about both of them. There's more going on than they've let on. Can you check the horses in about half-an-hour and text me if there's a problem? They should quiet down soon. I'll leave them in their stalls for now. Oh, and look after Kelly and Cooper again?"

"Sure thing. Lunch will keep till you get back."

"Thanks. Good. I'll be home soon I hope."

"Should I go to the track with that drawing after lunch?"

"No, it'll be too late in the day, and most people will have left. We'll go early in the morning."

* * *

Russell's farm has an aura of lifelessness. I can't see a vehicle in sight as I drive into the barnyard. But I didn't see Amy's car when I was here in the morning, so it could be behind the barn, if she's here. The door to the house is closed. Every time I've visited before, the door has been open and only the broken screen door was shut. I knock on the door. I knock again. I try to open it, but it's locked. I go around to the back of the house.

Weeds are thriving here and are taller than I'd expect for this time of year. While the rest of the farm has the appearance of being maintained, the back of the house must have been neglected for several years. I don't see much point in wrestling with the undergrowth but make myself do it, in case I'll be able to gain access to the house. There's a small porch and I wrench the door open, but it reveals a trapdoor down to a cellar and I can't budge it. I don't think it's been used for some time.

I fight my way back to the barnyard and enter the big old barn. There's no sign of human or animal life, except for the flapping of about ten pairs of pigeons' wings as the birds fly out of the doorway. Behind the barn is the old rusty red tractor I saw Russell driving when I came for my first visit.

I have to assume that the farm is deserted, and return home. I don't know what to make of Russell's behaviour.

Melissa has made two salads, one based on quinoa and one with mixed spring greens, with all sorts of interesting ingredients in both. We sit down at the kitchen table with glasses of water and ice, napkins and fresh rolls.

"This is rather sumptuous," I say as I pick up my fork.

"Simple really. Glad you approve." Melissa eats with relish, as if she hasn't seen food for a couple of days.

"I found out who owns forty-nine percent of Hector."

"William," she says with her mouth full.

"You seem to know more about what William's up to than I do."

"I'm sure I don't." She looks up at me with a frown. "I've been at his place for a couple of days and we chatted, that's all."

"It's okay. I'm fine with it."

"He's very nice. I hope he's going to be my brother-in-law."

"Melissa! I'm sure he doesn't want to marry me."

"You're sure. Mm."

* * *

After I've led Eagle, Bullet and Hector out, I put Speed in the round-pen. The other three aren't happy. Their whinnies make my ears ring, and it's almost as if the barn rattles in sympathy. But that's the way it has to be until everyone chills out. I only have one round-pen and it's not safe to set them free into a field yet.

I phone my neighbour Joanna. Ewert and Joanna rent from Russell.

"Joanna, do you have Russell's mobile number?"

"I didn't know he had a mobile. All I have are his landline numbers. I find him hard to get hold of."

"Numbers? He has more than one?"

"I thought I told you he has another farm, didn't I?"

"I had no clue."

"He has three properties, the one we rent, and two other farms. I found this out recently from Ewert's friend Austin. You remember Austin, who worked as a security guard at your place for a while?"

"Yes. I remember him well. Is he still seeing Linda?"

"I think so. He told me he knows Russell. Anyway, I can give you the other number."

I grab pen and paper and make a note of the number and the address. I relate the conversation to Melissa, who lets me know that she's unpacked and settled in and feels at home. At least someone is happy.

"I don't think you should go alone," Melissa says.

"There's nothing to worry about."

"But what if he's the killer, or Amy is? Or you could put Amy in danger, or Russell in danger."

"You might have a point."

"William's coming over for dinner and I'm making lasagne. You could go together afterwards. It would be safer."

"Okay. I'll take Kelly and we'll go to check out this other farm, but I won't go up the driveway. I'll just see if there are any vehicles or signs of life. I want to get there this evening before it starts to get dark, so I know the lay of the land."

It takes longer for Kelly and me to get to Russell's third property than I'd calculated. I should have used GPS. There's a wall of cedars along the road frontage. I stop at the end of the driveway, which is full of potholes. The house is hard to make out behind the dense growth of scrub, but I can see grey wooden siding, spattered with faint specks of paint, that joins at a sharp angle under the edges of the rotting roof. The asphalt shingles are curled up at the edges and look flimsy, as if they might take off in the next wind. There's a shed or garage set apart from the house, its roof crushed under a fallen tree.

Russell must have rented this out to tenants who didn't take care of the place, and he couldn't have had anyone to check on the farm or to undertake necessary maintenance while he lived abroad. And he's done nothing since he returned. It looks the picture of neglect and is in a much worse state of repair than the one he lives in.

Joanna and Ewert like him as a landlord, since he let them stay rent free at the farm near me for a while in return for doing major repairs, which allowed them to get back on their feet. But that deal also meant he got a lot of work done for a bargain price, increasing the value of the property.

I have thoughts of driving up to the house, but it looks sinister and uninviting. It's hard to imagine Russell and Amy being there, and there are no vehicles in sight, although there are fresh tire-marks visible in the muddy entrance. I turn around and head for home, disappointed that I haven't seen clear evidence that they're there.

* * *

Melissa's lasagne goes down well with the Italian wine William brought with him.

"I should have cooked some vegetables to go with it," Melissa says.

"It's got vegetables in it and we had the left-over salads. It was very good. Thanks," I say. "Now I want to connect with Austin about Russell. I'll give him a call."

"Who's Austin?" Melissa asks.

"He was a security guard who was here for a while. Long story," I say. "He's an ex-cop and apparently knows of Russell."

"That should be interesting."

I go into the family room with Kelly and Cooper in tow.

Austin remembers me and after a few preliminaries I get straight to the point of my call.

"Do you know Russell Stanley?"

"Owns three farms. He'd been an absentee landlord for many years. Returned a while ago, I heard."

"That's him." I'm surprised that Austin remembers him without more information.

"Why the interest in him?"

"There are some very odd things going on. There have been two murders at the racetrack, and now Russell's missing. And I think there might be a groom with him who's not been seen for about three days. And, although it might not be connected, some horses have been tampered with in various ways. That's it, in a very small nutshell."

"When I was a cop, he was on our radar screen. That was about fifteen years ago, but I remember because we were frustrated that we didn't have the evidence to charge him. We'd received three anonymous tips, but nothing substantial."

"About what?"

"Sexual assault. But none of the alleged victims would come forward. We just got those anonymous tips and there wasn't enough to proceed."

"Oh no. As I said, he might have Amy, a groom from the racetrack, with him. I think he's at one of the farms he owns just out of town.

"Phone the police."

"I will."

*   *   *

William and I sit in my pickup truck at the end of the driveway where I was before dinner. Flashing lights illuminate the scrub and the dilapidated house, which make the place look all the more sordid and sinister. William has just told me that, so far, they've found nothing. There are signs that someone was there earlier, probably today, but no-one appears to be there now.

"I have a hunch," I say.

"What do you mean?"

"There's a cellar in his other house. I have to check it out."

"No, you don't. I'll tell the police. I'm sure they'll look into it, given they have suspicions about Russell. But I do rather doubt that he'd go back there." William gets out of the truck and walks up the driveway. I guess he's been successful when two of the four police cars fly down the road in the direction of Russell's other farm, sirens blaring.

We follow. Kelly crouches behind the front seats. She must think there are fireworks going off or that we're in the middle of a thunderstorm. Whatever it is, she doesn't like it.

I don't attempt to keep up with the police cars. By the time we catch up with them at the farm, an ambulance pulls into the barnyard next to us. We walk towards the house. The wooden front door is smashed and open, the broken screen door is swinging with its spring dangling overhead. A police officer orders us out as the paramedics push us to one side in their dash for a small panel door being held open by the officer. We stand just outside the front door and wait, and listen to the tramping of boots on the cellar steps, the clatter of a collapsible stretcher, and police radio messages. I'm sure they've called in the forensics team. They won't find anything outside since the traffic, both human and vehicular, has surely annihilated any clues.

Without my saying a word, William knows I want to see what condition Amy is in. So, we wait. My guess is that she's still alive and not in serious danger. The house throbs with action but no-one is shouting. There's an energy, a vibration, which suggests that she's there and there's hope. A sudden clang and then the sound of wheels. I rush over to her as they push the stretcher into the back of the ambulance.

Amy is hooked up to an IV drip, but her eyes are open.

"How are you feeling?"

"I'm fine. Don't worry about me." She shuts her eyes as the back doors of the ambulance close.

"William, what do you think that meant?"

"Putting my lawyer hat on, my best guess is she won't be a co-op-erative witness to whatever occurred here."

*   *   *

Just after midnight I leave Kelly on the bed and tip-toe down the stairs so as not to wake Melissa, but she's sitting at the kitchen table with Cooper on her lap as she stares into a mug of hot chocolate.

"I hope you don't usually have trouble sleeping," I say.

"Sometimes. Do you?"

"Often."

"Bad dreams?"

"Yep. What about you?"

"My mind won't stop going over stuff, like this thing with Amy. What happened to her must be linked to the murders and the horse stuff, too. Right?"

"It seems likely. But we should be wary. If we assume they're all linked, we might miss something. And we might lose precious time."

"So, what do we do?"

"You should take that sketch to the backstretch tomorrow, like we said. Make note of who you show it to, and what their reaction is. I'll chat with Neal because Linda says he's uptight, and she thinks he might talk to me about it. I'm not sure after that."

"What are you going to do with the money you got?"

"How do you know about that? Don't tell me, William told you. And how did he know?"

"You'll have to ask him."

"I haven't thought about it, except that I now don't have to worry about the training expenses for Speed, Rose and Hector. I'll give you something to…"

"Staying here is more than enough. I'd feel real bad if you gave me money. I was thinking about those unwanted horses, Fay and Basil. I know you could lose all the money you'd have to put into them, but I just wondered if you're thinking about it."

"It wouldn't be responsible of me to have five racehorses on the go. It would cost a fortune to have them all in training at the same time."

"Can I work it out? Would you let me make up a plan and a budget?"

"I suppose that wouldn't hurt. It would have to include help for me when they're at home, and all the farm expenses that would go along with their time here, as well as the track expenses of course."

"I know. Would you like some hot chocolate? I can make some."

"That would be nice. I'll sit in a recliner in the family room and see if I can get a few hours' sleep."

"I'm going back to bed. Can I borrow a book?"

"Frank built up quite a collection. There are lots in the family room and more in his office. Help yourself."

The landline phone rings. We look at each other, puzzled.

"Who calls at this time of night?" I pick up the phone.

"Hello." Pause. "It's me." I recognize my mother's voice.

"You've forgotten the time difference between here and England. And it's only about six o'clock in the morning there. Why are you up so early?" I mouth the word 'mother' to Melissa.

"Oh dear. How silly of me. One of those awful senior moments they talk about. Did I wake you?"

"No. Melissa and I are having some hot chocolate."

"Ooh, I'd love some of your hot chocolate. How nice that Melissa is there with you."

"She's staying here. How are you doing?"

"Much better. That's one of the reasons for ringing you. I'm much steadier on these pegs of mine. And I can read and watch television." She stops. I'm sure I can hear sobbing.

"What's wrong?"

"I'm as miserable as a duck in a desert. I'm as lonely as a honeybee that can't find its hive. I'm as grumpy as…"

"I get it. So, when are you coming to visit?"

"Oh, I thought you'd never ask."

"I've told you many times that you're always welcome here."

"That's good, because I've just booked a plane ticket for next week."

"You've booked?"

"Yes. I can't wait. I'm so miserable."

"You're well enough to travel?"

"I am."

"You can get health insurance?"

"Costs an arm and a leg, but I arranged it through this place which runs a seniors' club of sorts so I got it cheaper."

"Okay." She gives me the details of her flight and I note the time when I need to pick her up from the airport before I hang up. Melissa has figured out what's happening.

"She must think she's dying again," Melissa says as she puts her mug in the dishwasher.

"Do you think she's dying? Because I don't."

"I suppose I don't know, really."

"She sure is a complicated person and full of contradictions."

"Well, she lies, if that's what you mean, and can put on an act, such as crying on the phone."

"Are you able to forgive her? Sometimes I think I've forgiven her and other times I think I'll never be able to."

"I try not to think about it at all, but that doesn't always work."

"She usually asks about William. I wonder why she didn't mention him?"

"I told her you were back together. It cheered her up, she said. She really likes William, doesn't she?"

Communication is going on all around me. It seems peculiar and, I admit, it disturbs me that this can happen, without my knowledge and without my being included, when it affects me or is about me. Perhaps I'll get used to it?

"Let's get some sleep, if we can," I say as I pick up my mug and walk into the family room. Cooper follows but Kelly must be fast asleep on my bed.

13

Misleading Picture

Melissa and I go into the office at the entrance to the backstretch, and I sign her in as a visitor. She seems keen to help with this investigation, so I might have to arrange for an ownership licence for her. Neal signed her in the time before. But it's a big inconvenience for him to have to walk over to the security office from his barn.

The heavy, hot air hits us as we walk down the steps. It hasn't been spring for long, and it's only mid-morning, but this feels like a muggy summer day. Melissa has put the copy of the sketch that Des drew into a clear, thin plastic folder she found in Frank's office. She said it would otherwise be in tatters before she's finished with it.

We part ways. Melissa says she'll make her own way back to the farm. She wants to drop off her resume at a couple more veterinary clinics before going home. She's adept at using public transit. She told me she used it all the time in England and gets frustrated here sometimes because the service is much more limited. I like my own transportation, especially since I can bring Kelly along, which I do more often than not.

Linda has already cleaned two stalls at the farm much earlier this morning, and I know she has a full load here as well. As I pass her in the aisle, she tells me that Neal is in his office. I find him eating a sandwich. He waves me in. I can smell the fishy aroma of tuna mixed with the clean scent of saddle soap.

"Have a seat. Thanks for coming. Linda said you might come here. Did the horses settle in okay?"

"They're doing well. I wish I had at least one more round-pen, but I think I'll be able to let them out into the paddock and small field tomorrow."

"Linda said they looked fine. I can't really believe it, but she thinks they've improved already."

"I'm glad she thinks that. I'm sure some grazing will do the trick, and being away from whatever's going on here, of course."

"Whatever's going on here is making me anxious. I wish I could figure it out."

"You must have heard that Amy was found?"

"No. Where was she?"

"In Russell's cellar. Alive, thank goodness."

"What? You've got to be kidding."

"I don't know the circumstances. William is going to reach out to a couple of his police services contacts to see if he can find out more. And I plan to see if Amy will talk to me. She's in hospital but I don't think it's anything very serious."

"Russell?"

"I haven't seen him. William and I were at the farm when the police were there, but the only person we saw was Amy and she just said 'don't worry about me'. Very odd."

"I've been trying to contact Russell. Oscar and Philippa bug me about Fay and Basil at least twice daily each. I can't handle it.

It's like harassment. They both say the same things. They want the horses back at the track, in training, and in races asap. I don't get that Philippa doesn't understand the time it takes and that you can't race horses that aren't fit and well. She's been in the business for a long time. But it doesn't surprise me that Oscar hasn't got a clue."

"It is odd that Philippa is creating so much fuss. Isn't she worth a bit?"

"It's rumoured that the property is worth a lot, but I don't know if she has cash. You know, I bet she doesn't. Something's happened, and she's skint. That has to be it."

"I'll see if I can find out."

"Can you talk to both of them and get them off my back? I sure would appreciate it. I can't focus on what I'm doing. I feel like a failure. It won't solve everything, but I'd feel better."

"I'll try. What else can I do?"

"Find the murderer. It's changed the atmosphere around here. No-one wants to admit it, but I think most of us are scared because we don't understand the motive and wonder who's going to be next."

"I'll do my best. I wish the police would see these cases as murders rather than suicides, but apparently they haven't changed their position."

"No-one here thinks either of the deaths was a suicide. That isn't even a consideration."

"I'm on it. Melissa is assisting, as well as William when he can. And it's a great help that Linda is coming to the farm every morning. Thanks for that."

* * *

When I reach Philippa's dignified stone house, I'm surprised that she answers the door herself this time. I remember a uniformed maid opened the door when I last visited. And there are no fresh flowers in vases on the tables in the sunroom today.

"Thanks for seeing me on such short notice," I say as I sit on a wicker chair with a view of the fields. The weeds are already making their presence felt even though winter isn't all that long behind us. My guess is that the fields couldn't have been mown for several years. Broken rails dangle, and the gate by the barn is off one of its hinges. I can't imagine how Philippa must feel: surrounded by her beloved property with all its memories, and watching it deteriorate into an unkempt, unlived-in ruin. It would break my heart to see my farm sink into such a state of disrepair and with no animals to give it life.

"Yes, the ghosts haunt me," she says as she hands me a glass of water. Philippa must have noticed my eyes as they wandered and guessed at my thoughts.

"I'm not one to beat around the bush. You must have fallen on some hard times?"

"Being a pensioner has its challenges." Her voice is more subdued than when I've talked to her before. She looks out at the fields with watery eyes.

"But that's not the whole story, is it?"

"Why are you here?" She turns to face me, one tear under her left eye. I wonder if she knows it's there.

"I had a chat with Neal this morning."

"He wants me to stop calling him."

"Yes."

"I will."

"He said he was surprised you were putting pressure on him when you know the racing business so well."

"Ah. Yes. He would be."

"Is there something I can do to help you?"

"I doubt it."

"By the way, did you know Amy was missing for a couple of days but was found yesterday evening in Russell's cellar?"

"That's my fault."

"What do you mean?"

"I talked to Amy this morning. She's going to be okay."

"How did you know where she was?"

"Amy called me. She knew it was my fault."

"Please tell me what you mean. How can it be your fault?"

"I hope I can trust you. I don't want you to do anything about this without my knowledge and approval."

"I won't break the law or knowingly withhold evidence."

"I would deny it to anyone else anyway. But you might be able to stop this nonsense without the police being involved, so I'm willing to give it a shot."

"Okay."

"My husband had an affair. I knew it. I put up with it for the sake of appearances and because I love this place and the way we lived. I didn't want to leave, and I suppose I still cared about him. But what made it harder for me was that his fling was with one of our staff, a maid called Flora. And the result was Amy. My husband agreed to a lump sum payment. Flora and Amy left the province. After Flora died, Amy came looking for her father. I told her he was dead. I gave her a couple of his things including a framed photograph."

"So, how could Amy being found in Russell's cellar be your fault?"

"I'm getting to that. Be patient with me. This is difficult. Amy asked me to help her find a job. She doesn't have an impressive resume but seemed keen. She had a couple of reference letters with her. Not that I have much faith in them. I noticed she'd worked at a riding stables and asked if she'd be interested in working at the track. I said she could enrol in the grooming course. She asked who she should talk to and the only person I remembered from our racing days was Grayson."

"But I assume this isn't the end of the story."

"No. The next thing that happens is that I get a call to talk at that racehorse ownership session. I didn't want to do it, but they said they had no-one else willing to speak to the breeding side of the business. I reluctantly agreed. I was shocked that Russell, my husband's business partner, was there. He took me aside, holding my arm, which I found offensive, and said that, if I didn't become a member of the syndicate he was setting up, he'd tell the world that my husband was Amy's father. He said he was sure I wouldn't want that spread all over the newspapers."

"But."

"I know. I've still not explained the cellar incident. Amy told me that Russell was stalking her."

"Amy met Russell because she was working for Grayson, then."

"Yes. Amy told me that Russell and Grayson were checking out horses for a syndicate, and Russell often hung around the barn. But later, Amy called me and told me she was afraid of Russell. And, at about the same time, Russell approached me for money. Cash only. Not only did he threaten to go to the media about my husband but also threatened to hurt Amy if I didn't pay up or if I went to the police."

"So, you paid up."

"Yes and no. I have simply run out of money. I get a small pension, but my husband was an independent businessman, he didn't have a pension. There wasn't much in the way of savings and it didn't take long for the nest-egg to go. Being part of that disastrous syndicate hasn't helped. It's made me a lot more anxious. I've lost many a sleepless night over that."

"Funny that Russell wanted you to be part of it."

"To continue the saga. A couple of days ago, I told him I had no more money. He didn't believe me. People assume we have pots of money. They always have. But we weren't all that well off. He said if I didn't hand over the cash, he would abduct Amy and I'd be lucky if I saw her alive again. I tried to play tough and make out I didn't care about Amy, after all she's no blood-relation of mine, but he saw through it and held on to his belief that I'd give him the money to save Amy from harm, and that I wouldn't go to the police."

"But you didn't have it to give."

"Precisely. So, he abducted Amy. Hence she ended up in his cellar."

"He must have contacted you after he'd taken Amy?"

"He did. I told him to ask Amy if I have any money because I decided, when she visited the first time, that I needed to make it clear the financial position I'm in. It seems to me, when one has money, people think up creative ways to have you part with it, for their own benefit."

"I've had that experience. I don't have a lot of money but, just like you, people assume that I have. It can present challenges and cause conflict sometimes."

"Definitely. I showed Amy my tax return, and I assured her I have no hidden money, like in the Cayman Islands or something preposterous like that."

"Right."

"She said she didn't want to look at it, but I made her sit down and review it. I told her the lump sum she and her mother Flora got, was it. There was no more. I probably offended her, but I needed to make it very clear."

"You don't feel that the reason for her visit was to ask for money?"

"I'm not sure, but I don't think so. Anyway, that's why, in desperation, I told Russell to ask Amy if I have any money. I don't know what happened after that brief conversation, but Amy called me from the hospital. Someone thought to call the police and have them check Russell's cellar."

"That was me. It was a hunch when we didn't find her at Russell's other farm. Have you any idea what drove Russell to blackmail?"

"Like any other blackmailer. Greed."

"He doesn't strike me as the greedy type. What was he like when you knew him previously?"

"I didn't know him well. My husband and I would see him at the club at the track, hanging around the bar, talking to the waitresses. Sometimes my husband would join him. I assumed they talked about horses, but who knows. We only went to the club about ten or twelve times each racing season. What are you going to do with all this information?"

"I have to find Russell and talk to Amy."

"She's leaving the hospital this afternoon. She was dehydrated, I think that was the main thing. Nothing serious."

"It would have been traumatic to be held captive, not knowing what was going to happen."

"She didn't sound traumatized."

"I don't suppose you know where Russell is?"

"No."

"I wonder if this is linked to the murders."

"I don't know. I just want Russell to go away. I'd like my money back, but I don't think that's going to happen for one goddam minute."

"Unfortunately, you might be right."

Philippa sees Kelly in my truck as I leave the house and tells me to let her have a run since we've talked for a long time and she's been cooped up. She says she'd like to see some living things in the fields, and we should stay for as long as we want.

We explore the edge of the extensive field that's overlooked by the sunroom. It seems a shame that all the lovely pasture, albeit now infested with weeds, is going to waste. It's as if the barn and fields are begging for horses to return. Their emptiness fills my heart with melancholy. Kelly's tail wags and she sniffs and runs, sniffs and runs. She enjoys herself, but I'm relieved to see the truck and, having waved to Philippa as she stands in the doorway, I drive as quickly as I dare, down her driveway and back onto the road, and leave the ghosts behind.

As I approach home, my mind flits from one thing to another because of what Philippa told me. She gave me quite a lot to think about.

Melissa has Cooper in her arms and waits for Kelly and me to get out of the truck. She has a smile showing shiny white teeth, and I can't help but feel brighter. Aromas come in waves and reveal something good is cooking.

"I thought you'd want something to eat before looking after the horses," she says as she puts Cooper down and pats Kelly, who wants some of her attention. "It's curry. Hope you like it. I didn't make it very spicy."

"Sounds great. You're getting more adventurous in the kitchen."

"I want to improve. I'd like to be a better cook. William's coming later."

"What did you find out today from that drawing?"

"You'll never guess."

"What?"

"I asked six different people and five of them said it looked most like the vet, Edwin, although I didn't see that much of a resemblance from what I remembered of him. So, I took the sketch to Edwin and told him that nearly everyone thought the sketch was a pretty good likeness. I explained that Des, the security guard, had drawn it, claiming to have seen this person coming out of Emma's trailer at the wrong time. He sure looked shaken. He handed the drawing back to me. His eyes went wide, and he let out a gasp. I was worried that he might have a heart attack, his reaction was that bad. We sat in his SUV, and after a brief chat I was convinced it wasn't him, so

I tracked Des down. He was in a coffee shop across the road where he hangs out a lot. I'll cut a long story short. He made it up."

"He made it up?" I choke on a mouthful of curry and grab my glass of water.

"He made it up. He told me he was so certain that Edwin sold ketamine to workers on the backstretch, and sold Testos to the trainers, that he wanted him caught."

"And you think Edwin has nothing to do with either?"

"I can't be sure, of course, but his reaction seemed genuine. I mentioned the Testos to Edwin, and he said, once he came up for air, that he would never use that drug under any circumstances because, not only is it a banned substance, studies have shown there can be adverse reactions. He doesn't think it's worth the risk and there are better treatment alternatives."

"I learned a fair amount from Philippa today. She was blackmailed by Russell."

I give Melissa the details of my conversation with Philippa as I clear up the dishes and clean the pots.

During our walk to the barn, Melissa asks what she can do to help with the investigation. I suggest she follow up with Amy since I want to talk to Oscar and Neal. I need to find out more about what was happening with the syndicate. I hope William can find out if the police are searching for Russell and if so, if they've got anywhere.

*   *   *

The sun is coming up, and the farm hasn't cooled down from the heat it radiated down on us yesterday. We're destined for above-seasonal temperatures again today. The ground is hard, the pasture's growth has slowed, the pansies are wilting, and the humidity weighs me down. Melissa seems energized by the heat, but Linda waddles into the barn with red cheeks and a sweaty forehead.

"I got carrot muffins and tea. I hope you like tea, Melissa."

"I do. I drink coffee mostly, but I like tea. Thanks. What's the damage?"

"My treat. It's a bribe. This way you'll give me a hand." Linda smiles, but it looks half-hearted, as if something's bothering her.

"Linda," I say. "Is everything okay at the track?"

"Sort of." She wipes her forehead with her arm. "Neal told me that someone scared the shit, sorry, the whatever out of Edwin. He was accused of going into Emma's office late in the day when she was killed. Neal says he looks like a ghost. He's worried about him."

"I'll talk to him," I say as I make a sign to Melissa not to say anything.

"The other thing," Linda says as she rubs some ointment onto the scabby patches on Fay's neck, "is that Neal found out Grayson reported Emma to the Vets' College. I don't know what for. Neal's pretty upset."

"You're upset too," I say.

"It's not the same in the barns 'cause we know there's a killer and there's someone who's hurting the horses."

"Could be the same person," I say.

"I don't get the link."

"You might be right, Linda. I must be careful not to assume. It could be something entirely different. Melissa and William are helping me. We'll do our best to find the killer and soon." I hope there was optimism in my voice despite the fact that I'm perplexed. I don't have solid leads to follow and can't think of an obvious motive.

14

Bizarre Behaviour

I drop Melissa off at the staff residence at the track, after we picked up a bagel and coffee for her to give to Amy. Kelly and I drive on to Oscar's condo. He said he'd meet me in the coffee shop on the ground floor before he goes to a meeting. He sits by the window and drums his fingers on the table as he swings his foot up and down.

"You're late," he says.

"One minute."

"I don't care by how much."

"Let's not waste time in an argument about my tardiness. I'll get straight to the point. I want to know why Russell's blackmailing you."

He uncrosses his legs, folds his arms and stares at me.

"What gives you that idea?"

"It's not an idea. Tell me about it. No more secrets. It could be linked to the murders, and it's critical that we find the killer before anyone else gets hurt."

"If I tell you some stuff, will you go to the police?"

"I can't guarantee anything. Once I find the killer, the police will do their own investigation and who knows how your secrets will play out in all this." He keeps staring. "I need to know, now."

"I knew Russell before that session, you know, the one when he twisted my arm, almost literally, to become a member of the damned syndicate. I had been in real estate then. I bought properties and then flipped them and made a fair bit at it. I seemed to have a knack for assessing the potential for quick turnover and prices were going up nicely. I borrowed money when I needed to."

"Okay."

"Trouble was, I sold a couple of properties that I didn't own. Short story is that there were complaints submitted to the Real Estate Council. I didn't get away with it like I thought I would. I lost my licence, but I settled out of court. Russell was involved with the Council somehow and learned of all this and threatened to make it public. It would not be good for my new internet banking business if I'm publicly exposed to be a shyster."

"Wouldn't this be on the Council's website, anyway?"

"My name and the fact that I had my licence revoked, perhaps. But at the time they weren't putting up details."

"Are you a shyster?"

"No. I got greedy. I won't let that happen again."

"Russell approached you about the syndicate?"

"It was a surprise that he asked me to attend the session. When I was there, he grabbed my arm and pulled me aside and told me that if I didn't become a member of the syndicate he was setting up, he'd make what I'd done public. I said okay, because I had to, and tried to make light of it by saying I'd bring him luck."

"Are you still paying him?"

"Yes, and it's killing me. It's not a lot of money each month, but with the syndicate going so badly it's tough. The big issue is the stress, and I can't see an end to this misery."

"You said that you think Emma killed Grayson and then committed suicide. Do you still think that?"

"I hate to admit it, but it could be Russell, couldn't it? If he's capable of killing, then heaven help me."

"Why do you think he wanted you to join the syndicate?"

"No clue. But the funny thing is that I got a sense that he was excited about the syndicate. That he really wanted to do it. He just needed members and I suppose he didn't have enough people so, because he has something over me, he could force me to join. And, after I got over the initial shock of it all, I didn't mind. I thought it would be fun. That was a mistake."

"Under normal circumstances, it should have been fun. Do you have any idea why the horses were having so many issues? Any theories?"

"No. I can't see how anyone would gain, even that Bryce guy. That's the real reason I talked to him. I thought he was the one messing around with the horses and that it would stop if he was their trainer. But I'm not so sure anymore. I can't see that the gain could possibly outweigh the risk. By the way, Emma didn't tell me he was a good trainer. I didn't tell you the truth. She told me he was not what he made himself out to be, just like Philippa told you when the three of us got together. He makes a thing about fairness and a level playing-field and all that, but his actions don't reflect his rhetoric."

"What makes you say that?"

"He reports trainers who have done nothing bad, just to cause trouble and put them under suspicion."

"Oh."

"I'm not sure if you should be looking for a killer who's been tampering with the syndicate horses, or if there are two different people, a murderer and a horse-hater. I gotta go, otherwise I'll be late for this meeting and I need to make a good impression."

"Don't be like me and make a bad one by being one minute late."

He laughs. "You got me. I feel better having told you what's been going on. But I'm stressed. I admit it."

*   *   *

Melissa has springs in her shoes. She virtually jumps on the spot as she opens the kitchen door for me. Kelly bounds out of the barn and almost collides with my legs. Her brakes don't work very well when she runs at top speed.

"What on earth is all the excitement?"

"I don't know what Kelly's excited about, but I can tell you what I'm excited about," Melissa says. "I'm really getting the hang of this sleuth thing."

"You've found out something important?"

"Sure have. I found Amy in her tiny flat next to the racetrack. We got talking about growing up and I shared some of my horror stories from the foster homes I was in. She opened up about the resentment and hurt her mother felt about being paid off by her father. Her mom was used and discarded."

"I'm making tea. Would you rather have coffee?"

"Tea's fine. That's not all. The worst bit's coming. Amy worked for Grayson, which you know, and Russell was a client, which you also know. I'll cut the long story short. Russell confronted Amy in Grayson's trailer when Grayson had taken a horse over for a race. Amy was scared. Emma happened to be looking for Grayson and had forgotten he was racing. She had some meds to deliver to him and wanted to talk to him about them. When she saw Amy in Grayson's office, she could see she was upset and they talked."

"Okay."

"No, it's not. During this long chat, Emma told Amy that she'd been raped by Russell. And to make it even worse, she ended up having an abortion."

"That's really dreadful. When did it happen? Recently?"

"No, a long time ago. Amy doesn't know when."

"That sure would have made Amy feel better."

"Amy was blown away and even more frightened. Emma warned her to stay away from Russell at all costs."

"How unnerving."

"Amy told Emma that Russell was stalking her. And that's what led them to cook up a scheme to get back at him, to get the upper hand. Sort of revenge, I suppose. They knew that money was important to him, so they thought they'd get him where it hurt."

"I see where you're going with this, but there were other members of the syndicate."

"I asked Amy about that. She and Emma thought the other members would get mad at Russell, because he's the one who got them all involved, and it would make his life even more difficult."

"But I thought Amy liked Grayson a lot. They would have been hurting him too, and it would have had more significant ramifications for him since he was both an owner and the trainer."

"I didn't ask Amy directly, but she volunteered that she's had a few sleepless nights about Emma's scheme and it hurting Grayson. She really got upset as she told me she's been worried sick that what they did to the horses led to Grayson's death somehow."

"Perhaps it did. The poor performances of the horses meant all members lost money, at the very least. And what about the innocent horses in all this?"

"Amy told me that Emma did what she could to impair their performance, but not make them suffer, or at least only in minor ways. She said she couldn't put into words how much Emma loathed

Russell and how much they both wanted to hurt him. I'm surprised he isn't the one that's dead."

"So am I. But this doesn't explain Grayson's or Emma's murder, does it?"

"I know. Amy's scared because we don't know who or why."

"Does she have any idea at all who might have killed Grayson or Emma?"

"I asked her and she said she's not sure. She can't think of a motive for Grayson's murder. She thinks Russell might have found out what Emma was up to and, if they had a confrontation, Emma could have told him she was going to the police to report his sexual assault on her, but she doesn't know. That would be enough of a motive, I guess, but there's nothing definite to go on."

"What Emma and Amy did, explains what happened to the horses, but doesn't explain Speed's condition and poor performance."

"Oh, yes, she mentioned him. That worries her because, after Emma was murdered, their interference with the horses stopped, of course. She can't explain it. She helped Emma, but she wasn't the instigator. She didn't know enough about the drugs and ointments and other stuff to do anything on her own."

"Does she know why Russell abducted her?"

"She thinks he's figured out that she helped Emma. But what makes no sense, is that she doesn't seem to be super-scared by Russell any more."

"If she's not frightened of Russell that would, perhaps, explain why she said she was fine, and that no-one should worry about her, when she was being taken away in the ambulance."

"It's odd. I get mixed messages from her. I think she's confused about Russell and can't figure him out. I sure can't."

"If he truly did sexually assault Emma, then I suggest he's someone to be feared."

"But Amy says she won't lay charges."

"Strange. She went, on her own, to his farm earlier, and it's not clear what happened to cause Russell to fall through the trapdoor. And then she appears to have been abducted by him. Amy's accounts confuse me. Despite her unwillingness to lay charges, Russell should be charged with sexual assault, blackmail, abduction and perhaps more that we don't know about yet. We need to get him arrested somehow."

"We will." Melissa smiles and jogs out of the kitchen. I wish I had that much energy and optimism.

She must have started to clean the kitchen before I got home. There are various cloths and cleaning products out on the counter. It makes me feel uneasy. I don't want disruption, but on the other hand our mother arrives in two days. I reluctantly admit that Melissa's right, we do need to tidy up and clean. I push everything to one end of the counter so that I have some room to prepare something for dinner, although I can't think of what.

"I've done it," Melissa says. She hops from one foot to the other, in a kind of celebratory dance.

"Got a job?" I ask.

"No. I've put a budget together for the horses. Easy peasy. You can buy those horses and have help to look after them and money left over. See!" She hands me a spreadsheet with numerous columns and a row for each month of the year. It's detailed and, just at a glance, it appears as if she's thought of everything. And the bottom-line annual cost, with no racing revenue accounted for, is not as horrific as I'd assumed from my crude mental arithmetic.

"Someone's got to buy them and give them a chance," she says. "And your barn and fields are large enough for them in the winter or for whenever they're not at the track."

"It's a lot of work."

"I've included one full-time person. I know it's only a twelve-month budget, but by then you'll know how many performers you have, and which ones will need to be given a chance at a second career."

"But it's a seven-day-a-week thing. How will I get someone to do that?"

"Hire two part-time. I would be one of them, and I'd work for free if you let me stay here. Free board in exchange for my help. That's what's in the budget. I'd learn more about horses. It would be great."

"What if you get a full-time job?"

"Part-time jobs are easier to get. And I think I'd like to work with a vet at the track. I'd be busier at work in the racing season when there are fewer horses here, and less busy in the winter when they're all at home."

"I'm willing to think about it. You give it more thought too. We're family, but we should work it out like a business arrangement, so that it's fair. I don't want you to feel that you're not being compensated properly."

"Oh, good! I hoped you'd be open to the idea." She skips out of the kitchen.

"Have you heard from William?" I shout after her.

"Didn't he say he'd come for dinner this evening?"

"Why can't I remember that? What are we going to eat?"

Melissa skips back into the kitchen, and Cooper runs in front of her with his tail bolt upright. Kelly appears to be oblivious to all the commotion, flat out on her side under the table. "I've got some stuff in the fridge," Melissa says. "I'll make a chicken dish. I hope it turns out."

"That's great."

"I've done nothing in the barn. Linda cleaned the stalls. I checked. It's nice of her to do all seven and then go to the track to clean out heaven knows how many there."

"That's so kind of her. I don't know how she does it. She should be as skinny as the rake she uses. I'll go to the barn and do the rest of the chores and put the horses in."

"I'll do a bit more cleaning until it's time to get dinner."

Before I enter the barn, I stop at the gate to the paddock, lean my two arms on it, and gaze at the seven horses. The heatwave is into its second day and the myriad of insects enjoy it more than I do. The horses swish their tails and shake their heads now and then in attempts to stop bites and stings. It amazes me how they can feel a fly on their thick hides and twitch a patch of their skin to get rid of it.

Kelly bounds down the driveway at the sound of the gate opening. I recognize the beat-up car. I haven't seen Joanna in a while, even though she lives close-by with her husband Ewert.

"Melissa said you were doing barn chores, so I thought I'd pop over," she says, as she greets Kelly with a face rub.

"I haven't quite made it into the barn. I was unwinding, watching the horses."

"You've got quite the herd."

"It's a long story. I'll tell you sometime if you're interested. I hope everything is all right?"

"Not really. That's why I wanted to talk to you. Russell's put the property up for sale. A real estate agent hammered a 'for sale' sign into the gritty ground at the end of the driveway. I'm in shock. Russell didn't tell us. As you know, he's been pretty decent to us. We've been living there rent-free in exchange for doing repairs and painting, which gave us a chance to get back on our feet, but this sure doesn't help. I don't know where we'll go. We love that place and put a lot into sprucing it up."

I give Joanna a synopsis of what's been going on with Russell and that he's wanted for sexual assault and blackmail as well as abduction.

"Oh, my god. What on earth? I've been alone with that creep on more than a couple of occasions. I wish I'd known." She stops patting Kelly and stands erect, her grey eyes wide and staring.

"I didn't know, either. I didn't pick up any vibes from him and I'm pretty sensitive to these things."

191

"Why do you think he put our place up for sale?"

"I don't know. I suppose he needs money. He set up a syndicate which owned five racehorses and it's done badly. But he must know that the racing business is very risky. He's been a racehorse owner for some time. I can't figure it out."

"Has he been arrested?"

"Not yet, as far as I know."

"Are the police looking for him, then?"

"I assume they are."

"How will he sell his property without showing his face and being arrested?"

"I don't know, but I expect there's a way. I'm sure people buy and sell properties remotely."

"Oh, that's awful. We're going to lose our home."

"I'm sorry."

Kelly and I walk with her to the car. Joanna looks wan. It's as if she's aged five years or more in a matter of minutes. Her mouth is turned down at the corners and the lines around her eyes look more pronounced. I tell her I'll try to find out more. But I can't see what I can do.

There's a deep rumble in the background and the light fades as dark grey clouds roll in like an unfurling blanket. Kelly slinks on her belly as we head for the barn. She knows a storm is on its way. I grab a lead rein and walk briskly to the paddock.

As I lead the seventh horse in, the raindrops have become large dollops which splatter on my head and shoulders and threaten to soak me to the skin in short order. I watch from the barn door as the wind plays with the rain, tossing it about. Sudden walls of water thrash at the plants and trees, making them bend and shudder.

But the sweet smell of soggy earth mixed with wet grass is refreshing, and the cooler air tingles my skin. The sudden dissipation of the heat leaves me energized but calm. Unfortunately, Kelly doesn't feel the same way. She's in the feed room, curled up with the barn cats, trembling.

By the time I've finished my barn chores, the sun is out and we're surrounded by sparkle and glitter as we walk back to the house. The ground has turned from hard to squelchy and the air has a nip to it.

"Wow, that was some storm," Melissa says as we enter the house. I go upstairs to change into dry clothes. Kelly isn't wet since she was smart enough to find refuge in the barn as I led the horses in. "Were the horses okay?" Melissa shouts up the stairs.

"They were good. I left Eagle and Bullet till last and they got a little wet but weren't upset. The storm wasn't doing much when I led the other five in."

My mobile rings just as I put a dry top on.

"Hi, Philippa. How are you?"

"Not good."

"What's the matter?"

"Russell had the nerve to turn up on my doorstep and demanded to stay here. I couldn't believe it. He pushed me aside and barged in before I could say anything." She coughs.

"What happened?"

"It was such good luck. I'd asked a real estate guy to come and assess the farm. And he showed up about two minutes later." I think she's stifling sobs. "I asked him to help me get rid of Russell, and I told Russell I would call the police if he didn't leave. I didn't know how he'd react, but he left. Sorry, I need a sip of water." I hear more coughs.

"That's okay. Take your time."

"I decided I can't live with his threats and him stealing my money, so I've just been to the police and told them everything, including about my husband and our maid Flora, and Amy." She sounds as if she's about to be choked up by tears.

"I don't suppose you have any idea where Russell went?"

"No. I'm frightened. If he finds out I've told the police every-thing he'll be as mad as hell." She takes a couple more gulps of her drink. "And if he thinks he still has a hold over me, he'll find me. I can't win. He must be on the run but it was stupid of him to come to my home."

"Not necessarily. He might have thought it was a clever idea since he believes he has you wrapped around his little finger, and that no-one would be looking for him there because he's attempted to blackmail you. What did the police say?"

"They said that I should stay with friends or relatives."

"Do you have somewhere to go?"

"I'm at the Vannersville Inn tonight but can't really afford it at the moment."

"Why don't you come here for a bit until things get sorted out?"

"A million thanks. That's so decent of you. I would feel much safer there and perhaps I can do something to help."

"Okay, just give me a heads up when you'll be coming so that I'm sure to be here."

She thanks me three more times with a voice that carries more vitality and less wretchedness.

15

Goings and Comings

Melissa, William and I sit at the kitchen table having eaten a spicy chicken casserole dish with rice. I've downed two glasses of water. In between gulps of the cooling liquid, I give William an update.

"Thanks, Melissa. That was great," I say as I clear the dishes.

"You're welcome. Sorry if it was a bit too hot. I like spicy foods."

"I expect I'll get used to it," I say.

"I'll finish clearing up. You and William go into the family room and chat. I mean it."

"But you prepared it. I should clear up," I say as I open the dishwasher.

"I want you and William to have a chance to talk. I'm fine with clearing up. And then I'm going out for a bit. Hope you don't mind if I borrow the truck."

"Of course not."

We do as we're told and take our glasses of water into the family room and sit in the recliners. Kelly settles by William's chair and Cooper curls up on my lap.

"Have you found out anything about what the police are doing to find Russell?" I ask.

"I was told that there's been a development. Two women have come forward who are willing to give testimony regarding allegations of sexual assault. I don't know why they chose this point in time to take action against Russell. Several years have lapsed. Their names have not been revealed yet."

"Are the police on Russell's trail?"

"I don't know. I don't think so because they told me they have a social media campaign ready to launch, probably tonight, with photographs, that they hope will enlist the help of the public to track him down."

"Change of subject. I know you're the one who owns forty-nine percent of Hector."

"I wondered when you'd find out."

"I found out a little while ago."

"Okay."

"Why did you do that?"

"I've always wanted to own a racehorse."

"That's news to me. Why the secretiveness?"

"I wanted it to be a nice surprise. A gift to you from me, to show you how much I care about you. I knew you very much wanted to own Hector, but that you were hesitating because of the expense. I thought I'd make the decision easier for you."

"But why didn't you tell me? I don't see why you would want me to find out rather than mentioning it yourself."

"I wasn't about to wrap him up in a bow, was I?"

"Be serious." I flop my head back and close my eyes with a big sigh.

"Okay. I wanted to choose the right moment to let you know. I wanted it to be special. But every time I was about to say something, there was either a distraction or you seemed to be pulling away from me. I admit it stung a bit that you didn't figure it out right away."

I make the recliner thump into an upright position and look at William.

"I'm messing this up, aren't I?"

"You just have to make up your mind about two things. One is whether you want a loving relationship and, if you do, whether it's with me."

I hang my head down. Why are we going down this path again, and why don't I say anything? It's as if I'm encased in concrete, making it impossible for me to move or breathe.

"I think I have my answer," he says as he stands up and walks to the kitchen. I break free of the stupor and gasp. I get up and follow him but, just as I'm about to catch up, he shuts the door behind him. He's gone. Instead of going after him, I sit on the floor with my head between my knees and my hands on my head. I don't have a clue what's going on. Every part of my body aches inside and out, and my chest has a truck parked on it.

The door opens, and my heart skips in hope. But it's Melissa.

"Would you believe I had to go to the grocery store on the other side of town for the power bars I like? What happened?" She dumps a grocery bag on the table and crouches down, trying to look into my face. I don't look up. "I can see Kelly's okay." Kelly pushes her nose in between my legs, trying to reach my face. "You said the horses were okay. Talk to me." She raises her voice and holds my arm, shaking me a little.

"William's left."

"He's left you, you mean?"

I don't answer.

"So, you've let him walk out of your life?"

197

Silence.

"And our mother is coming the day after tomorrow?"

"What does that have to do with it?"

"You let William, that wonderful, loving man, walk out of your life and you welcome our mother, who deserted us both, here at the farm. You won't invite William to move in, but you allow our mother to come and stay as long as she wants to." Melissa stands by the sink, her hands pressed onto the counter, her body taut, her voice sharp.

"I thought you had a good relationship with our mother." My words come out in sputters.

"I faked it, for your sake. You seemed to get on so well with her. She tossed me out of her life as if I was a piece of garbage."

"It would have been hell for you living in that house with Stan."

"She should have left him. Why didn't she love her children and care for them? Why did she stand by and watch you being abused, and why did she dump me? There's no excuse that holds up. It's cruelty. Our mother is a callous, uncaring person. You need to remember that. You've forgotten."

"I think she's changed."

"I don't. She's playing with you so that she can get money."

"She gave us both some of the proceeds from the sale of her house."

"That was peanuts. It was just an offering. She thinks you're going to get millions."

"I hope you're not right." I stay seated on the floor and hug my knees. I must look pathetic to Melissa. At this rate, I'll lose her too.

"William is loving, caring, compassionate and even good-looking to boot. He's intelligent, has a great job, helps you whenever he can. He adores you."

"Philippa is coming here tomorrow to stay for a while."

"What? You must be out of your mind. You invite a suspect to stay here!" She shouts at me as she walks toward me. "What is the matter with you?" She turns away, but almost immediately swirls around and glares at me. "I'm leaving. I'm going to stay with William until all these unpleasant and unwanted people leave. Then we'll talk." She bounds up the stairs, two at a time, and I hear her packing and mumbling. I look at Kelly. She sits under the table, ears pricked and head tilted to one side, with a quizzical look in her eyes.

Melissa stomps back down the stairs with her bags.

"And by the way, our wonderful mother didn't tell me the whole truth about my father." Her voice is close to a scream. She pumps her bags up and down as she stands by the kitchen door. "My father is called Joshua Kent, but he's not the person she said he was. He was a Canadian official working in the embassy in London, and it would have been a scandal. Our lovely mother put him first before her child."

I don't see her leave. I just hear the door slam behind her.

The relentless ticktock of the clock cuts through the silence, reminding me of every minute that I spend alone. Without thinking, I get up and empty the grocery bag onto the counter. There are some power bars, a large packet of oatmeal raisin cookies and a business card for Edwin, the vet at the track. Perhaps he's hired her. My eyes are watery and blur my vision as I refill my water glass and shuffle back to the recliner.

* * *

Philippa is on the doorstep just as I've finished over two hours of stall cleaning. Linda is sick and couldn't come. I've never known her to be ill before, and I'm worried about her. I miss her company and her competent, efficient help. The horses love her. It's not usual for horses to get noticeably attached to a specific person. They're not expected to be loyal and faithful companions to their humans in the same way that dogs are. But all seven horses respond to her voice, obey her instructions and appear to enjoy having her around, whatever she's doing.

Philippa has the appearance of an impoverished British aristocrat. Her expensive clothes must have fit her well at one time, but now they draw attention to the weight she's lost and the number of years she's worn them. Her leather suitcase is scuffed around the edges, and thirsty for nourishment much like its owner.

I show her to the room that was to be William's, although I haven't quite finished the painting. She says little as I give her a tour of the house and tell her where the things are to make coffee and tea. She takes a liking to Kelly and Cooper, and is eager to visit with the horses.

"I'm not in a position to pay you." She fiddles with her wedding ring as I rummage for the cups and saucers my mother had found during her last visit.

"There's no charge. You can help me solve the murders. That would be enough." I turn and smile at her.

"I'm not sure that I'll be any help. My head's spinning so much. And, to be frank, I feel my age these days."

"It must be hard to sell the farm."

"The hard part was making the decision. It doesn't do me any good being haunted by the vivid memories that the farm holds. I don't have much time left, so I should try to do something with it. I thought I might help with the thoroughbred adoption program."

"The one which adopts out retired racehorses?"

"Yes." She looks down at Cooper, who is playing with the tassel on one of her shoes, the shoes which she didn't take off when she stepped into the house.

"Tell me more about Russell. Did you know that he's likely facing charges of sexual assault? Did he rape Amy?"

Philippa's head snaps up.

"I've been told," I say, "that two women have come forward and are willing to testify against Russell."

Philippa's eyes widen, but she stays silent.

"I don't know how, but there must be a connection between Russell and your husband in this business."

Philippa's bottom lip trembles, but still no words come out.

"I think Amy's mother, Flora, told her that your husband raped her. Am I right?"

Philippa sits down with a thump as I place a cup of coffee in front of her. I even have cream and sugar in the house, thanks to Melissa.

"Yes, Amy told me." Philippa says. "She could see I was visibly shaken. My husband is a lot of things, but he isn't a rapist. This is another reason for my going to the police. I want them to have the truth, although I think that my loyalty to my husband is ill-placed."

"Going back to my thought that there might be a connection, do you think he and Russell could have had any kind of relationship to do with all this, like being involved in the sex-trade, perhaps?"

"How utterly horrible and reprehensible."

"But do you?"

"Do you have any brandy? I take some when my nerves are bad." Her cup rattles in its saucer as she places it back on the table.

"I'll get some. Do you? I'm determined to find out the truth, Philippa. You need to tell me what you know as well as what you suspect. People have been killed. I need all the help I can get with this."

"I know. It's just so hard." She fidgets on the chair. "Yes, I had suspicions there was something awful going on, but wouldn't let them penetrate much into my consciousness. I suppose I just couldn't face the possibility. But then Amy visited. I couldn't pretend any more. I decided to go through my husband's desk. I'd not had the courage before because I was terrified that I'd find something. But

Amy changed my whole attitude. I had to find out what I could." She almost snatches the glass of brandy from me and takes two sips.

"Did you find anything?"

"There was a ledger, some notes in a diary and a few phone numbers. I was too scared of what I might discover to do much digging, but I guessed that my husband and Russell were selling sex with underage girls. I think perhaps Russell continued after my husband died."

"You must be pretty upset."

"I can't understand anyone, let alone my own husband, exploiting young people in such a heinous way."

"Amy told Melissa that Russell was stalking her. Why do you think he would do that?"

"Mm. I've been seeing Amy regularly because I want to help her. I suppose it's my rather pathetic way of making a tiny bit of reparation for my husband's inexcusable behaviour. She phoned me and said Russell was stalking her. She was frightened. It made me angry, and I was concerned for her safety."

"You don't sound all that upset, considering. It's amazing Amy wasn't hurt while she was in that cellar of his. He should face justice before he does any more damage. Before any more women get hurt."

"He should." She takes a large swig of the brandy and then contemplates the little that remains in the glass as she slowly swirls it around.

"What's your husband's name? You never call him by name."

She throws back her head and finishes the brandy, setting the glass down with a thud, which makes Kelly sit up.

"You're persistent."

"I want the truth. So far you've given me a mixture of truth and lies."

She picks up the glass and holds it out.

"You might want some too," she says. "The truth hurts."

My mobile beeps, telling me I have a text message from Melissa. I can't resist picking it up. She tells me she's found Russell. I'm so relieved to hear something from her that I barely take in the message. I hover over my mini-keyboard, wondering what reply I can send that might encourage her to come back to the farm, now. But, before I can get my thoughts organized, another text pops up with just three letters: 'hel'.

I try calling her. It goes straight to voice mail.

I phone the police.

I leave a garbled message for William.

I give Philippa the gist of what's happening and, to my surprise, she insists on coming with me to Russell's farms. I don't have time for an argument, but I'm concerned for her safety as well as her potential to slow me down. She and Kelly follow me to the truck. Philippa needs help to clamber in.

I get out to open the gate and again to close it, just in case a horse breaks out, and curse it for using up precious time, although I don't know if I'm going to the right places in such a hurry.

A secret part of me hopes that Melissa being in apparent danger has a silver lining: that it will bring William, Melissa and me together again, and give me a second, or maybe it's a third or fourth, chance.

"I have to tell you now," Philippa says. "I have to come straight with you."

"About time." I'm in no mood for any nonsense.

"You asked what my husband's name is."

"Yes." My patience is running thin. I just want her to spit it out.

"Cecil."

"Okay. I suppose I could have found that out."

"But he's using the name 'Russell'."

"What?" I veer off the road onto the gravel shoulder. I'm going too fast for abrupt changes in direction. I get the truck back under control and grip the steering wheel so hard it hurts.

203

"You mean Cecil is posing as Russell?"

"I know, it's weird."

"Weird isn't the word I'd use. Why?"

"Amy is Cecil's daughter, as you know," Philippa takes in a sudden, deep breath, almost as if she's gasping for air. "My husband had an affair with the maid, Flora, and paid her to keep quiet. I knew. I made sure that Flora and Amy left years ago. I thought Amy, as she grew up, could be at risk of assault or worse from Russell, the real Russell, that is. I just couldn't bear that to happen."

It would have been smart for me to leave my mother and Stan much earlier than I did. If it hadn't been for my beloved dog Bertie, I would have.

"From what I know," Philippa says. "Cecil was in the human smuggling business and brought young girls into Canada. Russell was the broker, if that's the right term. He sold them to gangs who would use the girls in the sex-trade. Russell did pretty well out of the business, as far as I could tell, and bought properties with the profits, which he rented out. But the police were catching up with them, and they both left abruptly. I found out that they lived abroad in Thailand. In the meantime, I didn't tighten my belt enough and have gone into debt. That's it, in brief."

"But why would Cecil pose as Russell?"

"Money."

"I don't think you're telling the whole truth, even now. Amy got involved with Russell and Cecil somehow, didn't she?" I almost spit the words out. I'm fed up with lies and more lies.

"It's especially hard to talk about this part. How did you know?" She sniffs and finds an embroidered handkerchief in the bottom of her purse. She dabs her eyes and wipes her nose. "I was completely flabbergasted when my husband brought Amy home. This was several years after she and her mother had left. He'd found out where she was, or Amy found her father. I'm not sure which. Flora was sick and Amy was vulnerable. And she was attractive and quiet. I don't think Cecil brought her here with bad intentions. Russell virtually snatched her away from Cecil and offered her to a gang with some other girls. I can't understand why Cecil never stood up to Russell, not even to help his own daughter. I truly don't know why. I can't explain that. As it turned out, the gang didn't want Amy because she was sick. They were scared that she might have something contagious. It hadn't happened before. Fortunately, Russell didn't have anywhere to put her. He never used the same warehouse or storage facility twice, and he didn't want to put her with any other girls. I guess he used these places to house the girls temporarily until the deal was finalized and they were picked up by the gang who'd bought them."

"For someone who purports to be ignorant of what Russell and Cecil were up to, you seem to know an awful lot about what happened to Amy."

"I knew what they were doing. But I tried very hard to block it all out. It hasn't worked very well. I'm constantly haunted by all that went on."

I thought I was an expert at burying my head in the sand, but Philippa's right, you can't easily hide from reality. I grit my teeth. I must squeeze as much out of Philippa as I can right now, while I have this opportunity.

"I hope this is the truth at last." I raise my voice. "I must solve these murders before someone else gets killed, and I think there's a connection."

"I am. I promise."

"So, you nursed Amy while she was sick."

"I kept her in a locked room. None of the staff were allowed in. Cecil didn't want any risk of someone hearing about her. But as soon as she was well enough, I got her out of the house. I got my cousin in Alberta to help."

"Russell and Cecil must have been furious."

"That's an understatement. Russell said that she was his property, that he'd paid for her. Cecil said I'd been disloyal and made up a feeble argument about wanting to care for his daughter. I'm actually not sure of his motives. Did he really want to get to know his daughter? Or was he using this relationship to get at me, or in response to pressure from Russell? I don't know. It caused even more friction in our fractious marriage."

"We're almost at Russell's first farm."

"Amy agrees with me that we should try to get Cecil to justice, but she doesn't want to talk to the police. Perhaps she wants to administer her own justice. She mentioned the crazy and dangerous idea that she could blackmail him. That might be the reason she came here."

"Was he blackmailing you?"

"No, I lied about that. But he did say that, if I ever went to the police, he had evidence to prove that I was complicit in the business. I would be charged too."

"He threatened you."

"And when Amy showed up this time, he told me he'd hurt her if I didn't do as he said, which was to join that damn syndicate. I don't know why he wanted to set that up. And I don't know if he really would hurt his daughter. His behaviour is hard to predict. I shouldn't have married him. I was taken in by his charm. I was infatuated with him. But when we lived together, he often criticized me and put me down."

"You must have been relieved when he left."

"I was relieved that I could stay at the farm. It was bought with my family's money and is in my name. Despite his intimidation tactics, I'm proud that I was at least able to stand my ground on that. Now I have to sell, but it's for the best really, under the circumstances."

"This is the driveway. I don't see any vehicles."

I park the truck by the barn and ask Philippa to stay there with my mobile. I put Kelly on a leash and we walk towards the door of the house. The broken screen door is closed with the spring still dangling down. The smashed wooden door is open. As soon as we enter, Kelly pulls me to the bottom of the stairs. She looks up and starts to climb. We reach the top and she moves to one of the closed bedroom doors and sits with her head cocked to one side. She must hear something. I try the knob, but I can't move it. There's an old key hole under the knob. There must be a key somewhere. I scan the landing. There's a brown cupboard with a small jewellery box on top. It has one drawer and two doors. I yank the drawer open and bits and pieces are flung backwards. I drop Kelly's leash and pull the drawer out of its hole. I see two keys. The first one I try works in the lock, much to my surprise. I fling the door open. The knob on the inside bounces off the wall, and I hear a muffled groan. Kelly runs in and jumps on the bed. Melissa has duct tape over her mouth, and her wrists and ankles are tied to the bed with baling twine. What worries me the most is that her eyes are closed, although she's breathing. I rush downstairs to get a knife or scissors. I find a small knife with a serrated blade and leap up the stairs two at a time. Kelly's still on the bed when I get back.

I cut through the twine as fast as I can while taking care not to make her abrasions worse. Baling twine is tough stuff. As I cut each limb free, she shakes it. She moves her body slightly and then sits up. Meanwhile, I utter spurious gibberish in a feeble attempt to comfort her. I carefully lift a small corner of the duct tape, but Melissa grabs another corner and rips it off.

"The faster the better," she says in a whisper. Her face looks red and sore. It must have been painful.

"Don't move." I run as fast as I can to the truck, snatch the phone out of Philippa's hand and dial 911 for police and an ambulance.

*   *   *

Philippa says she'll stay at the farm with Kelly while I go to the hospital. I phone William as I walk from the truck to the house and give him a quick overview. He says he'll meet me there. He asks me a couple of quick questions, but I have no answers. I tell him I'll leave the farm as soon as Kelly and Philippa are in the house and the door's locked.

I shut the gate and put a padlock on it, which I'd bought previously, but didn't want to bother with until now. Extra precautions are called for.

16

Assault

A nurse tells me I can't see Melissa yet because the police are interviewing her. I ask her if she can tell me about her condition since I'm Melissa's sister and I was the one who found her. She looks over her reading glasses and says that the doctor has examined her and that she has abrasions around her wrists and ankles and irritated skin around her mouth. My frown is so deep, it's as if my eyes are squeezed closer together. And she finally gets to the point I'm most concerned about. She was not sexually assaulted. I feel dizzy, and rest my head on my arms on the high counter at the nurses' station.

"Tell me," William says, as he places a warm hand on my shoulder. I'm so glad to see him that give him a hug, and then stand back.

"I've made your jacket wet," I say, as I make a futile attempt to wipe away some of the tears shed for Melissa.

"How is she?"

"She'll be okay. I hope. She was not raped. The police are talking to her now, so we can't go in. She's in that room there." I point to the large door just opposite the nurses' station.

"God, that's a relief. I've been worried sick. Let's sit down." We find some chairs in an alcove a little further along the corridor. "They got her a bed quickly."

"Perhaps they do when it's a suspected sexual assault."

I tell William all I know. We're both puzzled that Russell, who I now know is Cecil, would go back to his farm, but perhaps he assumed it would be the last place anyone would look. I got lucky. For some unknown reason, his farm was the first place that I thought of. I then tell William all I learned from Philippa.

"I hope you can come back to the farm this evening? It would be great for you to meet Philippa and chat with her."

William looks at me for a second and then turns away. I mustn't blow this. How many chances can I have?

"William, the real reason I wish you would come to the farm this evening is that I miss you so much and I'd love to have you in my home again. It's not the same without you." This wasn't as difficult to say as I thought it would be, because it's the truth.

"In that case I'd be pleased to come. I'll bring takeout since no-one's going to want to cook. Is Linda going to be there? She must almost be a fixture in the barn with all those horses."

"No. She's sick. She's never ill, so I'm worried, but I haven't even checked with her. I must do that."

The nurse I talked to comes towards us and motions that we can see Melissa.

Melissa has her eyes closed and looks almost as white as the pillow her head's resting on. The bed has her propped up at about a thirty-degree angle. Her arms are stretched out along her sides on top of the white blanket that's draped over her body, and her feet are uncovered. I see bandages on her wrists and ankles. She's hooked up to an IV.

"Melissa, it's Meg and William to see you. I'm so sorry about what happened. How are you feeling?" She opens her eyes and looks more alert than I expected.

"Shaken more than anything. And tired. Those police officers wore me out with all their questions. I don't think any of my answers will help them get the guy."

"How badly hurt are you?" I ask, sitting down on a hard plastic chair near to the head of the bed.

"My injuries aren't serious. I got shook up. I wasn't sure what he was going to do." She turns her head away.

"Are you okay with us chatting with you?" I ask. "You look exhausted.

"I am tired, but I'd like you to stay for a bit. I'm glad you're both here."

"What made you go to Russell's farm?" I ask. William brings a chair from outside of the room and sits down next to me.

"Amy called me. She talked so fast I'm not sure what it was all about, but I think I heard she had a plan to blackmail him and it went bad. Does that make any sense?"

"It might, actually," I say.

"She asked me to do something, anything, to make him stay away from her. I didn't think he could be all that terrible, so I thought I could be a kind of mediator. You've visited him on your own a few times, so I wasn't worried. Anyway, I looked for him in the first place I thought of. I didn't think he'd be there, of course, but I thought I'd try to be a clever sleuth and gather clues about where he might have gone. And then I was going to tell William."

The little jab dares to poke me, but I don't pay it any attention.

"I wish you'd told me about Amy's call as soon as you received it," William says.

"I now know I shouldn't have gone alone. It was stupid."

"How did you get there?" I ask.

"I got a taxi to the end of Russell's driveway." She turns her head away from us. We wait in silence for a few seconds until she faces us again. "I walked up the driveway. I couldn't see a vehicle or any sign of life. I got bolder and thought I'd check around to see if anyone had been there recently. I heard a noise and thought I saw movement in the barn, and then Russell was walking towards me. So, I texted you, Meg, to let you know that I'd found him, because you live so close. I'm glad I did."

"So are we," William says.

"I wasn't afraid at that point. I was just going to talk to him about Amy. But, when I looked up from my phone, a hot, sweaty hand hit my mouth and stayed there while his other hand grabbed me round the waist. I kicked and struggled, but he half-dragged me upstairs to that bed and tied me down. I'm ashamed that I couldn't beat him off. I should have been able to."

"He's stronger than he looks, and a lot larger and heavier than you," I say.

"But I was able to text you again as he struggled with me on the stairs, although I had to send it before I'd finished."

"It was enough."

"As soon as we got to the landing, he yanked the phone out of my hands and stamped on it, cursing. He threw me on the bed and my head hit the headboard. I think that's why the hospital hasn't released me yet. I shouldn't have mentioned it."

"You were right to mention it," William says.

"There's more to this, isn't there?" I say.

"As he was tying my right wrist to the bed, I yanked on his beard and got him to look at me. I yelled at him, asking him why he was hurting me." Her eyes water up. "He straddled me with his knees on the bed and grabbed my left wrist with both hands and tied it to the bed as well. I could hardly breathe and I wretched. He told me to be quiet. That was my problem, he said, I talk too much. I poisoned

Amy's mind, and I think he said that I'd turned his daughter against him, but I must have got that part wrong. As he taped my mouth shut, I could feel and hear his phone vibrate. I thought Russell didn't have a mobile. He looked at it and left. I was saved by the phone, I guess." She reaches out for my hand, and I hold her icy fingers.

"William, is there another blanket somewhere? She's freezing."

He gets up and goes to ask at the nurses' station.

"Have you told Amy what happened?" I ask.

"No, can you text her? She should know that he's still around and that he's dangerous."

"Okay."

"What do you think's going on?" Melissa asks.

"I can only make wild guesses. We don't have enough to be sure. Perhaps it's a weird case of stolen identity. But it isn't enough to explain everything."

"What do you mean?"

"I've just learned that he's not who he says he is. He's Philippa's husband, Cecil, posing as Russell for some weird reason. And you probably know that Cecil is Amy's father."

"That would explain a lot."

"It explains some of Russell, or Cecil's odd behaviour."

"But he sure doesn't know how to be a father. But what would I know about that?" She turns her face away.

"Nor me."

William returns with two white cotton blankets, which we tuck around her. She asks us to promise that we'll find out what this is all about. Her eyes half-close, and she sighs. It's time for us to leave.

* * *

Having seven horses to care for with no help is a challenge. With Linda sick and Melissa recovering from her ordeal, I have a load of work to do. But if I do eventually own all seven, I must be able to care for them by myself. I can't be dependent on other people. Stuff happens.

What's wrong with Linda? I'll phone her as soon as I've finished the barn chores and had my shower. She's such a reliable, conscientious worker. She must be very sick.

*   *   *

My work in the barn is finished. The horses are out in the mist, which clings to the trees and hangs around the fields. The hazy sun barely makes its presence known and there's no breeze through the barn this morning. The stagnant air, combined with the humidity, has my clothes wet with perspiration.

The lukewarm water from the shower washes the sweat and dirt away, and although I'm wet, I'm refreshed. My clean, dry clothes have a crispness and a faint lavender scent, which would have brought a smile to my face if I wasn't thinking of Linda.

I call her as I fill up the kettle.

"Linda, is that you?" Her voice is muffled, so I wonder for a minute if I'm talking to her mother.

"Yeah. Are the horses okay?"

"They're fine. How are you? Hope you're feeling better."

"Yeah. Have you found the killer?" Her voice is flat.

"Not yet." I tell her what happened to Melissa and that she's coming out of the hospital today and that Philippa is here at the farm and that my mother is due to arrive this evening. "What's the matter, Linda? Are you crying?"

"Can I come to see you?"

"Of course you can."

"I want to talk to you in private. Can we meet in the barn?"

"When do you want to come?"

214

"In about fifteen minutes. Okay?"

"See you then. I'll wait there for you."

I pour a mug of tea, and Kelly follows me back out to the barn. The mist lingers, and its dampness seeps under my skin. I walk up and down the aisle and sip my tea. Kelly catches my agitation and paces with me, watchful. I'm sure she knows I expect someone to arrive.

Linda's little blue car stops just outside the barn door. She closes the large, sliding door behind her and walks into the feed room without a word, but she does pat Kelly's head. I close the feed room door behind me. Linda is dishevelled. Her cheeks aren't their usual rosy colour, her clothes hang as if draped over her, the holes in her jeans are frayed beyond the fashionable look, and her eyes are bloodshot.

"What on earth is wrong, Linda?" I walk towards her.

"I have to tell you something. I'm scared."

"What about? Are you very sick?"

"No. I'm not sick. It's about Russell."

"What about him?"

"Russell isn't Russell. He's Cecil."

"Thank goodness it's nothing more serious. I thought you were dying or something."

"It is serious. Don't think it isn't. Something about Russell has been bugging me and I've finally figured out who Russell and Cecil are. They both hung out around the backstretch a lot, years ago. They're evil."

"Linda, sit down. Would you like a coffee?"

"No." She sits on the edge of the old, rickety stool which I use to reach things from the top shelves. She puts her head in her hands.

"What makes you think they're so evil?"

"I don't think it, I know it." She lifts her head and stares at me with unblinking red eyes.

"Sorry, Linda. I didn't mean to imply that what you're telling me isn't important or isn't true."

"Cecil is Philippa's husband, and she knows all about their crimes. They're perverts and villains. I wish I'd figured it out earlier so you wouldn't let Philippa or Cecil into your house or let anyone near them." She gasps for breath, her cheeks now reddened and her fists clenched. "Before he got Melissa."

"Melissa will be okay."

"I really want you to listen. It's important."

"I'm listening."

"They're evil because one of them raped a hotwalker I was friendly with. I found her in the corner of the container thing where we store the hay by the barns. She was sobbing."

"He raped her in there?"

"No. She said he asked her out for a meal. He took her in his fancy car to a dumpy motel. She got scared, but it was too late. She said there were two of them and they talked as if she was an animal. She said they checked her over as if they might be thinking of selling her to someone or something. Then the one guy left. And that's when it happened. But she managed to escape afterwards. And she came back to work. But for a different trainer as far away as possible from where they had their horses. I told her it was stupid."

"No thought of telling the police?"

"You're joking, right? There were two of them. Her word against hot-shot racehorse owners. And if she said anything, they'd put her in that witness box thing and make out that she's the criminal because she looks nice. And they'd call it sexual assault, which sounds less than rape. She'd go through all that pain and they'd get off."

"Oh, Linda, that's awful. But how do you know that the two men were Russell and Cecil?"

"I just know. She told me, okay?" She glares at me. I've not seen this side of Linda ever before. My heart pounds and my palms feel sticky.

"When did you know Russell was Cecil in disguise?"

"A couple of days after Hector came to Neal."

"So?"

"I didn't tell you because he's evil."

"Isn't that a reason to tell me?"

"I wish I had, okay?"

"Did you think he'd do something to you or me?"

"He scares me. I don't want anything to do with him."

"But, if he really is a demon, we need to stop him. Do you have evidence of any kind that would help?"

"Just rumour and it's no good."

"Try me."

"Grayson saw Russell, who must have been Cecil, coming out of his office trailer. He went in and found Amy."

"I've heard that before, yes."

"That's why Grayson was killed. He must have known that Russell, Cecil, whatever, raped Amy."

"But I don't think he did."

"That's nuts. Of course he did." She stands up.

"Linda, Amy is Cecil's daughter. However evil he is, I can't see him raping his own daughter."

She sits down again and sobs. "I don't believe it. I don't want to go back to work. Amy already told me what happened to Melissa. It's too awful. I'm not going near any place Cecil's hanging around."

"I don't think for a moment he's going to be there. He's wanted by the police for his confinement of Amy, at the very least. He won't show up at the track. I think you're safe to go to work."

"But he went back to his farm when no-one thought he would."

"You have a point, but I still don't think he'll risk going to the backstretch."

"He might come here."

"I don't think so. Besides, I have a vicious guard dog." I look down at Kelly and smile, in a weak attempt to make light of it. "You're a good dog. You'll keep us safe, won't you?" Her silky tail wafts to and fro, almost in slow motion. "I admit I could do with your help, but most of all, I miss your visits to the farm."

"What about that woman, Philippa?"

"What about her?"

"She's lying about her husband. I wouldn't want her in my house. She's probably as evil as he is."

"Her staying here depends on her answers to my and William's questions and whether or not we believe her. We'll see."

She looks at me. "If I can come to the barn and don't have to go to the house or see that woman, then I'll come and help here."

"She'll not be permitted to come to the barn. The horses miss you." I touch her hand.

"I miss them so much."

I grab a piece of kitchen towel and hand it to her. She wipes her eyes and blows her nose.

"I want to see the horses," Linda says. "If you promise none of those creeps will be near the barn, I'll tell Neal that I'll help you starting the day after tomorrow, but I'm too scared to go to the backstretch."

"Thanks, Linda. I'm sure you'll feel better working with the animals. I always do. I'll give you updates on how my investigation is going, each morning."

"Okay."

I watch Linda get into her car. Her emotionally laden outburst about the heinous attack on her friend has shaken me, and the passion and intensity in Linda's face makes me think there's more to that story.

I squint at the glare as I leave the barn. The mist shrouding the house has captured some of the sunlight, but refuses to let it go, and radiates brightness. My skin is clammy and there are beads of sweat on my brow despite the less-than-warm air.

Philippa is not in the kitchen or the family room. It's nearly 11o'clock.

I call William.

"I just want to make sure you're coming to the farm this evening."

"Yes, I said I would and that I'd get takeout. You sound stressed."

"I am. I'm sure Philippa has been telling more lies."

"We'll have a chance to ask questions. And we shouldn't stop asking until we're satisfied. It will help having the two of us."

"That makes me feel better."

"I could leave work early," William says. "I can't stay late at the farm, but you're picking your mother up from the airport this evening, correct?"

"That would be great. Thank you."

"I'll be there about four."

"That'll work. How's Melissa?"

"Haven't got time to talk right now, but she's doing okay."

"Good."

As soon as I've said goodbye to William, I dial Melissa's mobile.

"How are you?"

"I'm fine. I had an appointment with that vet, Edwin, this morning and I went."

"Wow, you bounced back quickly."

"Yeah, I'm good. I'm pleased I could see Edwin. He was great. I think I have a part-time job working for him, which is just what I wanted. The vet assistant who was going to college in the fall resigned early."

"That's excellent. Congratulations."

"Thanks."

"When are you coming back to the farm? Don't forget that we have seven horses at the moment."

"I feel bad about not helping, but I can't come."

"Why not?"

"You know why not. Our mother is coming today. I can't face her. I don't know how you can have anything to do with her. And it's like you're not respecting how I feel. How can you possibly forgive her?"

"I don't know that I've forgiven her. I can't hate her. And there's part of me that feels some empathy for what she's been through."

"You know how I feel about that."

"Given how you feel, I'm probably asking the impossible, but do you think you could come for dinner tomorrow evening? Just the one meal with our mother. It'll probably be takeout because I'm so busy."

"If it's just one meal, I'll do it for you. As soon as she goes home, and Philippa's gone, I'd like to return to the farm and help with the chores. Hope neither of them stay long."

"Thanks, Melissa. That means a lot." I breathe a little easier, relieved that some of the tension has eased between us.

I congratulate her again on the job. She starts in one week's time. I hope we've found the killer by then.

* * *

William arrives on the dot of four.

"Philippa told me you were here," William says as he saunters down the aisle of the barn with his hands in his pockets. Kelly's standing next to me, and I can feel the breeze she's generating with her tail.

"You don't look dressed for barn work."

"I'm sure you can manage."

"Since you're here, I'll tell you about my conversation with Oscar."

I give him an overview of Oscar's claim that he'd sold a couple of properties that he didn't own and that he was being blackmailed by Russell, or Cecil rather.

"You don't believe him, do you?" William says.

"You're right, I don't.

I pull the hose down the aisle and start to fill the water bucket that hangs in Hector's stall. "You're not too well dressed to feed the barn cats and put out fresh water for them."

"Be happy to do that."

"By the way, it seems I'm going to receive some funds from Frank's estate. This doesn't include the Cayman Islands money that Murray has his hands on. From what I read in the lawyer's letter, there are proceeds from the sale of the horses that Frank had in Kentucky, and some cash in a couple of bank accounts. I'm not sure how much it'll be, but I think I'm going to do what Melissa suggested. I'll buy Fay and Basil. It'll be a lot of work, but I think that's what I should do."

"Your call."

"I think Frank would be okay with that. What do you think, though?"

"It could be fun to see them train and race."

"Could be, yes, and I'll be prudent. I don't want to just throw Frank's money away."

"Your trainer, Neal, seems to have a good head on his shoulders."

"I'll tell Neal that I'm thinking along these lines. Anyway, we ought to go back to the house. Philippa will be wondering who's getting her dinner."

"I don't think she has a right to make any demands. She's lucky to have somewhere free to stay." He strokes Kelly's silky head and we leave the barn. "I got some takeout, as promised. I popped it in the oven."

I'm glad that I finally gave William a key to the back door so that he doesn't have to knock or go to the barn to find the spare one. He, no doubt, thought this was long overdue, but for me it was a big step.

We enter the house and, as I shed my barn clothes, William dishes out the vegetable curry and rice, along with generous portions of Caesar salad. The three of us settle around the kitchen table with barely a word spoken.

17

Complicated

William makes coffee for himself and Philippa. I settle for a glass of water and we all traipse into the family room.

"Philippa, we need to talk to you," I say. "As you know, I'm determined to find out who killed Grayson and who killed Emma, and why, and the reasons behind Amy being held by Cecil in the farmhouse basement, and Melissa being tied up in the bedroom."

"I don't know how I can help any more than I have already."

"Last time we talked about all of this, you promised that what you told me was the truth, but it wasn't the full story. You left significant pieces out, didn't you?" I lean forward in my chair and look unblinking for a couple of seconds into her eyes. She turns her head away.

"I did. I mean, I left some things out. It's all so painful and awkward."

"People are getting killed. Think of the loss their families are feeling. You can help me get to the bottom of all of this if you tell me everything."

"Will William arrest me?"

"No," is all that William says.

"What for?" I ask.

Philippa leans back in the recliner, raises the foot rest and stares at the ceiling. Then she talks. Fifteen years ago, Cecil, her husband, and Russell, his business partner, made off for Thailand. They saw the writing on the wall: charges in the offing relating to allegations of human trafficking and sexual assault of minors. She conjectures that Russell must have kept ownership of his three farms, and acted as an absentee landlord, while they lived abroad.

"I don't know why they weren't arrested," Philippa says. "I didn't hear from them for over fourteen years. But then, out of the blue, Cecil called and told me Russell had died of cancer. He wanted to come back to the house, and I said no. It was a terse conversation on both sides. That was some time ago. I have to say I was shaken. He must have come up with the plan to assume Russell's identity after that call. As time passed, I managed to put the call out of my mind. But then I was invited to the session on racehorse ownership. I got a mailed invitation, a written reminder and three phone calls, pressuring me to attend and asking me to speak about the breeding side."

"Didn't you recognize Cecil's voice?"

"It was muffled. I often had to ask him to repeat. He just said it was a bad line. You know what these country lines are like, he said. But I suspected it was him. It was a shock that he was posing as Russell. I was pretty upset and confused."

"Why did you agree to go when you know what kind of person Cecil is?"

She sighs and looks down at Cooper, who's about to jump up onto her lap.

"I've been lonely. And I don't like to admit it, but I think I'm depressed. So, despite myself, I went. Even knowing what kind of cad Cecil is, I still have fond memories of the days we went to the races, and of owning racehorses. There's nothing more exciting than watching your racehorse win a race. It's exhilarating. But you'd know all about that. I don't have to tell you. So, I went."

"That doesn't sound like a sufficiently convincing reason for you to go," William says. "To go to a session to give a talk on an area you've not been involved in for at least fifteen years. Did Cecil threaten you?"

"He's not all bad, but he told me I'd go down with him if I said anything to the police about the human trafficking business, and it would be in my best interests for me to co-operate. To be honest, I didn't see much harm in going to the session, anyway."

"Did Cecil look like Russell, as you remember him?" I ask.

"Cecil didn't look like Cecil. But I couldn't say he looked like Russell either. I'd not seen either of them for about fifteen years. Cecil pulled me aside. He was agitated. He told me he'd assumed Russell's name and said that I mustn't tell anyone if I knew what was good for me. He didn't even ask me how I was or anything. I thought how ridiculous he looked with that beard and long hair. Then he told me I must join the syndicate. I would be in serious trouble if I didn't."

"What do you think he meant by that?" I ask.

"Oh, I don't know. He didn't spell it out."

"What made him so keen to set up the syndicate. Have you any idea?"

"He's always been passionate about racing. He once said to me that owning and racing thoroughbreds is addictive."

"Many people in the horse-racing business say that thorough-breds can get under your skin and racing can become a passion, even an obsession."

"It was for me, too, really. I missed it so much. I didn't have enough money to continue after Cecil left. It was as if I was in a vacuum. No family, no horses and nothing to do."

"Why did he want you to join the syndicate?"

"I don't know. Perhaps he couldn't find enough people and he knew he had some ability to force my hand. He might have erroneously thought I have some money. But it also crossed my mind that he was simply seeking revenge for the help I gave Amy in escaping. So, I played along, hoping to placate him and protect myself."

"Why do you think he returned to Canada?"

"I thought perhaps it was for revenge, as I mentioned, but how can you harbour anger for fifteen years? And why steal Russell's identity? I can't make sense of the man, even though he's my husband."

"He showed up on your doorstep. What did he say?"

"He said he'd come to claim what was his, whatever that meant. I told him I stood by what I'd told him on the phone. He couldn't stay at the house. Besides, it wouldn't make sense if he was posing as Russell. But he unnerved, me, I admit. So, I packed a few things and left as quickly as I could by the back door. I couldn't bear to be in the same house as him."

"It would be stupid for him to stay there."

"Perhaps he has some cash stashed away somewhere that I'm not aware of. I truly don't know why he wanted to stay at my farm, especially with the police on his tail."

"The police would be sure to check. You're right," William says.

"One thing I did which I think was the most regrettable thing I've ever done, was suggest that Amy connect with Grayson for a job," Philippa says. "But I didn't know that he'd be Cecil's trainer."

"Do you think Cecil murdered Grayson?" William asks, getting straight to the million-dollar question.

"No," Philippa says.

"Why do you say that?" I ask.

"Cecil is my husband and yes, he is guilty of human trafficking and selling girls into the sex-trade, but that's as far as it went. I don't believe he's guilty of sexual assault. Russell was the one who enjoyed pornography and had the connections to the gangs, and I believe he was guilty of sexual assault of minors. I don't believe Cecil did that. And I sure can't imagine him killing anyone."

"Where does Amy fit into all this?"

"He was angrier than I've ever known him when he found out that I'd helped her to escape."

"Ah," William says. "I think I can guess. Meg told me you originally stated that Amy is Cecil's daughter. And that was the truth, wasn't it?"

"Cecil had a short fling with Flora, one of our staff. He paid Flora a lump sum, but there was a condition: that they would live within an hour's commute so he could see his daughter. We have no children. It meant a lot to him to have a daughter. But Flora left the province. Eventually, after several years, Cecil found Amy and, I suppose he abducted her, or had someone do it for him, and brought her to our house. She was sick, that bit was true too, and she was missing her mother terribly, and was worried about her because Flora had colon cancer. So, even though I knew Cecil would be furious, I not only took care of her, but I also helped her to escape so she could return to her mother."

"Does Amy know Cecil is her father?" I ask.

"Yes, but she didn't know that Russell was Cecil in disguise."

"He wouldn't have sexually assaulted his daughter."

"Of course not. Cecil wouldn't have. I would swear that he's not a rapist. He's a lot of things, but not that. If you want my opinion?" Philippa wrings her hands.

"Yes, we do," I reply.

"I think Cecil was just trying to get Amy to believe that he is her father, and wanting to develop some kind of father-daughter relationship. But I suppose it went wrong."

"Sounds like he didn't approach it the right way, to put it mildly," I say. "But, if you're correct, and you're being honest with us this time, Cecil wouldn't have sexually assaulted Amy in Grayson's trailer, would he?"

"I know my husband. His business was a reprehensible one and I wish I'd never been involved with it. And he's not the best person you'll ever meet, but I believe he never assaulted the girls. I do really believe that."

"Perhaps that's what you want to believe," William suggests.

"I knew Russell was a cad, and Cecil knew," Philippa says. "And Cecil did nothing, as far as I know, to stop him."

"Philippa, he's culpable in the whole affair," William says. "He bought the girls and sold them into the sex-trade, he stood by while his partner assaulted some of them, and then took off with Russell when he thought the police were going to lay charges."

"I know. But even though he's not been a good and loving husband to me, I can't let him be wrongly accused of sexual assault and especially of raping his daughter." Philippa leans back in the recliner again and closes her eyes. It's as if she's signalling that she can't continue this conversation any longer.

"William, let's go into the kitchen," I say. "Have you got time to chat for a bit?"

"I can stay for a little while longer." As he stands beside me, he looks at me out of the corners of his eyes. It's up to me to make this relationship work. I touch his warm hand and it's enough to make him smile, as well as to spark a glow in my heart which lingers for a few seconds. But reality presses down on us.

"I have to pick my mother up from the airport in a couple of hours and I have some stuff to do before that, so I don't have long either."

"What do you think are the relevant kernels of truth in what Philippa said?"

"Once Russell died after they had been in Thailand for fifteen years, Cecil thought he could return to Canada. He wanted to build a relationship with his daughter somehow. I don't know how he knew she was here."

"Perhaps that was just fortuitous."

"Possibly. Once he faced the reality that he couldn't go back and live with Philippa, and realized that Russell had no relatives to leave his property to, he saw an opportunity to steal his identity and take over ownership of the three farms. Then he'd be able to find Amy and attempt to make a connection. But, being at the farm brought back memories of his horse-racing times and he got involved again. Perhaps he'd been involved in racing in Thailand and wanted to continue. I don't know. He hooked up with Grayson, and couldn't believe his luck when he found out Amy was working for him. He must have recognized her."

"He probably tried to strike up a friendship."

"But it sounds like he's lost any charm he might have once had, and she didn't take to him. But he was determined to have her listen and believe him."

"Did Cecil assault Amy in Grayson's trailer?"

"If Philippa told us the truth just now, I think they had an argument. That Amy didn't believe Russell was Cecil in disguise and got scared."

"What has Grayson got to do with this?"

"Who was the person who entered the trailer after Grayson left? It was the security guard. I'm wondering if he found Amy crying and upset and assumed that Grayson had assaulted her. So, when he had the opportunity, he re-entered the trailer and murdered Grayson. I'm certain he knows how to get ketamine."

"But wasn't he the one who told you that Grayson must have been murdered because they found the syringe on the wrong side of the body?"

"This might sound crazy," I say, "but perhaps he wants to be found out. Perhaps he feels he's done a wonderful thing for Amy."

"I suppose that's possible."

"Guess who I'm going to be talking with tomorrow."

"Did he murder Emma as well?"

"I haven't got that far yet. I'm not sure. I can't quite get a connection."

"There might not be one. It could have been a copy-cat crime, the murderer hoping that the police would either assume it was another suicide, or would incorrectly conclude that the same person killed both victims."

"It could be quite complicated."

* * *

The plane landed an hour ago, and my mother has yet to appear. She must be the last one to pick up her bags.

A wheelchair emerges through the automatic sliding doors, pushed by an airport staff member. The pallid occupant clutches a scuffed, brown leather suitcase to her chest. I walk towards her. She gives me a weak smile as the staff member, without a word, stops the wheelchair, takes my mother's suitcase and gives it to me. She offers my mother an arm to help her out of the chair, whisks the transport away and leaves us.

"Wheelchairs are worth their weight in gold around here," my mother says. "It took them half-an-hour to find that thing. And then there was no-one to push me from the luggage round-about gizmo. I had to wait. I feel as worn out as my suitcase looks."

"Never mind. You're here. Was the flight okay?"

"No. You know it's two o'clock in the morning at home?"

"What was wrong with the flight?"

"It was full. I was crammed in against a fat man who smelled of booze and who snored most of the way. The food was awful. The bread was as hard as rock. The stewardess was rude. Is that enough?"

"Quite enough. I get the picture."

As she heaves herself up into the truck, with some helpful licks from Kelly, her thinner legs dangle over the seat edge for a moment. Her raincoat hangs off her shoulders, making the sleeves appear to be too long for her. She's shrunk.

"So, how have you spent the money I sent you?" she asks, as we pull out of the multi-storey carpark.

"I haven't yet."

"Good, you're saving it to pay for the wedding."

"What wedding?"

"Yours and William's of course. Whose else would it be?"

"There are no plans."

"There should be. What are you waiting for? No-one better than him is going to come along."

"Perhaps, but it's between me and William."

"Well, by the sound of it, you have at least not broken up with him. I'll have to take solace in that for the moment." She closes her eyes and sleeps for the rest of the drive home.

Cooper remembers her. He rubs against her, almost tripping my mother up more than once. He purrs so much that drool drips out of his mouth. I tell my mother I'll make a decaf cup of tea, and take her bag up to her room.

When I get back downstairs, she's fast asleep with Cooper on her lap. I put a light-weight throw over her legs and another around her shoulders and decide not to disturb her or the cat. Kelly and I go out to check on the barn.

I need to leave the barn doors open wider. The heat from seven horses has created an almost sauna-like atmosphere, which isn't healthy for them. I underestimated tonight's outside temperature, as well as the heat that is given off by seven large bodies. I breathe in the heavy scents of manure, hay, feed and warm horse, and within seconds am more relaxed. I'd like to stay here for the night, escaping all that is to come, especially with my mother and Melissa.

* * *

Having cleaned the stalls this morning, I pause at the fence to gaze at the horses in the warm sunshine. The overnight rain freshened the air and perked up the grass. I love to watch and hear the horses as they tear at the bright green blades, but five of them should be back in training. Although a break can be good for a racehorse's mental health, every day a little of his or her condition, or fitness, is lost. Hector is restless sometimes. I sense he, in particular, would like to get back to work. Sending them to the track is one of several incentives which urge me on to find out the truth.

Kelly sniffs around the paddock as a robin sings an incredible repertoire of glorious melodies. I take a deep breath and savour the moment before we walk back towards the house.

Raised voices come from the kitchen and greet me before I reach the back door. I'd like to turn around and join the horses in the paddock, but think better of it. Kelly and I stand on the mat, motionless.

"Who do you think you are? You're staying in my daughter's house and acting as if you own it. You shouldn't be here at all as far as I'm concerned," my mother says with fervour. She must have slept well and regained some strength.

"It's none of your business. It's between Meg and me. You keep your nose out of it," Philippa says as her cheeks redden.

"It is my business. And, what's more, you asked me to make coffee as if I'm your maid. I suppose you're used to having a maid. But I'm not your maid. This isn't some posh house with servants, nor a hotel. You can get your own bloody coffee."

"I thought you'd be making some, that's all. If you're Meg's mother then you should be helping her to entertain her guests."

"Excuse me," I say. They both jerk their heads to face me. "Philippa, I thought I made it clear that I wasn't going to entertain you." I plan to say more, but my mother interrupts.

"You see, what did I tell you? You should be fending for yourself. You're just sponging off my daughter, taking advantage of the goodness of her heart. I don't suppose you've offered to cover any of the costs of your staying here?"

"No, but I don't have any money."

"Don't give me that rubbish. I can tell by looking at you you've got money. I don't believe you for a second."

"If this is about money, I'll pay."

"Oh, so you've suddenly got some money."

"Oh dear. I get myself into terrible messes."

"You're probably like me, and tell white lies now and again."

I don't know what snaps inside me, but laughter rocks me so hard that I have to pull out a chair and sit down. I grab a tissue and dab my eyes. Kelly looks at me with her head on one side as if she's trying to figure out what's so funny. And I can see Cooper as he pokes his head around the corner from the family room. He probably wonders if it's now safe to enter the war zone.

I glance up at them and see my mother and Philippa standing like statues with their mouths partly open, but I detect the trace of a smile emerging on Philippa's face. She moves towards the table and sits down.

"Meg, I do have some money. I'm not dead broke. I just thought I'd be safer here now that Cecil is back."

"Who's Cecil, when he's at home?" asks my mother, who's standing with her hands on her hips.

"Philippa," I say, "why don't you get my mother up to speed on everything you know while I have a shower. The truth, mind you. I have to get to the track before eleven to meet with someone." I don't have time to act as a referee, and my theory is that if Philippa tells my mother everything, the tension in the air around us will fade.

*　　*　　*

Amy answers the door to her small flat on the grounds of the track, almost before I've finished knocking.

"Thanks for seeing me," I say. "Before we start our chat, you should know that I don't want to hear anything that isn't the truth. I'd rather you say nothing than tell me lies. I've had enough of people making up stories which keep me going around in circles."

"I'll try." She sits down on a sagging sofa, the upholstery of which looks as if a cat has clawed at it for a year or two.

I sit on a brown, vinyl-covered armchair. The arms feel sticky to my bare arms. "Start by telling me what was really going on between you and Russell."

"Melissa told me that Russell is not Russell, but Cecil, Philippa's husband. It gives me the creeps just to think about it. Why would he pretend to be someone else?"

"Tell me about what happened between you."

"I'll call him Russell because that's who he said he was."

"Fine." I peel my left arm off the vinyl.

"Russell showed up one day when I was raking the shedrow. He asked me where Grayson was. After meeting with Grayson, he seemed to seek me out, which made me nervous. I couldn't think what his interest in me could be. We chatted about horses a bit, but I cut it short because I had so much work to do. Grayson told me later that Russell was interested in getting back into the horse-racing business and was considering using him as his trainer. Then I found out Russell had set up a syndicate, and he hung around a lot."

"Talking to you?"

"I tried to brush him off. I even mentioned it to Grayson, but he said he was a client and something like: he had confidence in my ability to deal tactfully with the situation."

"Mm."

"Anyway, the best way to describe Russell's behaviour is that it was like he was stalking me. He was at the track early nearly every day. He loitered at the security gate, waiting for me to come down from my flat, and then walked with me to the barn. Then he'd be in the cafeteria when it was my break. Then he got Grayson to agree that I could help at his farm, which I dreaded. I went there twice but then I told Grayson I didn't feel safe around him, so that stopped."

"Why were you there when Russell fell in the barn?"

"I went there even though I was scared of him. I know he's no good. I suppose my anger got the better of me. I was in a rage because I thought he'd killed Grayson. Russell was that mad about the horses doing poorly, and he's such a weirdo that I really believed he could have killed Grayson. I got so worked up about it. I wanted him to pay for what he'd done. Everyone was saying Grayson committed suicide. No way. I wanted to confront the creep." Her dark eyes are wide as she rubs her hands up and down her thighs.

"What happened?"

"When I found him in the barn's loft, he looked shocked. And I yelled at him. He stumbled and fell down a hole in the barn floor. He disappeared. I ran. I thought he might be dead, and I'd be blamed."

"You didn't think to call an ambulance?"

"I wasn't going to risk doing that."

"And how did you end up in Russell's cellar?

"I was letting myself into this pathetic hole of a home after work, when he came up behind me and frightened the bejcebers out of me. I dropped my keys. He said he had to talk with me, that it was very important. I wasn't going to let him in here, so I just stood there. He repeated himself and pulled at my arm. I was practically wetting my pants, I was so terrified. He asked me to walk with him just for five minutes. I agreed because I didn't know what else to do."

"You didn't scream for help."

"I thought if I screamed he might hurt me bad. We walked towards the small carpark this side of the security gate, and I don't remember anything else until I was in the cellar tied to a chair with him sitting in front of me."

"Do you think he drugged you somehow?"

"I don't see how. I think he must have hit me, or I might even have fainted. He sat in front of me and said he was glad I was okay. I said I wasn't okay. Anyway, then he blubbered on about not being Russell, but being Cecil. He didn't look much like the photograph Philippa gave me."

"But he was disguised as Russell."

"I suppose so, but I didn't know that, so I thought he was talking nonsense. I thought he was mad. He said he was my father and that he wanted to get to know me and wanted us to have a warm relationship. I felt sick to my stomach and almost threw up. He said he wasn't a bad man and that he could help me. That's when he thought he heard something. He left out of the door which is up a slope that goes to the outside, although he had a struggle to get it open. Then I heard heavy footsteps on the cellar stairs and a police officer crashed the door open. I told him I was the only one there. I was terrified he was going to shoot me. I've never had a gun waving around in the same room as I'm in before. It's not nice. But that's why I said don't worry about me. I realized he must be my father when I thought about all that had happened. So, by the time they were loading me into the ambulance I knew he wouldn't kill me."

"Philippa doesn't think he killed Grayson or Emma."

"All I know is that he mega-mucked up his attempts to develop a relationship with me. He's got no clue about how to deal with people. I never want to see him again. I'm ashamed that he's my father, and I can't bear to be anywhere near him."

"Are you back to work yet? Or are you going to look for something else?"

"I'm going back tomorrow. Melissa suggested I talk to your man, William, about a restraining order. He's started the process for me and isn't charging anything. Wow, he's a nice guy, isn't he? He said something about liking to do some bono work."

"Pro bono work. But it takes time to get a restraining order. It has to be processed in court."

"I know. Frustrating. But William has somehow got him banned from the backstretch. I don't know how he did it. He says that Russell won't want to draw attention to himself and he won't show up. Russell, or Cecil, I suppose I should call him that, could challenge it, at least that's what William says, but he's sure he won't want to push it if he's denied access at the gate."

"You must enjoy your job."

"I need the money, and I'm making a few friends. And Linda's been kind, but she's not feeling good at the moment."

"I know."

"Do you know what's wrong with her?"

"I have a hunch, but I'm not sure. I plan to look into it."

18

Misguided Vengeance

Desmond isn't here. I sit at a table in the corner of the coffee shop which is farthest from both the door and the counter. He's ten minutes late. I finish my tea and contemplate getting another when I see him arrive on a bicycle. The frame of his transport doesn't look strong enough to hold the weight of his tall, well-rounded body. He plods into the coffee shop, pushes past someone on their way out and goes to the counter without acknowledging my presence.

After a couple of minutes, he picks up his icy drink, wipes the sweat off his brow with his sleeve, and sits down in front of me with a thud.

"Got tied up," he says.

"Hi. I'll get straight to the point."

"Good."

"I want to know why you drew the sketch of Edwin entering Emma's office trailer."

"I came clean on it. I did it because I was sure that he was the one who was selling ketamine."

"That seems odd to me. Not only were you wrong, but I've been told that Edwin has an impeccable reputation, that he would be the last person anyone else would suspect of being unprofessional let alone of being a criminal."

"Peoples are entitled to their opinions, I guess."

"I'm being serious. You drew that sketch for a reason. I have a theory, but I'm going to give you a chance to explain."

"Wow. What have I done?" His hand shakes as he sucks up some of the creamy drink. His attempt at levity didn't work the way he'd hoped.

"It's best if you tell me the truth."

"I've told you. I could have made a mistake about who I saw, but I saw someone. I did the best with my sketch."

"I don't believe you."

"Too bad. I can't do anything about that." He gets up, grabs his drink, and leaves. He wobbles on his bike, using one hand on the handlebars, the other holding his drink as he sucks. His uncooperativeness confirms my suspicions. Next call, Amy. There's a lot more for us to talk about.

I text her I'll be outside her door at about three. I don't get an answer but show up, anyway.

"You're back," she says as she opens the door and turns her back on me as she walks into the dingy space.

"We have more to talk about, as you know. I've still not got the truth from you. It's frustrating and, more importantly, people could die."

"I doubt it."

"Why do you say that?"

She grabs a box of tissues, throws it on the bedraggled sofa and flops down next to it with tears running down her cheeks. Her eyes are red.

"Tell me everything," I say, as I sit in the sticky vinyl armchair again.

"The truth chokes me up."

"But it must be told. Take your time. I'm not in a rush. And start at the beginning, even if you think I've heard it before."

She tells me about her mother, Flora, and the story she was told about Cecil raping her. But she's not sure that her mother told the truth. Through social media, she linked up with one of the gardeners her mother had mentioned. Flora told her that Carl was a kind young man who knew a lot about plants, trees and birds, and that she used to talk to him as he worked in the vegetable garden and she picked herbs or hung out the sheets. Amy eventually plucked up courage to ask Carl questions about her mother and Cecil. The gardener thought the whole thing was a great lark. Flora had an affair with Cecil, which everyone knew about, including the lady of the household, and then got money out of him when she found out she was pregnant. Carl remembered she was incredibly relieved that Cecil didn't demand she get an abortion. In fact, he asked that he be able to see the child. Then Flora disappeared. Was she still alive? Amy gave Carl the sad news of her death from cancer.

After Flora died, Amy decided she wanted to see her father. Philippa told Amy that her father had died and gave her a framed photograph of a young man. She also gave her Grayson's name, suggesting that she might get a job with him at the track.

"And then this guy calling himself Russell shows up," Amy says. "I've already told you about him stalking me."

"But there's stuff you haven't told me yet."

"It's the hard stuff. On that terrible day, Grayson wanted to chat with me in the trailer about something important, he said. I was worried."

"Because of what you'd been doing."

"I'd been helping Emma. But I have to tell you first that Emma was taken in by Cecil's disguise. She possibly didn't remember exactly what he looked like, anyway. When I found out that Russell was Cecil, I just couldn't tell her. We'd gone too far. She wanted revenge because Russell had raped her when she was fifteen. She said she hadn't told anyone, ever. But she told me because I confided in her he was stalking me and I was afraid. That was before I knew he was Cecil and my father. She said revenge on Russell would be the best thing and asked if I would help. She did nothing really bad to the horses, just enough to have them out-of-sorts. Nothing permanent." She looks at me with wide eyes, as if pleading with me to excuse the behaviour.

"So, you think, when Grayson wanted to chat with you in the trailer, that he was wise to what was going on?"

"He asked me outright, and I confessed. I was a coward. I crumbled. He immediately emailed the College of Veterinarians about Emma. I just sat there in his trailer crying, knowing I'd betrayed Emma as well as Grayson. So many terrible mistakes. Then he asked me how could I hurt the horses? How could I be cruel to those beautiful animals? And then he fired me. I left the trailer sobbing my heart out. I'd lost my job and my boyfriend. Russell, I mean Cecil, was lurking at the bottom of the steps. It was the last straw. The next minute, I bumped into a security guard. I was so furious and so fed up with Russell pestering me that I screamed 'that man raped me', pointing to the steps where Russell was standing. And I ran."

"Ah. Des misunderstood. He thought Grayson had raped you. He probably didn't see Russell."

Amy's sobs rock the sofa. She sits up and puts her head in her hands.

"I think what I said killed Grayson. Des must have done it. I can't bear it. It's my fault that he's dead."

"Whatever you said doesn't excuse someone killing Grayson. But you will have to repeat all this to the police. You could be charged with cruelty to animals. I'm not sure what charges, if any, can be laid against you for what happened to Grayson."

"I lied about being raped."

"That's not good."

"I've thought about it a lot. It might mean that other women who really have been raped won't be believed."

"That will happen in any case." I pick up the box of tissues that has tumbled to the floor and hand it to her. "I have to ask you about Emma. Do you have any theories about who killed Emma?"

"All I can say is that I think it's got to be different."

"You mean Des didn't kill her. I think the same thing. Someone used the opportunity of Grayson's murder to copycat. Since the police believed Grayson committed suicide, the killer thought he'd get away with murder, literally."

"That's what I think."

"Have you got some friends you can stay with for a couple of days while all this gets sorted out?"

"Not really."

"I'll see what I can do and get back to you. I think you need some support while you go through the ordeal of talking to the police, and you start to recover from all that you've been through. Do you truly feel that you're ready to go back to work?"

"I suppose not. Thank you for helping me. I don't think I deserve it."

* * *

When I get back to the farm, Kelly greets me as if she thought I'd died and she'd never see me again. I couldn't get her to stop jumping up and licking my chin. Despite Kelly's rambunctious behaviour, Cooper rubs against my legs so hard I think I might stumble. Philippa sits immobile at the kitchen table as my mother puts the kettle on. I sense an uneasy truce.

"Philippa, there's something important I think you should do," I say as I give Kelly a biscuit and Cooper a couple of his treats: diversion tactics. Philippa turns her head towards me as if in slow motion.

"I've told your mother all that I know."

She looks exhausted. What little colour she had in her face has drained away and her mouth has drooped into a more sombre downwards arc. The emotional strain is showing. Perhaps I shouldn't ask her to do this, but I do anyway.

I give them an overview of what Amy said and tell them I'm concerned for her well-being, especially since she seems to have no-one to support her.

"Philippa, how about you go back to your house and ask Amy to stay with you? I don't think for a moment that Cecil will turn up again. I think he's gone into hiding, perhaps even back to Thailand. And I think you care about Amy, and she needs someone."

"I doubt she'd want to."

"Let's find out."

I phone Amy and ask her to come for dinner and arrange for a taxi. I don't tell her who'll be here.

I phone William and ask him to explain to Melissa that Amy and Philippa will be here, along with our mother. Then I panic about what to do for food.

"There'll be six of us for dinner. I need help with food purchase and preparation," I say. "And I have work to do in the barn and I have to bring the horses in."

"Isn't there somewhere we can pick up a lasagne, garlic bread and salad?" My mother asks. "That would do, I'm sure."

"Yes, I think it'll have to, under the circumstances. I'll order it and ask William to pick it up. He's getting used to that."

My mobile flashes a picture of Neal.

"Meg, we need to get those horses back in training. Are you getting closer to finding out who the murderer is?"

"Murderers. I believe I know who killed Grayson and I have a theory about Emma, but need to do a bit more digging. The horses won't be tampered with any more, I'm sure of that. By the way, do all your horses get the same feed?"

"Ah, no, they don't. Russell asked me to use a special mix that he has made at the Vannersville Feed Mill."

"Perhaps you should dump that feed?"

"I did that yesterday. I should have done it as soon as things began to go wrong, and I should have kept the feed locked up. A bit slow off the mark. It's locked up and will be from now on."

"A nuisance, I'm sure, but a good idea."

"So, when can we get these horses back?"

"As soon as you're ready."

"As soon as Linda's back, then."

"She'll be here tomorrow morning. I'll talk to her. She's having a rough time at the moment."

"Tell her she's left a big hole."

*   *   *

As I lead Hector into his stall, I realize that I'll miss him and the others, despite all the hard work and the time that gets eaten up each and every day. Just when I could have done with some help, Linda and Melissa abandon ship. Still, I've enjoyed watching the horses graze, seeing them kick up their heels and canter around the paddocks, and listening to their whinnies and snorts as they wag their heads in fun. At least Eagle and Bullet will be here.

It occurs to me, as I turn off the barn lights, that I should purchase Fay and Basil now, if I'm going to do it, before all hell breaks loose about Cecil having stolen Russell's identity. I hope the sale of the horses won't run into snags down the road because of it. I'll take my chances that it can get sorted out. I hope Neal has signing authority for the syndicate regarding the sale of the horses.

Melissa will be pleased. But I don't see her in the kitchen with William, as I expected. Just Philippa is here with him.

"Amy's here," William says. "We sent her into the family room to sit in a recliner. I've given her some hot chocolate. I have the feeling she's not been eating."

"Where's my mother?"

"I'm here." She walks into the kitchen. "I've just laid the dining room table. It feels like a hike to get there. Silly design. Should have it next to the kitchen."

"When Frank and I entertained we used caterers. I never even thought of it," I say.

"La-di-da," says my mother, but with a smile.

"I had a maid and a cook," Philippa says. "Those were the days."

"Go talk to Amy," my mother tells Philippa. "She's by herself in the family room, and you're no use to us in the kitchen." The truce is shaky. But Philippa does as she's told without objection.

"Where's Melissa?" I ask William.

"I'm not sure she's going to come. I did what I could."

"Uh oh," my mother says. "She doesn't want to see me."

"I thought you said you had a good relationship," I say as I transfer the salad into a large bowl.

"Just because I saw her several times doesn't mean it was good."

"Why don't you send her a message on my phone?" I say.

I help her send a text. She asked that the message say: "It's lasagne for dinner. Come help us eat it. Your mum." I don't think it's inspiring, but my mother is happy with it.

William pulls a huge, heavy, bubbling lasagne out of the oven.

"I thought it needed some heating up, but now it's a bit too hot," William says.

"You should leave lasagne to stand for about fifteen minutes before serving," Melissa says as she walks in. I must have left the door unlocked. I'm glad I did. I run over and give her a hug. William smiles.

"Thank you for coming," my mother says. I've rarely heard her thank anyone.

Melissa ignores her and goes over to William. They seem to be sharing secrets about lasagne. Melissa puts the garlic bread in the oven. I take the salad to the dining room and glance into the family room on the way. Philippa and Amy are each sitting in a recliner apparently oblivious of one another. This promises to be a challenging evening.

The clatter of forks on plates, the clink of wine bottles and the tinkle of glasses are the only noises that fill the large, echoey dining room. The dark furniture and grey walls reflect the sombreness of its occupants. I must say something.

"Melissa, I've thought about your budget and your proposition. I hope you still mean what you said?"

"You mean about the horses? Buying Fay and Basil?" she asks. Her eyes light up a little.

"And living here and helping with the barn chores," I say.

"I still mean it."

"Well, I decided today that I'll buy Fay and Basil, which as you know means we'll have Eagle, Bullet, Rose, Speed, Hector and then Fay and Basil."

"A herd! Awesome!" Melissa says.

"Oh no," my mother says. I brace myself for what she'll say next. "A string of racehorses is what you'll have. What fun!"

"I'm not sure 'fun' is the word that comes to mind," I say, thankful that she didn't make one of her cutting remarks, but out of the corner of my eyes I catch Melissa rolling hers. I don't think it matters what our mother says, Melissa will find fault with it.

"It might not be," Philippa says, "but it's just wonderful to have racehorses. I miss having them terribly. The syndicate was a mess, but I still have a yearning to be back in the middle of it all."

"Can't you buy a racehorse or two?" Amy asks.

"Now that I've decided to sell the house, it's as if I've been liberated. I'll get somewhere smaller, and yes, I'll have at least one racehorse. I'm already looking forward to being part of the next racing season. That's if I'm not in jail by then."

"I have to go," Melissa says.

"Can't you stay a bit longer?" my mother asks.

"I could, but I don't want to," Melissa says.

My stomach knots, and I'm aware of the fact that it's full of food. It's as if my digestion is shutting down. I fear what might happen next between Melissa and our mother, and wonder how I can prevent it.

"Can't we let bygones be bygones?" my mother asks followed by a chuckle, which sounds more like she's choking.

"Bygones be bygones? You've got to be kidding. You can't expect me to forgive and forget that you dumped me, your own daughter. You didn't try to contact me until I was an adult. You just tossed me aside like an unwanted piece of garbage, without a thought." Melissa is red in the face and stands with her hands pressed down on the table, and leans towards her mother. It's as if everyone else has been cast in stone. Silence hangs for one very long second.

"You don't know what I was thinking," our mother says, looking down at her lap which has her napkin on it, neatly folded in half.

"Clearly you weren't thinking about me."

"But I was. I knew I couldn't raise you."

"You didn't leave that brute, Stan. You left me instead."

"I didn't leave Stan, you're right." Tears pour down her face and drip onto the napkin, making large dark circles.

"Why the hell not?"

I am tempted to stop them, but my intuition tells me to let this happen. They need to do this, even if they're having a private quarrel in front of other people. If I cut it off, they might not confront one another again.

"Because Stan's threats were real to me. He said he would find me and murder me if I left him. He said he owned me, that I was his wife and I'd better obey him. He tried to kill you when he found out I was pregnant because he knew he wasn't the father. He went apoplectic and beat me so badly that I was amazed I was still alive the next morning and that I could feel you kicking. He beat me again several more times while I was carrying you, but he didn't hit my stomach. He punched me in the face and kicked my legs after he'd hit me to the floor. I didn't know about women's shelters and before you ask, no I didn't go to your father for help." She sniffs. "And Stan controlled the money. I couldn't do anything without him knowing."

"How come you had an affair then?" Melissa seems unmoved by her mother's account.

"It wasn't an affair."

"What was it then? And tell the truth for once," Melissa says.

"It was sexual assault."

"What?" Both Melissa and I ask at the same time.

"Is this the truth?" asks William in his calm, steady, professional-sounding lawyerly voice. My mother turns to him as if grateful to be answering him rather than having to face Melissa.

"The elaborate story about meeting someone in a grocers wasn't."

"I hope this is," Melissa says. "I can't stand any more lies."

"Truth. The whole truth." My mother clasps her hands and purses her lips. "One evening Stan said we were going out. I was shocked because we never went out. He said he'd joined this group and it involved wives, so I must attend with him. I found out it was a wife-swapping thing and I ended up with this Canadian official. I pleaded with him to leave me alone, but he wouldn't. I won't go into sordid details. You don't need to hear it. I don't suppose I suffered as much as his wife did with Stan. The result of that evening was that Stan got thrown out of the group and I got pregnant. There, I've told you. I didn't want to because none of us gain anything from knowing the truth. It just hurts us more. It's much better to make things up."

"I don't agree," William says with a voice like velvet which strokes our ears. "The truth is always better than lies. Facing facts might hurt at first but it leads to healing and peace of mind."

"I don't believe any of it," Melissa says. "She always tells lies. She's full of shit." Melissa pushes past me, knocking my chair, and slams the back door as she leaves the house.

"I'm going after her," William says as he trots out of the room. "I think she came by bike and I don't think it's safe on these roads in the dark."

"I believe you," Philippa says as she looks directly at my mother. "And William is right. Facing the truth can be hard, but it's the only way to move on with your life."

"Have you told me the truth about Cecil?" asks Amy.

"He is your father. He didn't rape Flora. They had an affair which everyone in the house knew about. I think he truly cared about your mother. Our marriage was difficult because of the business he was in, and because I hated it with a vengeance. But I felt trapped. The house belongs to me, bought with my family's money, so I'd have to get him to leave, which wasn't going to happen. I certainly wasn't prepared to hand it over to him. But Cecil isn't all bad, really."

"What? He sold underage girls into the sex-trade," Amy says, as she thumps her fist onto the table.

"I know. And I was the admin assistant, so I'm not much better."

"At least you helped me to escape so I could go back to my mother."

"You know, he just wanted his daughter with him."

"I don't know how you can possibly be sympathetic to him. I don't get it."

"I'm not sympathetic," Philippa says.

"I know what it is," Amy says in a calmer, softer voice. "You feel guilty. You blame yourself for not being able to have kids. Yeah. And when Flora had me, it made you feel worse. But it wasn't your fault. I bet you wanted kids, right?"

"It's best if I keep those things to myself. It won't help to open those old wounds."

"Did you hate me?"

"No. But it didn't help my relationship with Cecil. When he heard of your birth, he wanted desperately to see you. I've never seen him like that."

"But he didn't try to protect me from the sex-trade he and Russell were running."

"I've fretted over that a lot. The only rational explanation, and I know this to be true, is that Russell had a strong hold over Cecil, but I don't know why. I considered Russell to be a psychopath. And I believed him to be dangerous. I never thought of Cecil as dangerous, just weak and driven by greed. He wanted to be wealthy like my family once was. But neither of them was good with money and it didn't help that Cecil became so extraordinarily passionate about horse-racing."

"You're not making me feel better about my father. And he didn't consider my feelings at all. Just his own, I reckon. It's as if he thought he had some right to ownership. Still does. He sees me as his rightful possession. It's sick."

I'm glad that Philippa and Amy are talking, but I'm not in the slightest bit optimistic that they'll sort things out between them.

"Okay," William says as he walks into the dining room, breathing a little heavier than usual. "I had to run after her." He touches my mother on her shoulder. "Miriam, will you come with me? I'd like you and Melissa to chat, and I think it would be best if you came with us to my apartment." He looks at me.

"That's a great idea," I say.

My mother stands up. At least she's willing to try.

"Amy," Philippa says. "I wonder if you'd be willing to talk some more with me, privately?"

"You can use this room if you like," I say. "I've got some clearing up to do in the kitchen."

"Let's help you out with the dishes first," Amy says.

"Thank you," Philippa says to me as we each pick up items off the table.

I listen for raised voices as I load the dishwasher. I handle each plate and glass as if it's made of eggshells. Kelly lies on her side under the table and isn't picking up any unusual sounds. Cooper licks his tail with vigour, seemingly oblivious to anything else. Once I've dealt with the dishes and put all the left-over food away, I put on the coffeemaker and plug in the kettle. Unfortunately, they each make a racket. I've not given much thought to the noise that the heating of water makes until now. It means that I've no chance of discerning if a battle is brewing in the dining room. I walk towards the closed door and hear a faint mumble, so retrace my steps. William comes through the back door just as I re-enter the kitchen.

"I came back to help with the dishes," he says, shaking out a large, black umbrella. "Melissa's bike's on the verandah, by the way."

"Are they talking?"

"Your mother is making an effort to reach out to Melissa, but she's tired. We can only hope that Melissa responds positively."

"The trouble is, our mother has lied so many times that we don't know whether to believe anything she says. It makes it very difficult."

"Melissa knows who her father is and how Miriam met him. I think she's finally been told the truth about that, and it's a start. Oh, good, there's coffee. I'd like to tell you what I uncovered today while I have a mug or two."

"I hope it's something good. By the way, I think I know who killed Grayson. And I have a pretty good idea who killed Emma. Let me go first."

"Fine. I can enjoy my coffee while I listen."

19

Pointed Attack

I give him the run-down: a rather quick one because I want to hear what he's discovered. He agrees that Des, the security guard, is a likely suspect in Grayson's murder, and also concurs that someone else probably murdered Emma. I say I have an idea who but am not ready to share yet. I need more to go on. He doesn't push me to reveal more of my thoughts.

"My turn," he says. "Oscar lied, as we guessed, about the real estate deal. He didn't, in fact, sell a piece of property he didn't own, and therefore that wasn't the card that Russell, or Cecil rather, had up his sleeve. I found out that, sixteen years ago, when Oscar was about twenty, he was charged with having sex with an underage girl. The charges were later dropped because there was insufficient evidence. The girl backed down. Perhaps Cecil has proof of the incident."

"I have a crazy thought."

"What is it?"

"What if Russell kept records of clients?"

"I thought his clients were gangs who sold the girls into the sex-trade."

"Perhaps they weren't all gangs. Philippa might have been told that, but there could have been individuals as well, and Russell kept records and maybe even photographs and videos. Oh, crikey."

"What?"

"I bet that's the sort of thing that happened to Linda. You know how to keep a confidence, at least most of the time."

"Don't remind me of the only time I've divulged a confidence: when I told you what your mother had confided in me about your abuse."

"I don't want to be reminded either. I shouldn't have brought it up. Back to Linda. Linda was sexually assaulted."

"That's shocking to hear."

"It truly is. And I know only too well how it leaves a deep, angry scar for life. Anyway, two things come to mind. First, she said there were two people in the room. I thought that odd, but perhaps she was being delivered to the client. Second, the person who brought her could have set up hidden cameras."

"From what Philippa has told us, Cecil and Russell were operating different sides of the business. Russell bought the girls from Cecil, who ran the human trafficking side. Russell then sold the girls to gangs, or sometimes to individuals, and this fits with what Linda told you."

"From what I've gathered, Russell assaulted a few of the girls himself," I say. "Why would Cecil disguise himself as Russell, when Russell is facing the possibility of being charged with sexual assault? Perhaps there are even charges outstanding."

"I've done some more digging into Russell's background because of Amy's ordeal in the cellar. My police contacts tell me that charges have not been laid on Russell in the past. I was told that the police were sure he was involved in the sex-trade, and desperately wanted to stop the assaults on underage girls, but they were frustrated by the lack of proof. They said there were plans for an undercover operation developed at about the same time the two of them left for Thailand."

"Remember Austin said we should contact the police immediately? When he was in police services, he must have been aware. Perhaps he was involved in the plan to launch that undercover operation."

"Could be."

"How come they left for Thailand if no charges were laid?"

"I have to think that Russell and Cecil were tipped off that the police were after them. They might have thought that the police had evidence against them. Are Philippa and Amy still talking, by the way?"

"I hope so, and I hope that my mother and Melissa are."

"But the police might now have something on Russell, if not Cecil himself," William says. "So, why do you think Cecil risked coming back?"

"I can only guess that he must have missed Canada and the horse-racing business here. And he was short of money. He saw an obvious solution when Russell died: steal Russell's identity and assume ownership of his properties."

"That's an enormous risk to take."

"Yes. You told me that there's now no limitation on the time between when an assault occurred and when charges can be laid."

"He could be unaware of the change in the law, especially since he's been out of the country for so long."

"There's now more support for victims and even more women could come forward. But perhaps Cecil was oblivious to Russell's assaults. Perhaps he gambled that the police, since so many years have passed, could not lay charges against Russell for selling under-age girls into the sex-trade."

"That's possible."

"Another thing, when Russell died, Cecil could have accessed his computer files and found compromising photographs and videos of clients. I think he was in a bit of a financial squeeze, so blackmail could have looked like a promising plan."

"If what you say is accurate, Russell would have been working that angle from Thailand. Why couldn't Cecil have picked up where Russell left off, without leaving Thailand? I still think he took an incredible risk coming here."

"Perhaps. But it might have been harder for him to assume Russell's identity there."

"He must have known it wouldn't be easy here either."

"You know, when I think about it, the stronger driving force could have been his daughter. We shouldn't overlook that. He was free of Russell's control or power over him, whatever form that took, and took the risk of coming back here so that he could find her. And imagine at how amazed he must have been when he found her working in the backstretch. But, as we know, he messed that up entirely."

"He can't be too smart if he's taken these huge chances just so he could reach out to a daughter with whom he's had no previous relationship. And why the syndicate?"

"Cecil's passionate about horse-racing. By Philippa's accounts, it sounds as if she, and particularly Cecil, were avid breeders and racers, and their home reflects this: with the barns and paddocks, pictures and awards. He didn't want to put the limited funds he had into one horse. It would have been too risky. So, he used the leverage he had with Oscar and Philippa to get them involved. Emma was possibly genuinely interested. And it's not unusual for the trainer to have part-ownership. And once he found out that Amy was working in the backstretch, he wanted to have a reason to visit often. Having several horses justified long visits."

"The timing is interesting. It might not have been a coincidence that Amy was working there. You say that Philippa gave her Grayson's number? I suspect Philippa is more involved than she's revealed."

"We might never know for sure."

I hear the dining-room door open and Kelly lifts her head, only to put it down again. Cooper yawns and stretches, ambles over to Kelly and licks the dog's ear.

Philippa and Amy walk into the kitchen. They both look tired.

"Coffee or tea?" I ask. They both settle for coffee, which William pours for them. He refills his mug as the clock's ticking seems to get louder by the second. I get myself another mug of tea. I don't want to ask questions, but I'm bursting with curiosity. All four of us sit down at the kitchen table. Amy breaks the expectant silence first.

"Philippa told me she's sorry that Cecil had an affair with my mother. She wishes she could have stopped it. She believes Cecil did care about my mother. He was cut up when she left and made her promise he'd be able to visit his child, me. He'd always wanted children, apparently."

"And so have I. But it wasn't to be," Philippa adds.

"And Philippa said that she's appalled by Cecil's behaviour towards me since his return from Thailand."

"But he isn't a rapist or a murderer, of that I'm sure," Philippa says.

"I've taken up Philippa's offer of a home with her, at least for now."

"I'm selling the house and plan to find somewhere where I can have a couple of horses and get back into the racehorse business. Amy says she'd like to be part of that."

"Where do you think Cecil is now?" I ask.

"All I know is that the relevant agencies have been alerted," William says.

"I'd really like to know why he tied Melissa up," I say. "That one puzzles me."

"It had something to do with her asking Amy questions," William says.

"I'd like to find out," I say. "I hope I get the chance."

Philippa tells me she'll stay the night at the Vannersville Inn so my mother can feel comfortable staying here. The truce is still on shaky ground and perhaps there's nothing I can do about it. Amy says she's going back to her place to pack. They both plan to stay at the house until they move to their new home. At least that relationship is moving towards a mutually beneficial resolution.

"I'll give each of you a lift," William tells Philippa and Amy. "And then I'll pick up your mother, Meg. I hope it won't be too late for her, especially since she'll be suffering from jet lag."

"It's two o'clock in the morning in England, so I expect she's very tired."

"Why don't you pick her up and we'll take a taxi," Philippa says. "I've made up my mind that I'm taking out a loan so I don't have to be so frugal. Once the house is sold, I'll be fine."

"If you don't mind, that would be helpful. Thanks," I say. "I'd rather not leave at the moment."

William returns with my mother looking ashen and with eyelids that look as if they're weighted down with lead. She wobbles as she walks through the back door, and I take her arm and help her up the stairs. She says she'll be okay and closes the bedroom door.

"When are you going to talk to the police about Grayson's murder?" William asks.

"When I've confirmed to myself who murdered Emma. I've an idea who did, but I'm honestly not at all sure, so I don't want to tell anyone yet."

"Not even me?"

"Who do you think killed her?"

"I don't have the benefit of all the intelligence that you've gathered."

"But you're smarter than I am. You don't need as much."

"That's not true."

"We could argue about it."

"Let's not. I'd lose."

"Who?"

"I'll make a stab at it then," William says. "That's not an appropriate phrase to use under the circumstances."

"No, but Emma was injected with ketamine, not stabbed."

"What about motive?"

"The motive gives it away."

"That's what I think," William says. "So, we might be thinking of the same person."

"Amy is in potential danger, although I've not said anything because I've not been sure."

"She's by herself in that awful flat you told me about."

"But they have some level of security around."

"You know it's not enough."

"Now you've got me worried."

"Let's bring her back here."

"I'll go. I'll text her first. Can you stay with my mother?"

"Sure."

No answer to my text.

William wants to come with me, but I insist on going alone. My mother can't be left with no-one in the house. She probably just has jet lag, but her face was drawn and looked as if something was weighing her down, literally. I'm concerned. I'd love to know what she and Melissa said to one another. I get the sense that it wasn't the healing, liberating exchange that I hoped for.

William is not convinced that I'll be fine with Kelly by my side. I point out that he shouldn't underestimate my dog.

But it isn't without some trepidation that I turn into the road that leads to the apartment blocks close to the security office. The latter is in complete darkness. One racetrack vehicle sits outside, but I don't see any sign of activity. Opposite, only a couple of flats have lights on. It's late for backstretch workers, since many of them will have to get up before dawn to feed the horses their breakfast.

Outdoor metal stairs lead to a long outdoor landing. Amy's door is one of several identical ones lined up in a row, each concealing a bachelorette. Kelly doesn't like the sensation of treading on the stairs, nor the tinny noise they make as I run up them. But she doesn't want to be left behind, so she makes a dash for it, and reaches me in three bounds. There's a light on, so I knock. I can hear something, but no-one comes. Kelly tilts her head, her ears pricked, and scratches at the door. She wants in. I turn the knob and the door opens, revealing dim light from a table lamp. I see someone leaning over Amy who's slumped in the vinyl armchair.

I yell something. Kelly growls and lurches at the man, and grabs hold of a leg of his jeans and pulls in jerks. He looks up and, sure enough, it's Bryce. He has a syringe in his hand, but it looks as if he's not yet administered its deadly contents. Things couldn't have gone as smoothly for him as they did with Emma. I pick up a mug that's on the coffee table and chuck it at his head. It hits him in the eye, and it must have hurt because his hand flies up to his face.

Amy sits up and kicks him in his crotch.

Bryce screams. Kelly yanks his jeans with extra effort and sends him off balance. He stumbles and drops the syringe, which I grab almost before it hits the floor. Amy passes out. I hope that she's fainted and nothing worse.

Bryce is still on his feet, so Kelly keeps hold of his jeans and jerks hard, growling. Bryce tries to shake Kelly off, but loses his balance and falls onto the sofa. Kelly sits by his face and snarls as if to say, 'don't you dare move'. I phone 911 and then I dial the racetrack security office. A sleepy voice answers, but as soon as I report, in a high-pitched raspy voice, that there's an intruder in one of the apartments who has attempted murder, he's alert, and says he's on the way. I see lights come on in the security office as I talk to him. He must have been hanging out in the back. I hope he hurries because I can't think of a way to restrain Bryce. He hasn't moved since he collapsed on the sofa, but if he tried to make a run for it, I don't think I'd be able to stop him.

Kelly continues to snarl at him. I grab the table lamp and stand out of reach but ready to hit him if I have to.

Heavy footsteps clang up the metal stairs, and the sound reverberates around me. The security guard appears in the doorway and nearly fills its frame.

"Have you called 911?" He asks, his face red and sweat beading on his brow.

"Yes. Can you help prevent this man from escaping? I must tend to Amy."

"Sure thing. Being a big man has its advantages." Bryce doesn't appear to exhibit any desire to escape or resist, but the security guard doesn't take any chances. He turns him over on the sofa, so that he's face down, and pulls his arms behind his back and ties them up with his belt. For a large man, he can move fast. Kelly increases the pitch of her growl as she holds her ground, her eyes fixed on Bryce, her lips curled to reveal her pearly-white teeth.

I'm not sure if she can hear me, but I talk to Amy while this is going on, to divert her attention away from Bryce.

"She's a cruel, hateful woman." Bryce's shrill voice is muffled by the cushions. "She hurts animals. She doesn't deserve to live on the same planet as them. She's got to go."

"Enough talking," the security guard says. "I'm sure the cops will want to hear all you've got to say down at the station."

"They should lock her up and throw away the key. It would better if there was capital punishment for the likes of her."

"I think you're the one who's going to be in the slammer."

Kelly decides that Bryce isn't going anywhere, so she joins Amy and me, and sits by the vinyl armchair, and leans against Amy's legs, panting.

"Stop shaking me," Amy says with a groggy voice and eyes half-closed.

"It's just Kelly, trying to help," I say.

"I thought it was Bryce."

"I'd like to help you lie on the floor." Amy doesn't respond. I try to soften her landing as she half-falls onto the worn, dingy carpet that might have had some pile at one time.

"I can hear sirens," the security guard says.

"Good," I say. "Amy, I'm going to lift your legs up onto this." I yank the seat cushion off the armchair and put it under her lower legs. "I'm going to get a wet cloth." I find a washcloth in the bathroom, wet it with cold water and put it on Amy's forehead.

About three minutes later, her tiny home is invaded by paramedics and police officers. The paramedics ask me a few questions about Amy as they check her vital signs. They put her on a stretcher and wrap a white blanket around her that matches the colour of her face. I call Philippa at the Vannersville Inn and she says she'll get a taxi to the hospital. She sounds alarmed despite my reassurances that I think Amy will be fine.

I'm sure it will take time, though.

The police pick up the syringe, which I must have put on the coffee table, and ask me several questions, including why I was at the scene. I'm to report to police services in the morning. They talk to the security guard and give him his belt back. Bryce is in handcuffs.

I text William to say I'm okay and will be back soon.

Kelly lies next to the armchair with her ears down, no doubt hoping no-one treads on her.

The police let me, Kelly, and the security guard leave after what seems like half the night.

A few of the other occupants of the apartment block are standing outside their doors and I hear one say that it must be a drug bust, that they saw it coming.

* * *

Kelly and I rush into the kitchen. We're greeted by William, who hands me a glass of brandy. I put the drink down and give him a quick hug.

"Wow, it was that bad, was it?" he asks.

"If you hadn't got me thinking, I wouldn't have gone, and Amy would be dead."

"You caught him in the act, then?"

"Kelly was amazing, by the way. She grabbed hold of his jean leg and pulled and pulled, and growled."

"She might have got hurt."

"I don't think so. Bryce cares much more about animals than he does people. This is what it's all about. He couldn't bear to see horses hurt by Emma and Amy."

"How's Amy?"

"I think she'll be fine. Philippa is going to the hospital, which is great. Although I think Amy will take time to recover from the emotional trauma she's been through."

"She'll realize that all the facts will come out in Bryce's trial and that no-one will give her a job at the track caring for horses."

"No, and I don't blame them. To be honest, I wouldn't hire her to look after mine. Animals depend on us, trust us, and are innocent and vulnerable. How anyone could deliberately harm an animal is beyond my comprehension. But I could tell you some stories from my days at the humane society."

"I don't want to hear any of them, thanks."

"And we don't know where Cecil is. Let's sit in the family room and I'll give you a detailed account of what just happened. I have to give Kelly a treat first, though. She's a hero again. The security guard was helpful too, once I stirred him into action."

William's not sure if there'll be sufficient evidence to convict Bryce of Emma's murder, but he says the police should be on solid ground with his attempted murder of Amy. We chat about the circumstances of Grayson's death. William's uncertain that the prosecution will be able to prove, beyond a reasonable doubt, that Des is guilty.

I need to talk to Des again.

"I'm now rethinking Des being guilty of Grayson's murder," I say.

"Ah."

20

Likely Suspect

Linda arrives just as dawn breaks, with tinges of pink, orange and purple on the edges of the clouds that hover above the horizon. She hands me a tea and a bag which holds the inevitable carrot muffin. I've fed the horses but they haven't quite finished their breakfast. We sit on a couple of bales of hay, which I've left in the aisle of the barn.

"Linda, we need to talk."

"I know."

"It was you who was assaulted, wasn't it?"

"I shouldn't have said anything."

"You should have. You know that there's no limitation on the time after which you can report it, don't you?"

"It makes no difference."

"Are you sure that Russell and Cecil were the culprits?"

"Those guys scare me."

"Russell's dead and Cecil's not a rapist. He's not going to do anything to you. Tell me about it."

She sips her coffee and turns away. "Russell got me to go to the motel. I knew him from the track. I've thought about it a lot. I'm not real sure the other demon was Cecil. It was all so awful, and I didn't want to see his face. That was dumb."

"Don't blame yourself for any of this. Linda, look at me. You're a wonderful, kind, caring person. You're not the problem." She sighs as Kelly puts her head on her lap and looks up at her with soft, dewy eyes. Linda strokes her silky coat. "I'm pretty sure that your attacker was not Cecil. Although he's not a nice man, to put it mildly, there's no evidence that Cecil is a rapist or ever has been, as I told you. We think he ran the human-trafficking side of things and Russell supplied the girls to clients and gangs."

"Great." She sniffs.

"Remember, Russell is dead. We don't know where Cecil is at the moment, but I don't think for a minute that he'd have a clue who you are, because you weren't part of his side of the business. My guess is that Russell picked you up himself for one of his clients, and it had nothing to do with his arrangement with Cecil. He must have felt confident that you wouldn't report it, and you didn't."

"It's hard."

"It's very hard. I understand only too well. You love working at the track, and I honestly think it's safe for you to return to your job. I'm not as sure as I was about who killed Grayson, but I'm sure there's no danger to you. Bryce must be an animal rights extremist, and we believe he killed Emma because he found out she was harming the horses. She was doing it as revenge against Russell, who'd raped her when she was fifteen, and she used Amy as a willing accomplice. She didn't know that Russell was, in fact, Cecil. It's all very tragic."

"God, that's awful. How could a vet harm horses?"

"I ask myself the same question. She seemed compassionate and professional whenever I talked to her. But I understand how incredibly traumatic it is to be raped."

"But I'd never hurt the poor horses. I couldn't."

"I know."

Linda sobs. I put my arm around her for a couple of seconds. She is such a good, special person with the warmest, kindest heart. I hate to think of her being violated.

"How can you understand?" she asks.

"Understand what?"

"You said you understand about being raped."

"My stepfather abused me."

"Rape?"

"I have a hard time using that word when I'm talking about myself."

"I'm sure glad I asked, though. People think they know, but they don't, until it happens to them. I reckon it would be worse with it being your stepfather."

"Okay, enough," I say. "Let's get these horses outside. Then you can go to the track and talk to Neal about getting back to work. I'll clean the stalls."

"Are you going to buy Fay and Basil?"

"If Neal gets the ownership papers, I'll sign them today. I expect that the part owned by Cecil will be held in limbo until things get sorted out, but I'll have majority ownership."

She stands up, wipes her hands on her jeans, sniffs again, and purses her lips as if a smile is in there somewhere.

"Will you send them back to the track soon?"

"Tomorrow, if Neal can do it. I'm sure the horses will be safe now. Neal will definitely want you back at work with five more horses to look after, and I'd like to know they're in your good hands."

"I'll make sure the stalls are ready," she says. "Thanks for your faith in me, and for understanding how I feel."

"You're special. And the horses love you too."

She turns and faces me with a faint smile, which brightens her face.

We let the horses out onto the dew-laden grass to a loud chorus of tuneful birds. The air is still, holding the scent of lilac mixed with the smell of horse. The flower bed is almost overrun with cheerful blue of forget-me-nots, which will soon be overpowered by the hostas that are poking their bright green noses up into the spring sunshine.

Linda looks more like her old self as she leaves in her little car. I turn back towards the barn.

"Kelly, it would be really good if you could wield a pitchfork." She looks up at me and shakes. "Where's Melissa when I need her?" Seven stalls to clean out. I enjoy this work, but a myriad of thoughts whirl and clash in my mind. I want to solve Grayson's murder, and then I can focus my undivided attention on William, Melissa, and my mother.

William had little more to say about my mother's chat with Melissa, and I was up too early to take her a cup of tea and find out.

I've set up another meeting with Des, the security guard who reportedly found the bodies, and who I suspected of murdering Grayson. I'm relieved he agreed to see me again. I take this as a good sign. He's back at work after only a brief break, which is also good. We're to meet in the cafeteria.

* * *

I sit on a plastic chair holding my Styrofoam cup as the aroma of hot chocolate wafts under my nose. It's too hot, so patience is required.

Des has shaved and his uniform is neat and clean, which makes him look trimmer. He even offers his hand with a half-smile. Something's shifted.

"Thanks for meeting with me. I'm glad you're back at work. It must feel good," I say.

"It does, and it doesn't."

"I need to ask some more questions because my theory of who killed Grayson has changed."

"You should never have suspected me."

"How do you know I did?"

"Linda told me. She went to see Amy in hospital. Amy told her. Linda says she was real miserable. Amy blames herself for what happened to Grayson. But Linda told Amy that I wouldn't hurt anyone. That you'd realize that I'm innocent."

"I'm surprised Linda went there, and that she said that. She's not one to chat or gossip." I squeeze my cup and its contents rise to the top, threatening to cascade on to my jeans. I release my grip just in time. I'm not sure if I believe Des. Perhaps it doesn't matter.

"Don't get angry. Linda's a good person. She takes good care of her horses. Everyone who knows her says she's a good horsewoman."

"She is."

"When she heard that the horses Grayson was training were getting sick, she was that upset that she asked me about it. I said I'd look into it. She thought something odd was going on. I couldn't argue. It did sound sort of peculiar."

"What did you do?"

"I hung around Grayson's barn a bit more on each of my shifts and kept my eyes peeled and my ears open."

"Did you hear or see anything, then?"

"Nothing that I could say for sure, but Emma and Amy were often together in the barn and I thought that was odd. Usually the vet deals mostly with the trainer. And, if Grayson was around, he'd ask Emma a lot of questions and seemed uptight about things."

"Do you suspect Emma or Amy of killing Grayson?"

271

"I don't. I'm getting to that. I saw someone else skulking around. Someone who should have been in his own barn minding his own business."

"Let me guess. Bryce?"

"You got it."

"What's your theory then?"

"It's more than a theory. When I was near Grayson's trailer one evening, Amy ran head-long into me and screamed something about being raped. This might sound awful, but I didn't believe her. Something about her body language and the way she yelled it. It was more like she was in a rage. But I thought something must be up. So, I went to Grayson's trailer, and he said it had been a bad day, but he had some stuff to do before he left. He offered me a coffee if I came back in half an hour. He said he was going to have one to keep him awake on the drive home."

"So, you went back?"

"I saw someone running down the steps of the trailer just as I turned the corner. It was Bryce."

"Why didn't you tell anyone this before?"

"I like Bryce. He cares about the horses. He said that the horses around here deserve to be treated humanely. He thinks some trainers just want to win and don't care about the animals. They'll do anything to get their share of the purse. He was sure that Grayson was one of those trainers. He was wrong. That's the terrible part."

"So, his plan is to kill off all the trainers he thinks aren't doing a good job of caring for their horses?"

"When you put it like that, it sounds gruesome."

"It is. And you knew what he was doing?"

"No, I didn't. But then there was Emma."

"She's not a trainer."

"Bryce was determined to get justice for the horses, his words. I reckon he had it in for anyone who wasn't nice to the animals."

"What on earth made you lie about Edwin leaving Emma's trailer?"

"That was bad. I did it because I thought Edwin was selling ketamine, but I now know that wasn't true."

"I still don't understand why you didn't tell the truth about what you saw at Grayson's trailer. Emma might have been saved."

"She might have been saved so she could go on hurting horses."

"That's what the College of Veterinarians of Ontario is for. Grayson was doing the right thing by reporting her conduct to them. And he was disciplining Amy. It was not at all appropriate for Bryce to murder Grayson and Emma. It's outrageous. Explain why you sat by while this went on?"

"You're not being fair. I didn't know that Bryce was going to kill Emma."

"Why didn't you tell me about Bryce?"

"I don't know."

"Anything to do with Linda?"

"Linda told me she wanted the nasty people who were hurting the horses to be caught and punished."

"I can't imagine for one minute that she meant someone should kill them."

"No, I'm not saying that. Don't put words into my mouth."

"I still don't understand why you didn't report Bryce to someone."

"Because he's a friend. And he cares so much about the horses. Linda admires how he puts the horses first and doesn't do so well in the races."

"You realize that makes no sense, don't you? The thoroughbreds that are here are bred and trained to race and are competitive. They know when they've won and feel good about it. Having a stable of horses that never get a chance to win because of poor training, including putting them in the wrong races, is not fair to the horses. This whole thing is beyond ridiculous."

"When you put it like that, I see what you're saying."

"Des, use your head. I know Bryce is your friend and you respected him for his apparent concern for horses' well-being. He's probably convinced himself that the horses that win have been maltreated. But that's abject nonsense. As an owner I'm certain that my horses enjoy both the attention and care they get here, as well as the work they do. You know you can't force a horse to race. They have to love the game. I can only conclude that Bryce is a bit soft in the head."

"Nuts you mean?"

"I'm not sure what I mean exactly, but his behaviour is bizarre. If I had to guess, I'd say he's an animal rights extremist."

"I feel bad. What should I do now?"

"You should give a statement to the police. The sooner you report this, the better."

"I was so goddam relieved to hear that Amy is okay."

"She could have been the third dead body. Would you like me to come with you to police services?"

"No. Maybe."

"When? Think about it. He's a murderer and should face justice. He could get bail if you don't give a statement."

"Okay. I'll go see my boss. I'll come back here."

"I'll drive you."

* * *

My mother says that she didn't get up until about noon, even though it would have been early evening in England. The chat with Melissa exhausted her, and that's all she'll tell me. She doesn't want to talk about it at the moment. She says I should go look after the horses and that she'll make dinner. She's invited William. When I ask her what she found in the kitchen to make dinner with, she answers that there was nothing, so she asked William to order groceries on-line and had a taxi service deliver it all. She points to a pile of boxes which sit on the counter, staring me in the face. Cooper pops his head out of one. I hope that my mother has already emptied it.

Kelly and I go to the barn. I should be excited about my five racehorses going back into training, and relieved that I won't have so much barn work to do, especially since Melissa's promise to help has gone off the rails before it even started. Nevertheless, I will miss these beautiful animals with their big, kind eyes, their whinnies, their trust and their honesty. I can see why some people say they love animals more than they do people. Sometimes I think I do. But I know deep-down that people have to come first. If only they were just as truthful, genuine, and kind as our animal friends.

After I've led Hector into his stall, he dives into the feed bucket for his carrots. His coat gleams. None of them have had much grooming, but grazing has a magical effect. Grass is their natural food and I've noticed all seven horses have beautiful dapples in their shiny coats. They'll miss the pasture, but they'll enjoy being put to work again, and I'll have fun watching them exercise and, hopefully, race.

The barn cats are curled up together in the feed room as I shut the door. I leave the radio playing the classical station, as well as a light on, to discourage racoons and skunks and other unwanted visitors. Kelly walks towards the door, knowing that we've done all the chores for the evening. I'm pretty sure she'd let me know if I forgot something.

I do not know if my mother can cook. I can't recall what I ate as a child. I should be able to remember something, but all that pops up into my mind is baked beans on toast. I hope that's not what she has on the menu, but I'll be thankful for anything: 'fuel', as Linda said.

* * *

William arrives almost at the same time as I walk downstairs after having had a long, warm shower.

"You look tired," I say.

"Thanks. So do you."

"There's a glass of sherry each in the family room," my mother says with her back to us. "I'm better if I'm left alone in the kitchen to do my thing. We'll eat in here. I can't make the hike to the dining room."

"That's perfectly fine," I say. "William, I think we should do as we're told."

"Not difficult. A glass of sherry will go down very well at this point."

"Have you had a hard day?" I ask as I settle into a recliner with Kelly at my feet. Cooper can smell fish, so he's helping my mother.

"It's your fault. I've been juggling too many balls."

"I know you've been assisting, but I didn't realize it was that onerous."

"It's not really. It's just that I decided to find out if there've been any developments regarding Cecil's whereabouts. I connected with my contact in the RCMP to make sure they're aware of the situation. They have connected with officials in Thailand, and with border security, local police services, and others. There appears to be universal abhorrence among officers for people like Cecil who are in the underage human-trafficking business, feeding the sex-trade."

"And so there should be."

"I also found out that Bryce has confessed to the murders of Grayson and Emma and to the attempted murder of Amy."

"That was quick. I can't get my head around the fact that he believed that justice for horses meant killing anyone he thought was hurting them."

"And also, the local police discovered that Bryce, using a different name, is an active member of the Vannersville Animal Rights Army.

Bryce belongs to a subgroup of ardent members who do undercover work."

"That would explain a lot, but it puzzles me that he posed as a racehorse trainer. I'm sure that animal rights activists do not support horse-racing or any sport which involves animals. Even people having pets is frowned upon. How he could involve himself directly for so long is very odd. He's an enigma."

"Apparently he has a blog that he told the police about. His belief was that he was going to change the horse-racing business from the inside."

"That's ridiculous. How could he do that as a trainer? He must have realized that he wasn't getting very far. And he was a hypocrite because he trained horses and entered them into races."

"The police are searching for evidence as we speak. My guess is that they'll find videos and photos on his phone and computer which he was going to use in an attempt to have animal cruelty charges laid against several people, including Grayson, Emma and Amy."

"But we know that the animal cruelty laws are not tough. I think they need to be a lot stronger. And he must have thought the same way. My bet is that he became enraged about Grayson's horses getting sick and took the law into his own hands, instead of following VARA's usual protocols."

"Could be. If you're right, the police might not find much other than what's already posted on his blog."

"He was wrong about Grayson, and he realized that after he'd murdered him, but it didn't stop him going after Emma and Amy. I can't understand his behaviour. I love animals, but I can't see myself murdering someone who abuses animals. I'd report them and hope they got convicted of animal cruelty, even though the law is weaker than I'd like. At least they wouldn't have got away with it, and the abuse would stop, and the animal would get care."

"I feel the same way. As a lawyer I believe in using the justice system. I don't have the power to create laws and to administer punishment."

"Bryce thought he had that power. And he must have a lot of patience. It takes some time to become a trainer. You can't get a licence overnight."

"I did a bit of research on him and found out that his father was a trainer. He grew up in the business."

"That would make it easier for him. Perhaps he'd even been an assistant trainer with his father."

"Could have been. I didn't check."

"Perhaps his father's treatment of horses made him think of becoming an animal rights activist."

"I've seen two video clips on his blog of people at the track being unkind to horses, but I saw nothing that would stand up to the scrutiny of the court, in my opinion, although I'm not familiar with the definition of animal cruelty under the law."

"Wow, you've been busy."

"They showed me when I popped into Vannersville Police Services. Anyone can access the blog."

"I should have checked. I don't know why I didn't think of it."

"We didn't know the name he uses on-line."

"I don't pretend to believe that nothing bad happens to horses at the track," I say. "I'm sure it does. What I do believe is that those incidents are a very small part of the lives of horses there. After all, there are witnesses around all the time. And the people working with the horses have so much invested in them. I'm still shaking my head over the fact that Emma and Amy did harmful things to the horses in their care."

"Amy could face charges of animal cruelty. It depends if there is enough evidence. I suppose it's doubtful because Grayson is dead, Cecil is absent, and Bryce is an accused murderer. The prosecutors might be reluctant to bring a murderer to the witness stand to testify against her. And if Cecil were to turn up, he's her father, so that could pose a problem."

"Anyway, I hope they find Cecil. I think several people will sleep easier if he was found," I say.

"Talking of finding people, where's Melissa?"

"She's not at your place?"

"She took her bags and left this morning."

"I've not seen her, nor heard from her, since she left here with you and our mother. Now I'm worried. I'll text her."

"She's an impulsive young woman. She needs somewhere stable to live, where she feels wanted and valued."

"Don't we all?"

"I don't think she's had much love in her life."

"She can join the club."

"Meg!"

I look up from my phone as William gets out of the recliner with his teeth clenched and lips pursed.

"Don't go," I say as I drop the phone, waking Kelly with a start. "I didn't mean it."

"What didn't you mean?"

"I was just being flippant. I didn't mean to sound as if I don't feel compassion for her."

"I know you were subjected to unspeakable abuse under you stepfather's roof, but Melissa suffered as well. Recognizing this and understanding her pain doesn't diminish the significance of what you experienced."

"There's no need for a sermon. I want to reach out to her. She's my sister. I want us to feel like family. But it's become much more complicated than I ever imagined it would be with our mother showing up. Obviously, their talk didn't go well."

"Your mother was so tired that Melissa thought she wasn't listening. That was about all I caught of the conversation because I shut myself in the kitchen area."

"Uh oh. I'd hoped there'd be a little melting of the ice between them."

"There's still a large iceberg looming."

"No answer to her text. I'll see Edwin tomorrow. She's to start work next week, I think, and perhaps he's been in contact with her. I plan to go to the track later in the day anyway, because all five horses are leaving here in the morning and I want to make sure that they're settled in their stalls in Neal's barn."

"Okay. And I'll text her tomorrow and let you know if she responds."

"I hope I shouldn't be reporting her as a missing person."

"She probably just wants to be alone for a bit."

"But I can't think where she could have gone."

"She took her things, so she's probably found somewhere to stay for a few days."

But my stomach flutters. I'm unsettled by the mystery of Melissa's whereabouts. Why hasn't she answered my text? Is her relationship with our mother bad enough to prevent her from communicating with me at all? She's not happy with me for inviting our mother, but surely that doesn't warrant her shutting me out of her life? As William dozes in a recliner, I work myself up into a lather as my imagination creates several scenarios, none of which I like. I can't wait until tomorrow, so I pick up my phone and text Edwin to ask if he's had any contact with her. His quick response is negative. Fortunately, he doesn't ask questions. I text Amy, just in case she's connected with her. No answer.

21

Desperation

My mother summons us to the kitchen, so I walk in and sit down with my phone in my hand.

"I was hoping we wouldn't have phones eating with us," she says. "This is salmon steak with white sauce and cauliflower and asparagus. And there's a salad of sorts. I don't want any complaints. I've found cooking quite a challenge. I think they must have damaged the part of my brain that's necessary for this business." She smiles and sits down.

"Thank you," William says. "I'm grateful for anything I don't have to prepare."

"That goes for me too," I say, although I look at the fish and queasiness stirs. I pick up my fork and brace myself.

"Tastes good, Miriam," William says.

His enthusiasm spurs me on, and I eventually eat half of the meal.

"Despite what you said, William," I say. "I'm worried about Melissa. I texted Edwin, and he hasn't heard from her, and I texted Amy and there's no response. My intuition is niggling at me. I just wonder if something is wrong."

"I don't think there's anything to worry about," William says as he takes the plates to the counter. "I'll make coffee. No, I mean tea."

"I wouldn't say no to a coffee," my mother says.

The calmness around me fuels my agitation. I phone Philippa on her landline.

"Philippa, this might seem odd, but have you seen Melissa? I haven't been able to get hold of her."

"Oh, Meg, I'm so worried. I'm sure something's wrong." She coughs.

"Why?"

"Because Melissa came here. She asked to stay for a couple of days. She looked stressed but didn't say what was wrong."

"Is she there now?"

"No, that's what I'm worried about. Melissa offered to help Amy get some of her things from that awful flat at the track. She's given her notice and needs to vacate it. There's a waiting list for that terrible place. They've not come back and I can't get hold of either of them."

"When was this?"

"This morning. Quite early. I hadn't even had my coffee. I kept thinking they'll be back any moment, but I was just about to call the police when you phoned."

"That's a good idea. I'll go check Amy's flat just in case they're there."

I give William and my mother a synopsis of the phone call and tell them I'm going to Amy's flat. Neither of them appears to share my anxiety. William says he has work to do, preparation for an important case, but says he'll stay to help my mother clear up. The latter phrase carries an emphasis that I choose to ignore.

Kelly and I reach the track in near darkness. The outside lighting gives me the sensation of going back in time. It's dull and yellow, like an old, sombre movie scene. But there's no action. Stillness and silence greet us as we get out of the truck. A shiver travels down my spine. As I walk towards the metal stairs, a sudden clatter shatters the quiet. It comes from the opposite end of the outdoor landing on the second floor. Three silhouetted figures lurch and stumble down the steps, as if drunk. Perhaps they are. I can't make out the shapes. Kelly barks and runs towards them as they reach the ground. I follow with as much haste as I can muster. Kelly knows who they are, or must know at least one of them.

"You keep back," Cecil says as he waves what looks like a gun at me. Melissa and Amy have duct tape over their mouths and they must have their arms taped together behind their backs. As the dim light catches her face, I see sweat from Amy's forehead running down her nose. "Stop that dog's noise or I'll shoot her."

"You won't. You love Kelly. I know you couldn't hurt her," I say. "Besides, the noise would raise the alarm. The security office is just over there." I look towards the dark building and imagine the guard asleep inside.

"No-one's there," he says as he turns to look. Melissa seizes the opportunity and kicks him hard behind the knee. He buckles just as Kelly tugs on his pant leg and drops the gun. I leap forward with speed I didn't know I had and step on it. Cecil doesn't react. I pick the gun up. It feels light, as if it's made of plastic.

"You should mind your own business," he says. His eyes flit from one side to the other. "If you hadn't asked your stupid questions and snooped around, none of this would have happened."

"I was investigating Grayson's murder," I say.

"But you poked your nose into my business. It's your fault that my daughter doesn't like me."

Amy groans and grumbles as Cecil grabs her elbow and yanks his pant leg away from Kelly.

"You're coming with me," Cecil says. "You're my daughter. You should have some respect for your father and we should be together."

But Amy kicks his ankle, causing him to loosen his grip on her elbow. Melissa and I look at each other and both of us lunge at Cecil at the same time. He falls to the ground with all three of us on top of him, holding him down. Kelly sits at his head and snarls, baring her white teeth and looking menacing. She's figured out that he's a threat, even though he befriended her. Kelly must be the smartest and most loyal dog there is.

I pull the duct tape off Melissa's wrists, which have only partly healed from the baling-twine burns. She rips the duct tape off her mouth as I peel the tape off Amy's wrists. We continue our group sprawl on top of Cecil's back and legs. He puts up little resistance.

"I think he's crying," Melissa whispers.

"He should be," Amy says. "He's a low-life loser and I don't want anything to do with him."

"He must be desperate," Melissa says. "He must want you in his life so much. I can't imagine having a real father, let alone one who wants you that badly."

Amy turns her head and glares at Melissa.

A different security guard bursts out of the office and sprints across the road towards us. He asks a couple of quick questions. The name 'Russell Stanley' registers with him as someone banned from the backstretch. He takes over and pins Cecil in some kind of contorted wrestling hold.

The three of us stumble up the metal stairs, which rattle and make my ears ring. Amy and Melissa don't appear to have been harmed physically, except that Melissa's wrists and face look fiery red, and she has a deep frown. They both shiver as they sit down on the tatty sofa. I pull the faded quilt off Amy's bed and hand it to them.

No-one speaks.

The police show up to Amy's flat, again, closely followed by the paramedics.

"I'm never, ever coming anywhere near this place again," Amy says as she leaves with Melissa in the ambulance.

I text the people who I know will want to hear the news. William says he'll meet me at the hospital for the second time.

* * *

"I sort of feel sorry for Cecil," Philippa says. She puts a plate of cookies in front of me, Melissa and Amy, as we sit in her house surrounded by cardboard boxes, most of which are partially packed.

"Sorry for him!" Amy says. "How could you?"

"He so desperately wanted children. In those days when we tried, there weren't the advances in reproductive therapy that we have now."

"Good thing. He hasn't got a clue how to treat a daughter," Amy says.

"My mother hasn't a clue how to treat daughters either," Melissa says. "She just tossed me aside as if I was an unwanted rag doll."

"But she isn't a bad person like my father is," Amy says.

"Let's not make this a contest about whose parent has been the most neglectful or abusive," I say, as I put my cup and saucer down on the coffee table.

"We know," Melissa says as she turns her head to face me with a flick of her long hair. "You suffered the most. You had the worst of it. I've heard it. I don't want to hear any more. You don't understand how I feel."

"I think it's impossible to appreciate completely how someone else feels about something," I say, as I get up from my seat.

"You sure have no clue. You invited our mother to the farm and ruined everything. I thought we had a deal that I'd help with the horses in exchange for staying there. And then she waltzes in. Her being there spoils it all for me."

"I hear your anger and resentment and hurt."

"There's lots of all of that."

"I get it. But…",

"There are no 'buts'."

"There are some 'buts' from my perspective, according to my feelings."

"Touché," says Philippa, who receives a steely glare from Melissa.

"For instance," I say, "you let me down when I needed you. As you said yourself, we had a deal. I respect that you have serious issues with our mother, but she's my mother too. It's my farm, and you agreed to help. It's fortunate that the horses have gone back to the track and, hopefully, I won't need your help for a while. But you ran away when I needed you. I think we both should stop running and see what we can do to develop some kind of workable relationship with our mother, warts and all."

"She has enough of those to fill Hector's feed bucket."

"We all have some."

"But you don't understand. To be tossed aside and then have your mother show up in your life over twenty years later, and be expected to greet her with open arms, is surreal." Melissa tosses her long blond hair and stands up. Tears trickle in silver streaks down her cheeks. She turns and jogs to the door. "It's bullshit. It hurts. I don't owe her anything. She's a waste of space. I can't believe you invited her to the farm. I was so looking forward to being there. And you've made it impossible for me to avoid her." She slams the door behind her and a picture falls off the wall.

Amy gasps, trots over to the painting and picks it up.

"Don't worry about it," Philippa says. "It's just something I did years ago."

"You painted it?" Amy asks as she holds it up at eye-level.

"I wanted to have a portrait of my favourite horse. I used to ride. That was a long time ago."

"I'd love to ride," Amy says as she puts the picture back.

"Perhaps we can work something out when we're in the new place."

"I do like horses. I care about animals. What I did was wrong." Amy turns to face us as tears run down her face. All this crying.

"It was wrong," Philippa said. "But I don't think you're a cruel person. Let's put it behind us and look forward to happier times."

I'm slumped in a chair as I look out at the already overgrown fields, wishing that this cordiality was contagious, so that I could infect my mother and Melissa. Instead, I seem to have made matters worse.

"Meg," Philippa says as she sits in a chair next to mine. "Why don't I ask Melissa to stay here until she starts work at the track with Edwin? She and Amy can help me get things organized for the move. Perhaps Melissa needs some time. Just for a few days."

"I thought she had a good relationship with our mother. I was mistaken of course."

"I can see that she has a short fuse, and her anxiety is showing. Perhaps she was more traumatized by being tied up by Cecil than she can admit. And then he tapes them both up and waves a gun around. I know it was fake, but they didn't know that."

I turn to speak to Amy, but she's stretched out on the sofa, fast asleep.

"Amy's been through a lot," I say.

"Yes, she has. And I think she needs time to heal, just as Melissa does."

"You might be right. Staying here for a few days could help Melissa. And I'll keep our mother away."

My already sombre mood on the drive home is further damp-ened by the relentless drizzle and lack of sunshine. This is not a

287

typical short-lived spring shower, and I fear that my grey mood has also settled in.

I get out of the truck and walk to the kitchen door, counting on Kelly's greeting to give me a boost. But she's not here. Cooper's curled up on a chair and takes no notice of me. He might have opened an eye for a split second, but I can't be sure.

My palms are sweaty as I pull out my phone and I drop it. The clatter echoes around the empty room. I pick it up and see that I've three text messages and a voice mail from William. He's taken my mother to the hospital and didn't want to leave Kelly on her own. My mother had a dizzy spell and felt nauseated. I respond with tears in my eyes. I realize that my primary concern is for Kelly. But I should be focussed on my mother. After all, she's a human being, not an animal.

*   *   *

William's old Jag is in the parking lot, near the end of a row and, sure enough, Kelly wags her tail as she sees me walking towards her. All four windows are open about three inches and I talk to her and tell her I'll be back. I haven't got a leash with me, so don't transfer her to the truck.

William greets me in the emergency department with the news that my mother has been prioritized because she has had a recent operation for a brain tumour.

"I expect they'll want to do scans and other tests. I can't imagine she'll be leaving soon," he says, as he pulls back a privacy curtain that doesn't live up to its name. My mother has lost all the colour she gained and her hair has gone frizzy, but the expression on her face is not what I expect.

"Meg, you have to do something about it," she says, as she pushes herself up on the pillow.

"About what?" Does she think I can get her a magic cure for whatever is the matter with her?

"About me and Melissa, that's what."

"What do you mean?"

"You're being a bit slow on the uptake, and I'm the one lying in a hospital bed."

"That's not fair."

"Okay," William says as he places two small orange plastic chairs that he's managed to pilfer, near the bed. "Let's go back to the beginning." He turns to me and takes a deep breath. I think we're trying his lawyerly patience. "Miriam says that Melissa's apparent inability to forgive her and unwillingness to attempt a reconciliation has caused her a great deal of stress. She contends that this stress has caused her to fall ill."

"William," my mother says as she flops her head back onto the pillow. "Sometimes it's best to just get to the point. Meg, you need to do something so that Melissa listens to me."

"That is going to be very difficult," I say.

"No, it's not. Just tell her I'm dying. We're all dying, so it's not a lie. And tell her I've something I must tell her before I go."

"You didn't have a dizzy spell, did you? I thought you'd stopped the lies."

"It's only a white lie, to help get my daughter back."

"Melissa is having a very hard time forgiving you. She feels more abandoned and betrayed than I do, and that's saying a lot."

"How long do I have to go on being punished? When are you both going to stop blaming me for everything? We're family. Surely that counts for something?"

"I think you underestimate the harm you've caused," William says, "with both your action and lack of action. We're referring to babies and children and their relationship with their mother. And I am doing my best to be objective here."

"No-one asked you," my mother says, almost spitting out the words.

"I'm still going to speak, and you're going to listen. It's important to understand both sides of any situation and to hear what each has to say."

"To think I thought William would make a good husband for you, Meg."

I stare at her in disbelief.

"To continue," William says, in a quiet, steady voice. "Melissa believes you made the choice to stay with Stan rather than raise her. Meg believes you did nothing to help her. You knew Stan was abusing your daughter, but you made the choice to stay with Stan, rather than leave and raise Meg on your own. So, while the situations are different, both feel abandoned and betrayed by their own mother, you. Is this a fair summary, Meg?"

I nod. Words don't come.

"You're making it sound much worse than it was," my mother says.

"I don't believe I am."

"Children should show respect towards their parents. Neither of mine does. They're both hard-hearted and unforgiving. I don't want to see either of them again. They're suited to each other, those two."

"I think…"

"I don't need or want your opinion," she says.

"This is sad. You'll regret this, Miriam."

She turns her head away from the side of the bed where we're seated.

"We're going to leave," William says. "I'm going to reserve a room for you at the Vannersville Inn, and make sure your bags reach the hotel as soon as possible."

William reaches for my hand. His warm, gentle touch makes me sigh. I look at my mother. She's lying motionless with her head still turned away from us. Her behaviour is incredulous.

"Let's go," William says.

We walk out to the carpark and stand by the ticket kiosk.

"Don't cry, Meg."

I didn't realize that tears are streaming down my cheeks.

"Why is she doing this?" I ask. "I thought we'd built some kind of relationship. What's going on? Is she sick? I should go back in."

"If I were you, I wouldn't go. Let's go to the farm. I'll text Melissa and let her know that your mother is staying at the Vannersville Inn. You and Melissa should talk. But first we need to take Kelly home and have something to eat."

"Thanks, William." I squeeze his large hand, which I realize I'm still holding. "I'll check with the Vannersville Inn tomorrow to make sure my mother has arrived there safely."

* * *

William insisted I sit in the recliner while he makes some sandwiches, and I'm doing my best to relax. So far it hasn't worked, despite stroking Kelly's soft silky head, and the warmth of Cooper's furry body curled up on my lap. I can't believe my mother's behaviour.

I slam the recliner into its upright position and the cat tumbles off, but recovers well.

"William," I shout. "I know what my mother's up to."

"What do you mean?" He asks as he walks into the room wiping his hands on the kitchen towel.

"She wants me and Melissa to get on, to be sisters. And she knows Melissa is angry with me because I've been building a relationship with our mother and she sees that as forgiveness and Melissa just cannot forgive her. She believes that our mother doesn't deserve forgiveness from either of us. My mother is deliberately turning me against herself, hoping that Melissa and I will make up."

"That sounds rather far-fetched."

291

"No, I'm right. And I'm going to fix this."

"Uh oh. What do you plan to do?"

"Don't worry. It'll be okay." I say this with more confidence than I feel. "But I will leave it for a couple of days. We all need time to cool off."

22

Sparkle

William and Kelly want to come with me and I can't say no to either of them. All three of us show up at Philippa's house and we're welcomed into the kitchen. Dogs aren't allowed into any other part of the house and we don't want to leave her shut in William's car.

The kitchen has an overwhelming expanse of ceramic tile on the floor and walls. Its shiny cold practicality offers no comfort, and we sit on hard, scratched wooden stools which surround a stained marble centre-island. Philippa isn't sure that she'll be able to convince Melissa to show her face, but she says she'll do her best. Amy says she'll help.

We sit in silence, almost motionless. The warmth from William's body next to mine stops my mood from plummeting, and his rhythmic breathing helps to calm my nerves.

Kelly lies on her front with her head between her paws. She can't get traction on the shiny tiles, so she's not inclined to move. She lifts her head as Melissa appears in the doorway.

"Thank you, Melissa, for joining us," I say. I pull a stool out for her and wait for her to sit. Her skin is almost the same colour as her blond hair, and her face in expressionless. As she sits on the stool, she fixes her gaze on her clenched hands held in her lap.

"Melissa, as I mentioned on the phone yesterday, I'm so glad that you're my sister and feel lucky to have a family, finally. You and William mean so much to me. I don't want to lose either of you. It's important for me to say this because I'm not good at demonstrating love. But that doesn't mean I don't feel it. You are very special to me. I want you to be happy. I'm going to keep talking until I've said my bit. Then you can tell me how you feel. Okay?"

She nods and sniffs without lifting her head. At least she didn't barge out of the room and slam the door behind her.

"What I'm going to say may cause you to get upset, but it's not intended to. I think you should know, that's all. It's about our mother, so bear with me. Okay?"

She nods again.

"Our mother faked a dizzy spell and had William take her to the hospital. She told William it was brought on by stress, by your apparent inability to forgive her and unwillingness to attempt a reconciliation. When I think about it, the dizzy spell might have been real, but, during our visit, she thought on her feet and made us both so angry that we booked her into the Vannersville Inn, and delivered her bags there. But, making us mad at her was deliberate. She has said to me right from the beginning that she wants you and me to get on, as sisters. That's all that's important to her. She can see, because I've been a little more willing to forgive than you, that there is a wedge between us. The fact that we're not getting along is tearing her apart. She wants me to be angry with her, to turn my back on her, so that the two of us can be sisters."

"How can you be sure?" she asks in a raspy voice. "If that's the truth, that would be a laugh."

"I believe I'm right. And, you should know that while I can't forgive her entirely for what happened to me, I'm willing to provide her with a little support and comfort. I think she's racked with guilt and regret and doesn't like herself much. We're all she's got. Family should be there for you through thick and thin."

"She wasn't there for us, though, was she?"

"You're right. She let us down. And we'll never really understand what made her take those decisions. But she wants us both in her life and for us to be sisters."

"I can't be in her life."

"Okay. Perhaps I should have used different words for what I mean."

"Time for the lawyer to butt in," William says, as he puts his palms down on the cold stone surface. "A suggestion. Miriam is the mother of each of you. That's not in dispute. You care about each other and want to help each other and that's what Miriam wants to hear more than anything else at this point. So, we can tell her that. Agreed?"

We both nod.

"Miriam is staying at the Vannersville Inn and returns to England tomorrow, so that you can come home, Melissa," he says.

"That sounds so nice," Melissa says. She buries her head in her hands.

It sounds nice to me as well.

"Because," William says, "you want to live at the farm more than anything, right?"

I'm taken aback. I didn't realize how important living at the farm is for Melissa. I put my arm around her, and she puts her head on my shoulder. Tears pool in my eyes, blurring my vision. I don't recall ever having someone lean on my shoulder like this. And I don't want to push her away. I want to be close to her.

William's told me before that Melissa's desperate for a family. To belong somewhere. And she thought she'd found it with William and me, but my mother showing up made her question my allegiance. She believes that I have to choose between my mother and her. To make it worse, she can't comprehend how I can forgive our mother for what she did to us. And I can understand that.

"William's living at the farm now. The three of us are family," I say.

William stands up and puts his arms around us both.

"Our mother is our mother," I say, "but she's not part of this family. We can't pretend she doesn't exist, though, and I might want to see her now and then, but it doesn't mean I forgive her entirely, or that I care about her more than you. I hope you'll come home with us."

Melissa slides off the stool and gives each of us a kiss on the cheek. More tears run down her face, but they have a different sparkle. She claps her hands and chases Kelly around the room. The dog skids on the slippery tiles and yips as she catches the excitement.

"Let's go home," I say.

CPSIA information can be obtained
at www.ICGtesting.com
Printed in the USA
BVHW060019231221
624661BV00008B/196